Conte

1914

**Book 1 in the
British Ace Series
By
Griff Hosker**

1914

Published by Sword Books Ltd 2014

Copyright © Griff Hosker First Edition

The author has asserted their moral right under the Copyright, Designs and Patents Act, 1988, to be identified as the author of this work.

A CIP catalogue record for this title is available from the British Library.

Dedication

1914 V: The Soldier

If I should die, think only this of me:
That there's some corner of a foreign field
That is for ever England. There shall be
In that rich earth a richer dust concealed;
A dust whom England bore, shaped, made aware,
Gave, once, her flowers to love, her ways to roam,
A body of England's, breathing English air,
Washed by the rivers, blest by suns of home.
And think, this heart, all evil shed away,
A pulse in the eternal mind, no less
Gives somewhere back the thoughts by England given;
Her sights and sounds; dreams happy as her day;
And laughter, learnt of friends; and gentleness,
In hearts at peace, under an English heaven.
Rupert Brooke

To the fictional soldiers like Doddy and Tiny, as well as the real heroes like Wilfred Owen, Rupert Brooke and Siegfried Sassoon. To those pilots like McCudden, Roy Brown and Albert Ball who pioneered combat flying. They died for the country and they should be remembered. To the families who lost sons, brothers and fathers. This is dedicated to you all.
Thanks to Ian Ritchie for supplying the gaps in my research.

1914

Chapter 1

They call it the Great War now but when it all started we thought it was a lark. We pictured a war like Dad had been in, the South African War; a few months away and then back home with a suntan and some strange souvenirs. We never thought that it would last so long and kill so many good men. We just did our duty and followed orders. That was how we had been brought up. We were in for a shock when it lasted four years and took away so many of the boys we had grown up with.

We were nothing special as a family. We lived, as many people did back in those days, in a cottage on Lord Burscough's estate. We had two bedrooms and there were seven children. It was not remarkable in any way and the family adapted to four big lads in one bedroom. We were better off than the girls; they had to share a room with mum and dad. Even when we had grown up and were earning money we still had to share the bedroom. That was the way of the world. You had to work long hours and the money you were paid was coppers. There were some who went on about socialism and how the high and mighty had too much money. I heard lads say as how we ought to take what they had and share it out. We never said that in front of mum and dad. We would have been out on our ear. They had both worked for the Burscough family since they were old enough to work. Serving the aristocracy was in their veins.

Dad, John Harsker, was the chief groom for Lord Burscough. He had worked for him since he was a lad. His father had been a groom too. It was where he had met mum, Mary, she had been a below stairs maid. They had married when she was sixteen and dad was eighteen. The two up two down cottage had been their first home and we still lived there. It was on the estate and life was pleasant. The village of Burscough owed everything to the Burscough family and it was an extension of Lord Burscough's domain. When we went into Wigan or St.Helens or even Liverpool for a night out we saw the dirt and the crime. The estate the was; it was a peaceful place. Some considered it boring but we were happy.

My name is William and I was the fourth child to be born into the family and the third boy. It meant I got the clothes that John and Tom had outgrown. Poor Albert, my younger brother, had to have them third hand. I felt sorry for Bert.

I was the only one of the lads to survive the war. My dad had four brothers and all of them lived to be old men but my brothers all died before they were thirty. Poor Bert died before he was twenty. They didn't see much of life. And the funny thing was, I was the one who was in the army first and I was the only one who saw the end of the war and lived to

1

1914

talk about it. I still wonder about that to this day. Why? What was so special about me?

John wanted to be off the estate as soon as he could. There were fewer jobs now that we had more steam traction engines on the estate. The day he turned fourteen he left home and went to Manchester to earn a living. There was good money to be made in the factories of Manchester. With the new railways, it was not a long journey but we had no money to go to see him. It was not a good parting. Mother and father still hoped he could do something on the estate but John was pig-headed. He knew his own mind and he went. He wrote and, every holiday, he visited. He was still the same big brother who had given me such a hard time growing up but he seemed worldlier now. When he came home on the increasingly rare Sunday he was different. I know that my mother frowned on his new habit of smoking and the jaunty way he wore his cap. I thought he looked sophisticated but to Mother, he was being polluted by the city.

Of course, the direct effect was that Tom wanted to join him and the minute he turned fourteen he upped and left too. The lure of money and a little equality with others suited them both. I knew what they meant; on the estate, we had to tip our caps and say, "Yes sir, no sir, three bags full sir!" to almost everyone. Mum and dad never minded, it was the old way and they were used to it. However, John and Tom had seen the new world and they wanted some of it.

That left my sister Sarah as the eldest girl and me as the eldest boy. I was always close to my sister Sarah. I think because I was the next one to her she had someone to care for. I think my mother was with child almost every year. She accepted it and seemed to think that was her role. She was always a mother; a homemaker and someone who deeply cared for her children. We were her reason for living; along with her deep love for my father. The closer I came to fourteen the more nervous and worried became my mother. I think she thought I would join my big brothers. She needn't have worried. I liked the life on the estate and that was because I loved horses.

Dad was a quiet thoughtful man. He used his pipe as a way of meditating and it gave him time to think. As I grew up I realised that more men should pause before they speak. It would save many arguments. He had never tried to dissuade my brothers from leaving home. As he had said to me, "It's this way lad, a chap will be happier doing what he enjoys. You canna make a man like working on the land. Me? I'd hate to be in one of them factory places but each to his own."

I agreed but my motive was different. I wanted to be around horses. This was not the cart horses who pulled the ploughs or the working horses who pulled the carriages, these were the hunters that Lord Burscough and his son, Master James, rode. I had shown an ability to ride from an early age. There was a time I thought I might have been able to be a jockey but I grew too tall. Still, Lord Burscough liked me and liked the way I looked after his horses. He let me ride his hunters. There was one, in particular, Caesar, who was special to me. He had been the first horse I had seen born and I looked after him when he was growing. I schooled him and I was the first to ride him. Lord Burscough encouraged me to ride him every day. As he said, "Fine animals like that deserve to be ridden as often as possible."

That suited me down to the ground. Every day I rode Caesar and I rode him as fast as I could. Sometimes I would ride two or three a day. It was the speed I liked; I liked the wind rushing through my hair and the thrill of making instant decisions. I would not be working in the factory I knew that. I would be working with the horses on the estate. I began working when I was twelve. I was too young really but my father and Lord Burscough thought it was a good thing. The money was coppers but I was frugal and I could save. Besides, had they but known it, I would have worked for nothing.

I think that made up for the disappointment of Tom and John leaving home. Mother became much happier when she knew I would not be leaving the nest. My brother's visits became increasingly rare. When our Sarah began working as a scullery maid in the *big house*, as we termed it, then order came into our house once more. The departure of the two big lads had also made the house a little bigger and we enjoyed that.

I worked happily for the next four years learning about horses and becoming a bigger man as I filled out my frame. Caesar was now the only horse for me. He too was big and we made a fine pair; at least I thought so. I suppose the most important event that happened was that Lord James Burscough joined the Lancashire Yeomanry as a lieutenant. He was only four years older than me but had been to University and was a well-educated man. He wanted and needed a servant and the logical choice was me. It appealed to me, too. The Yeomanry did not serve abroad and was a part-time unit. There was a dashing ceremonial uniform and a fine regular one. We paraded more than we worked and were only needed when the police had a riot to deal with. Ironically the one time I did have to draw ammunition was when the factories in Manchester had a protest. I get ahead of myself; that was some time in the future.

I was sixteen when we joined the Yeomanry and Mother cried when she saw me in my dress uniform. The tears were of pride; the war and tears of despair were two years away. I know that I was lucky to be joining as an officer's servant. The colonel of the regiment was Lord Burscough himself and so his son was afforded a great deal of both latitude and tolerance. The troop sergeants shouted at the other troopers who were no more incompetent than I was but as the servant of the lieutenant I got away with things. We trained and drilled just like the regular cavalry and we were paid for the time we served.

The troop sergeants had all served in regular regiments: the 17th Lancers, the Dragoon Guards and many others. They had joined when they retired as the pay allowed them to drink more than they would otherwise have been able to do. I think they were all career soldiers who could not face life in the outside world. The ordered world of the soldier appealed to them. Many of them told sad tales of comrades who had left the service only to end up drunks or in the workhouse. That was no way for someone who had served their country to end their days.

Having said that I could get away with things the fact of the matter was that I didn't. I enjoyed being a trooper and the things that the troop sergeants liked, such as smart tack, a well-presented horse and an immaculate uniform, were not a problem. My problem was keeping at the same pace as the others. I forever wanted to gallop off. The sergeants did not like that. However, they did admire the way I rode and the control I had over my horse. We had to provide our own horses. Normally that would have been impossible for the son of a servant but Lord Burscough and his son liked me and they allowed me to ride Caesar. All of the horses were named after great generals. Bizarrely it didn't matter if they were a male or a female; they were all granted a grand title. There was no doubt that I would ride Caesar.

Caesar was one of the bigger horses. I had grown into a big lad and I knew there were few others who could ride him. Lord James was much smaller. Caesar was jet black with a white blaze; he had one long white sock and three short ones. However, the best things about Caesar were his speed and his ability to jump fences.

During one of the obligatory training weekends, luckily held on the estate, we had competitions. I won two of them: the long-distance race and the steeplechase around the estate. While other horses baulked at, even the smallest fences, Caesar soared over them without blinking. I was really proud to win those two cups. They were not enormous and they were not valuable but to me and my family, they were the highest accolade anyone had ever received. That day changed me. I decided I would knuckle down and become the best trooper in the regiment.

The troop sergeants, especially, Sergeant Armstrong, were not only amazed but pleased. The old grey-haired sergeant who had charged at Omdurman took me to one side. "You know, lad, you could join a regular regiment and do this full time." He waved a deprecatory hand around the others. "Most of these are just fannying around and will never make cavalrymen. You can ride and this change in attitude is impressive."

I was flattered but I knew it was not for me. "You see, Sergeant Armstrong, I am going to be a groom here on the estate, just like my dad."

"That is admirable in many ways, son, but there is a whole world out there and it looks better from the back of a horse." He could see I was not convinced. "Well, keep on doing what you are doing and you'll soon get a promotion."

I did as he said. I became an expert with the Short Magazine Lee Enfield with which we were issued. I confess I was never much good with the sword they gave us but I became known as the best shot in our squadron. I was proud of that too.

When John and Tom came home that Christmas in 1912, the peace of the home was shattered. There had been order in the house. We all knew our places and got on well with each other. My younger sisters, Alice and Kathleen were preparing for a life of work and Albert was dreaming of the day he would leave school. There was balance. It ended the day my two brothers came home for Christmas.

I think I blamed myself. My mother insisted that I wear my uniform for Christmas dinner. That did not please Tom and John. It caused bitter comments. It was not helped by the fact that the two of them took themselves off to the Blacksmith's Arms for a drink which turned into a two-hour drinking session. They arrived back barely in time for dinner. Mother had been given a fine goose by Lord Burscough that year. She lavished much attention on it. Fortunately, it was not ruined although in light of subsequent events it might have been. There were rules in our house and one of them was that when mother said dinner was ready then you were at the table. We all adhered to that rule.

When they had left for the pub I was dressed in my ordinary clothes. Mother told me to get changed when she took the goose out of the oven. She was keen to make the occasion a special one. All of her chicks were home. My three sisters oohed and aahed when I came down the stairs. I just blushed. I was not used to the attention.

"Eeh our Bill, what a handsome one you are."

"If you go down to the village tonight you'll have to beat the lasses off with a stick."

"Look at the shine on those buttons."

I saw a tear in my mother's eye and she came and gave me a hug. "I'm right proud of you son."

Young Bert, just fourteen years old looked wistfully at the uniform which was bright and colourful and unlike the drab grey and brown clothes everyone else wore. The red jacket had barely been worn and there was no sign of fading. I knew, from Sergeant Armstrong's uniform, that the red soon faded to a rusty colour. It was a sign of service, but mine had only been worn a handful of times.

Even my father, sat in his armchair by the fire with his pipe puffing away looked impressed. He was proud of me as a horseman and now he was proud of me as a soldier. He had worn the same uniform in Africa. He understood what it was to be a cavalryman. He had served with Lord Burscough and he valued the red tunic. I couldn't wait for Tom and John to come home and see me.

The goose had just been placed on the table when we heard them coming up the lane. They were singing some rude ditty and I saw my mother frown. She hated smut of any description. That should have been a warning, I suppose, of the storm that was about to break.

We were all smiling when they entered but they took one look at me and their faces turned to scowls. "Who the bloody hell is this? General Lord bloody Kitchener?" It was not banter and not intended as humour. It was an insult.

Mother pointed the carving knife at Tom and said, "Language! This is Christmas Day!"

John ignored the warning in mother's tone, "All dressed up like a dog's dinner. Mister La-di-da Fancy Pants!"

I felt stupid and I muttered, "Mother thought I should wear it."

"Aye well, it's blokes like you that keeps us working men down. It's time the likes of you and his lordship who oppress the working man were thrown out on their ear once and for all."

"You are right John and one of these days we'll have a revolution and their days will be over!" Tom always agreed with his big brother.

Mother looked shocked but I could see that dad was furious. You did not attack the upper classes in his earshot. Neither did you insult the red uniform he had worn with pride. He was, like me, more than happy with the status quo. He stood and tapped his pipe out on the fireplace. He glared at his two sons. In the silence which followed I could suddenly smell the beer on them and their clothes. They were drunk. I had never ever seen dad drunk and this would be another reason for his anger.

"Now you two listen to me. You are my sons; my flesh and blood. You are welcome under this roof. But if you express sentiments like that again I shall not have you here. Do you understand me? And I will not have bad language in front of the ladies. You should apologise now and then sit down so that we can get on with celebrating this special day."

This was the point at which they should have nodded, apologised and sat down. The old Tom and John would have done so but these were not the same brothers who had gone off to Manchester. John put his face in my father's and said, "This is a free country despite what your precious Lord Bloody Burscough would have us think. An Englishman can express his views and there's nowt you can do about it!"

I saw tears coursing down my mother's cheeks. Our Sarah was bright red and clenching her fists. Poor Albert didn't know where to look. I stood next to my father. My brothers were bigger but if it came to blows then I would stand shoulder to shoulder with dad.

Dad nodded, went to the door and opened it. "There's the door. Either you apologise and sit at the table or leave and never come back."

I am not sure if John intended to hit dad or if he just lost his balance but he put his arm out and caught dad on the chin. I just reacted. I was a strong lad and could use my fists and I was sober. I spun John around and then hit him an uppercut. More by luck than anything else, he fell backwards out of the open door.

Tom snarled, "You little toe rag!"

He put his hand on my shoulder. I turned and hit him hard in the solar plexus with my right hand. He was not as fit as he had been; he smoked too much and he was drunk. He doubled up. Our Sarah had had enough too and she put everything she had into a blow to his chin so that he ended up lying on top of his brother.
Mother went to dad, "Are you hurt?"

I could see he was not but he was shocked. "I can't believe it! They hit me! If I had done that to my dad...."

Mother dabbed her eye, "Well the fact of the matter is you wouldn't have, nor would Bill or Bert. It's that town that's done it. I don't recognise them!"

Kathleen and Alice had been shocked too and they now went and filled two pails with cold water, throwing the contents on the two brothers. They spluttered and looked up at them. The girls put down their pails and picked up a pan and a rolling pin from the kitchen cupboard. Our Alice had a sharp tongue on her. "And if you try anything again I have a rolling pin and our Kath has a frying pan. Now clear off. You aren't my brothers anymore."

They both staggered to their feet and glowered belligerently at the girls but when they saw the weapons in their hands then discretion took over and they both stormed off. John turned and roared, "You can keep your poxy goose too. If I ever catch you on your own our Bill, I'll give you the hiding of your life."

I was not worried about John now. I had stood up to him and won. I just shook my head and turned back into the cottage. As the door closed it was like the end of a way of life. My parents were never the same after that. The five children who remained became closer and John and Tom were like strangers to us.

I don't think either of them intended to cause such distress and to ruin Christmas Day and I cursed the fact that I had triggered the conflict, well my uniform had. I didn't realise until that moment the power it had.

That was not the end of it, of course. Fate has a way of throwing you into situations you could not possibly imagine. The regiment was called up in March of the next year and ordered to ride to Manchester where workers were rioting. Major Harrison was in command and he made sure that none of us had live ammunition in our guns. He was a teacher, normally, and most of the men called him 'Uncle', affectionately. His calm demeanour was matched with an iron discipline. Most of the troopers, me included, had been in his class when we had been schoolboys. He did not have to work at discipline, he had it naturally. He addressed us before we left.

"Men, we will need great self-control today. These rioters will try to intimidate you. Do not let them. You have live ammunition in your bandoliers but I do not want us to use it. Today we will use our horses to control them. These workers are misguided that is all."

I rode next to Sergeant Armstrong and just behind Lieutenant Burscough. The veteran turned to me. "The Major might be right, son, but be under no illusions, there will be some nasty pieces of work out there. They might try to hurt your horse so watch out."

I was appalled. I was happy enough for me to be hurt but not Caesar. If anyone tried they would have me to deal with.

The streets leading to the square where the rally was being held was congested. As we rode along I could see policemen, some of them bleeding and hurt, being carried away on stretchers. Eventually, we came to a thin line of blue and the Chief Constable, in all his finery, was there. He had a very serious look on his face.

"Ah Major, thank God you have arrived! They have been throwing bottles at my chaps. Perhaps your guns can sort them out."

I was close enough to hear the conversation. "No, sir. My men will not fire."

"But I have read the Riot Act!" He seemed to think that the simple reading of a document would allow us to shoot on our fellow men.

"Well, sir, what would you like us to do?" The policeman looked confused. Major Harrison was used to explaining things to boys and he sighed. "What will make the situation calm sir?"

"I need those workers moving out of the square and for them to go home."

That seemed to satisfy the major. "Thank you, sir, now leave it to us." He turned to Lieutenant Burscough, "I want us to make an arrow behind me. You and the sergeant and then three more and so on. Just follow me and have the men keep their hands to themselves. We do not want to provoke them. We will use the horses to force them from the square. When I give the command we spread out in a single line."

Although the order had been given to the lieutenant it was the sergeant who organised it. I found myself behind the lieutenant with Doddy Brown next to me and, on his other side his brother Tiny. They were both farmworkers from the estate and so big they made me look small. All three of us had the biggest horses in the regiment and I could see why the sergeant had placed us where he had. He wanted us to frighten the rioters.

When we were in position he said, "Move slowly forward and wait for me to signal halt. Forward!"

We moved towards the mass of humanity. They had been drinking and there were crudely drawn placards. They had the same sentiments as those espoused by my brothers. When we were thirty yards from them he held up his hand and every rider stopped instantly. I had to admit it was impressive.

The major used the voice which could still a schoolyard full of boisterous children and it worked on the rioters too. "Gentlemen, you have all been read the Riot Act and asked to disperse. I ask you to comply with these instructions."

One large rioter stepped forwards. I saw he had a cudgel in his hand. "Or what, soldier boy?"

I could hear the smile in his voice as the teacher said calmly, "Or we shall move forward and shift you," he paused, "forcibly." I saw him nudge his horse forward and he leaned down to speak with the man. I was still close enough to hear his words. "And if anyone offers us violence then, I have to say, that my men are not policemen, they are soldiers and unlike the police, we are armed." He sat upright in the saddle and said loud enough for all to hear, "However that is your choice and your decision." He turned and waved his right arm, "Lancashire Yeomanry, forward."

Once again I felt pride in the regiment as we moved as one man. The crowd watched on in eager anticipation. They had dealt with the police; they thought all men in uniform were the same. The police weren't soldiers. They didn't have the discipline we had nor, I suspect, the courage. The mob began to move towards us.

I heard Sergeant Armstrong mutter, "They need a little persuasion sir!"

Major Harrison glanced around and nodded. "Regiment, draw sabres!"

The sound of three hundred sabres all being drawn at once is a very menacing sound. There is a hiss which chills the bones. As the shiny weapons were all held with the tip on each trooper's shoulder the sun suddenly flashed on them. It was a magical moment. I was close enough to the rioters to see the fear in their eyes. The belligerent man with the placard was next to Sergeant Armstrong who leaned down again. Caesar was almost next to his mount and I heard every word and saw each reaction from the rioters.

"Now then, sonny boy, if you want to use your cudgel, here's your chance. But remember this my sword is sharp enough to shave with and I guarantee that if I use it you'll bleed like a stuck pig so do me a favour and piss off."

The fear was absolute in the man's eyes. I could hear the threat in the sergeant's words. Most of the rioters were there because they thought it would be safe. They could bait the police and go home feeling like men. Suddenly they were faced with three hundred armed men on, what must have looked like, huge horses. The ones in the front row began to slink back through the lines of the rest of the mob.

Major Harrison saw the movement and shouted, "Single line! Walk!"

I put my horse next to Sergeant Armstrong and felt one of the Brown boys put his next to me. When I turned to look at him I could see that he was grinning from ear to ear. We moved forward, slowly at first but, as the line grew in width the mob began to speed up and so did we.

"Walk, trot!"

There was real fear in the eyes of the men before us. They had not bargained for this.

"Trot!"

When three hundred horses began to open their legs, the mob lost all cohesion and fled the square as quickly as they could. We reached the buildings and Major Harrison yelled, "Halt!" In an instant, we were stopped. We heard cheering. It was the police behind us. The riot was over and no one had been hurt.

Chapter 2

It had hardly been warfare but it showed us that we had the discipline to face up to men who were many times our number and we would not back down. After we had handed the square back to the police we trotted home. There was elation amongst the troopers; we had done our duty and even drawn our weapons! I was not certain if I could have used my sword but it had not come to that anyway.

Lieutenant Burscough was particularly pleased. One of the factories which had been targeted by the strikers had been his father's. I knew nothing of the politics and I didn't need to. Those, like the major and the lieutenant, would make all the right decisions and I would just have to trust them.

That was the last occasion we were called upon to do such service and our duties, from then on, were largely ceremonial. I had thought of what the sergeant had said and it did appeal. I liked being in the cavalry, even though it was part-time, and I seemed to be born for it. I still enjoyed working with the horses but they were less exciting than when I was being in the Yeomanry. Perhaps it had been the speed and excitement of horses which had drawn me towards them. When we exercised in the Yeomanry we got to gallop the horses. When I worked with my father we just groomed and walked them. I had heard that they now had railways and steam trains which could go even faster than horses. That would not suit me. I liked being in control of the speed. When you had to adjust what you were doing to suit the terrain and the horse then that was when I enjoyed riding the most. I was not a great fan of the sword except when we had the practise sessions and had to charge at a line of marrows stuck on sticks. I was the one who managed to hit more than anyone else. Perhaps that was why I was leaning to a life in the cavalry.

Life went in at the same pace during that summer of 1913. My father gradually gave me more responsibility in the stables as my confidence and skills improved. Then something happened which changed everything. It was like throwing a small stone into the village pond; the ripples kept on going outwards. They became smaller but they still affected everything they touched. Lord Burscough had a stroke. It was not a major one but the left side of his face appeared frozen and he could not use his right leg. I did not know, at the time, what the effect would be.

The young Lord Burscough came to see me a week after it had happened. "I am afraid Lord Burscough can no longer be colonel of the regiment." I waited in anticipation. Would he be the next colonel? He answered me in the next breath. "It appears that an outsider is to be appointed and I am leaving the regiment."

I was shocked. There had always been a Burscough as colonel of the regiment. I suspected there was more to this than I knew but my first thoughts were selfish; what would happen to me? "Should I resign too, sir?"

He laughed, "There is no need for us both to fall upon our swords, besides everyone thinks highly of you. You shall carry on in the regiment."

I bit my lip, "And Caesar sir? Will I have to return him?"

He put his arm on my shoulder. "Caesar was always my father's favourite. Consider him a gift to the regiment and you."

"What will you do then sir? Join another regiment?"

We began to walk towards the stables. "It is either, join a regiment, or run the estate and young Roger seems to be doing a damned fine job of that. " My father saw us approach and he came towards us, removing his hat as he did so.

"Morning your lordship."

"Morning Harsker. I've just been telling young William here that as I am leaving the regiment and father won't need him we are giving Caesar to him."

The smile on my father's face went from ear to ear. "That's very kind of you, my lord."

"Now the thing of it is father needs some form of transport to get around and he has taken it into his head to get one of these new-fangled automobiles."

I could see that dad was confused. "I know nothing about machines my lord."

"I know which is where young William comes into it. He is a bright lad and my father wondered if he might learn how to drive one and then be the driver for his lordship."

The look in dad's eyes told me that I had to comply. If Lord Burscough wanted me to learn how to drive then I would have to learn how to drive. "Certainly sir, I am willing to have a go but I am not sure if I would be any good at it."

His lordship smiled as he said, "We shall learn together. I intend to get one too."

I felt relief course through my body. This would not be so bad. "In that case, sir, when do we start?"

"Capital! Saddle our horses and we'll ride to the station and pop into Manchester this morning. Strike while the iron is hot."

When we were at the station waiting for the train I asked his lordship why his father was not choosing his own car.

"Ah well he will do but we'll get one for me first for us to learn in and then we can drive the old man into town to get his own." He leaned in conspiratorially, "He doesn't want people staring at his face and his limp. He has his pride you know. This way he retains his privacy."

We separated when the train arrived, he went to the First Class and I walked to the rear of the train and Third Class.

This was the first time I had been to Manchester since the riot and I was a little wary. There were so many people around I felt intimidated. If I saw twenty people in a day then that was a crowd. In Manchester, I saw a hundred in the first five minutes. His lordship seemed quite happy and oblivious to the memory of that day. We took a taxi to the showroom which had recently opened. The automobile we looked at was something called a Singer 10. I did not think it would suit his father at all for it was a two-seater and rather small. The salesman drove him around the outside of the showroom and the local streets. To me, it sounded as noisy as one of the steam engines we had on the estate but it was fast. His lordship fell in love with it straight away. "I shall have one! When can I pick it up?"

I think the salesman was a little surprised at the speed with which the decision had been made but that was his lordship's way. He was always impulsive and decisive."Er by the end of the week, possibly, your lordship."

His lordship fixed him with a stare. "It will be the end of the week. Have it delivered to the estate and we shall want some instruction in operating it too."

"That will be extra, your lordship."

"I can assure you it will not. You can have the payment when the vehicle is delivered."

With that, we turned around and headed back to the waiting taxis. "Some of these fellows don't know their place, William, that is the trouble. Jumped up little chap! Now I shall drop you at the station and then I think I'll have a few hours in the city." He winked, "Do a bit of business and suchlike."

"Shall I wait at the station for you sir?"

"No, just take the horses back to the stables and then return for me in the carriage at eight this evening."

It is only now that I can look back on that world of 1913. It was a world which was about to change and we could never go back.

I was worried about the automobile and I went to see Harold; he was the man who drove the traction engines. I say drove them but he only drove them to the field and then winches were attached to ploughs and they did the work of twelve horses. They had had no attraction to me because they were slow. The Singer had been faster than Caesar! I thought, however, that the principles might be the same.

Harold laughed and shook his head. He tapped his short pipe out. "Nay, young William, they are as different as your Caesar and a donkey. You will be driving a petrol engine automobile. We had to fire these up with coal. Yours will have brakes and the steering will be easier, still, I can show you how it works." He tapped his nose, "Master will expect you to keep it running as well as driving it. They think it is the same as it was with horses." He shook his head. "Your dad is lucky because horses are easier than these temperamental beasts."

I was glad I spent the time with Harold. The principles helped me when the first automobile arrived. It would be a little like riding. A good rider used his hands, arms, legs and knees as well as his head. He had to use them all at the same time and I suspected it would be the same with the Singer.

Despite his words the salesman did turn up with the Singer and another automobile; a four-seater. As soon as he saw the house he became more deferential. "Here you are my lord. Delivered on time as promised and we have brought the Crossley. It is slower but much easier for you to learn how to drive it."

The young master looked a little more nervous than he had done. He pointed to me, "William here will be driving too so I shall sit in the back while you instruct him."

I thought the salesman would object but he just shrugged. As he took me through the controls and pedals I knew why I had been chosen to go first. I would make all the mistakes and his lordship would learn from them. My speculation was ended when I sat behind the wheel and tried to make it go forward. We bounced along the driveway like a mad rabbit. I nearly demolished one of the old statues which stood in the turning circle for the carriages. Everything seemed to happen too fast and it was so easy to make the engine cut out and then we would have to start it again. Starting involved the salesman leaping out and turning the starting handle. Stopping was not as easy as it looked either. When I had to use gears I thought that my head would explode. After an hour, however, both his lordship and the salesman were impressed. His lordship couldn't wait to get behind the wheel.

I was dismissed, "You go and stand over there by the Singer and watch!" If he thought he was going to impress me he was wrong; like me bounced along the drive and stalled it so often I thought the poor salesman would break his back starting it. His lordship managed to scrape the car next to a tree. I suspect the salesman was grateful it was not the new Singer. I found myself bored and, instead of watching I began to examine the Singer 10. The steering wheel was smaller but the gearstick was in the same place as were the pedals. It looked to be much smaller than the Crossley. I couldn't see old Lord Burscough squeezing into it.

Finally, the car was driven by his lordship without mishap and he came to the Singer. The salesman wisely allowed his lordship to drive it alone. Perhaps he was overconfident, I don't know, but the car leapt forward as though propelled from a cannon. He managed to stop it before he demolished the statue but I could see that he was shaken.

"Are you sure there isn't something wrong with the damned thing?"

The salesman hid his smile well, "No sir. It just needs handling differently."

"William, you have a go. I'll sit in the passenger seat."

I was terrified. If I wrecked this car then my new career could be over before it had even started. I just concentrated and tried to imagine that it was Caesar and not a mass of machinery. I barely moved my right foot and the vehicle moved slowly down the drive. The gears were actually easier to use and soon we were travelling quite quickly. I was aware that the main gates were looming up and I slowed down. There was a large turning circle at the end of the drive and I turned around.

His lordship looked impressed. "How in God's name did you manage to do that William?"

"Concentrated sir and barely moved my right foot." I took a breath, "Why not drive back sir? There's no one around."

He flashed me a look to see if I was mocking him but my innocent face reassured him. "Very well."

I turned, in the passenger seat so that I could see what he was doing. I immediately spotted that he was not using his right foot for the brake and the accelerator. As soon as I pointed it out to him he began to drive more confidently. When he pulled the car up next to the Crossley he beamed at the salesman. "I have to say, old chap, that William here is a much better teacher than you are. However, I am satisfied so come into the house and I will give you the cheque. William, familiarise yourself with the engine."

I had been dreading this part but I did as I was asked. The man who had driven the Crossley was standing nearby smoking a cigarette. I opened the bonnet and looked inside at the mass of tubes and machinery. "Excuse me, what does this do?"

Fortunately, he seemed an affable chap and he took me through the wires, pipes and pistons. He explained it quite simply and I picked the basic principles. I knew it would take me some time but I was confident that I could come to grips with this horseless carriage. I was hooked. The brief burst of speed had put Caesar's gallop into the shade.

By the time his lordship came out, I had been given the manual for the vehicle. I would ask if I could read it. I didn't think, for one moment, that his lordship would be bothered to read the tome.

"So you'll bring the other automobile at the end of the month. It has to be crimson; Lord Burscough loves the colour."

"Yes, sir."

As the Crossley drove away he clapped me on the back. "His lordship doesn't need to go into town. They will deliver here."

"But sir, how do you know he will like it?"

"Oh, he will like it. I asked for the one which looked the most like a carriage. This one has a separate compartment for you as the driver and it can seat five. He will like it."

And he did. He cared nothing about the workings of it but it was comfortable and it even had curtains for him to close for privacy. The first time I took him out in it I was almost shaking with fright. I needn't have worried. The suspension was better than his best carriage and he had me drive him all the way around the estate. I had my new job and I was happy. I still got to ride Caesar with the Yeomanry. My duties as a driver were not arduous and I learned to understand both the Lanchester's and the Singer's engines. That proved to be advantageous for the young Lord Burscough did not understand simple ideas such as putting petrol in. As for making sure it had enough oil… suffice it to say I had to check both vehicles every morning and evening. It did result in a pay rise for me for both of them were happy. My father could not believe I was getting more money than him. He could not resist a dig at his two elder sons. "If them two daft buggers hadn't gone off to the factories they could have had a nice little job like you and mother wouldn't be all upset like she is."

He was right. The family at home were close but there was a void where my brothers had been. Life was good and I looked forward to 1914 with great optimism.

Chapter 3

The war got in the way of all of our plans. When the Balkan Wars began again the regiment believed that it was too far away to affect us. I felt that something was in the air when young Lord Burscough joined the Royal Flying Corps. The automobile had given him a taste for speed and he did not want to go back to horses. I liked speed but I still loved horses. We found that the air of unease led more men to join the Yeomanry. The increased numbers led to my promotion to corporal; although they used the term Artificer the NCOs would not use the title and so I was Corporal Harsker. Sergeant Armstrong was delighted but he still thought that I should have joined a regular regiment.

When the Archduke was assassinated in June there was a noticeably tense atmosphere everywhere. The papers were full of talk of war. We knew that Germany had been building up a fleet and an army. As we sat around the table mother fretted away. "Why do we have to have all this talk of war? You can't go into a shop without someone having an opinion."

Sarah shook her head. She had blossomed into a beautiful young woman and one of the deputy butlers, Rogers, had shown an interest in her. They were now engaged. A marriage would put them in a good position when Carter, the head butler retired; he was seventy and it showed. "Don't worry mother. It'll come to nothing. These politicians just like to talk. They are like a bunch of old women."

Albert looked disappointed. He was seventeen and worked in the gardens. He had green fingers. "I think we should go to war. Germany is getting too big for its boots. It's time we showed them that we still rule the waves."

"All this talk of fighting. My brother Jack was killed in the Zulu wars. What good did that do us? We had to go to war a few years after with the Boers and the Zulu War was fought to help them. We should mind our own business." Mother's views were not to be gainsaid.

My father was silent. I watched him as he finished his meal and placed his knife and fork on the cleaned plate. "I don't want any British soldiers to get killed, not least of all young William here but you cannot let bullies get away with this sort of thing. If we stand up to Germany then they'll back down. You mark my words."

Once father had given his views on any subject then mother would never argue with him. She might disagree but she would always back him up. She was as loyal a wife as a man could wish for.

Our new colonel, Colonel Mackenzie, arrived and he came like a whirlwind. He was only in his forties and, from his suntan, had served in the tropics. We heard he had been in India and he was a fine horseman. We only found information second hand but one piece of information we had directly from his mouth was that we could expect to be mobilised by the middle of July. The married men began panicking about their families while the single ones like me were just excited. It seemed to us that this would be fun. We would swan over to France; rattle our sabres and then there would be peace again. It would be a lark.

Sergeant Armstrong took me to one side. "A word to the wise; I think we will be on duty every weekend until we are mobilised. We are getting a shipment of ammunition next week and the new colonel is keen to give the troopers and the horses the experience of live firing."

That was an eye-opener; live ammunition suggested they were taking things seriously. We did fire our guns but it was always at the practice range. I could not even remember firing when there had been a horse within four hundred yards. I wondered if that was a mistake. They would need acclimatising if we were going to war.

We were too small a regiment to have different messes for sergeants and corporals and we shared one. Those who lived in the barracks all the time kept it well stocked. I liked to sit, nursing a pint of beer, and listen to the old sergeants talking. It was where you learned what was likely to happen.

The Quartermaster-Sergeant, Harry Grimes, was the oldest soldier we had and the most experienced. I had no idea of his age; one of the lads joked that he had been at Balaclava but I didn't believe that for a moment. What he did have was authority. When he spoke then everyone, even Sergeant Armstrong listened.

"You lads will have to make sure the troopers practice firing dismounted. We learned that fighting the Boers. It isn't as easy as they might think. There'll be no charges like Omdurman in this war. We also need a couple of sections training for the two machine guns we are getting next week."

The shock statement made everyone look at each other. Machine guns meant a fixed position and we had always believed we would be mobile. I turned to Sergeant Armstrong, "I don't fancy that sarge."

"You are too good a horseman to waste you behind a static gun. I think that Major Harrison will impress on the colonel that we need to use the likes of you and your lads as scouts. Find the enemy, that will be your job."

"Someone said that we can't serve outside of Britain."

"And that is right but they are changing the law to allow it. To be honest it was always up to the colonel of the regiment or the Lord Lieutenant. They are happy for us to serve and so we probably shall."

"But where will the war be fought? Will they send us to the Balkans?"

He swallowed some of his beer and shrugged, "I doubt it but it could be anywhere. Russia, Italy, Austria and even Turkey are all taking sides. It could be anywhere." I must have looked worried for he smiled and said, "Listen, son, it doesn't matter where they send us; we just do our duty. It's what the British soldier has done for years. The thin red line, the charge of the Light Brigade, Rorke's Drift they are all places where British soldiers followed their orders and that's what we will do."

He was right. The politicians might not be trustworthy but the generals were dependable and we could rely on them. Lord Kitchener and the others would make sure that we prevailed. If there was a war then I was sure that we would win.

Mobilisation came sooner than thought; it was the second week of July. Our goodbyes had to be hurried. Because of my position I had to tell his lordship first. He was torn; he knew the regiment had to follow orders but he hated losing me.

"I took the liberty, your lordship, of showing young Albert, my brother, how to drive. I am sure he could drive you when necessary."

Albert was delighted as it was a cleaner job and he received more money. Since my brothers had left I had become something of a hero to him. Sarah told me one night how he modelled himself on me. It was flattering but I was no hero. Dad was the hero. Still, I knew that I had looked up to John right until the moment he had threatened the family. That was the reason I had used his opinion of me to make him into a driver; it might keep him safe. Mother was tearful. We only had two days to get ready and say our goodbyes. She kept wringing her hands every time she looked at me and her eyes were permanently puffy and red. It did not help when all of the newspapers were full of Balkan atrocities. It was not the Germans who worried my mother, after all, they were related to our Royal Family, and it was these other foreigners. The fact that they came from somewhere so far to the east also made her suspicious.

"I might not even be going to the Balkans. We'll probably just be sent to somewhere down south."

"And that is just as bad. I can't abide southerners. You should stay here in Lancashire! You can trust northern folk."

The thought that the people in the south of Britain were somehow different from us made us all laugh and parting a little easier.

Dad took me to the stables to pick up Caesar. "Just do your duty son, that's all anyone can ever ask." He patted Caesar affectionately, "And look after this old boy. He's a good 'un." He shook my hand. We didn't go in for hugs or great shows of affection. It wasn't our way. "And try to write. Your mum would like that. I know you might not have time but you know women."

"Aye, dad. I'll be alright you know?"

I could see him becoming a little upset himself and he just nodded and said, very quietly, "I know son but… well, you best get off to the barracks then eh?"

As soon as we were issued our kit we knew we were not going to sunny climes. It was the heavy woollen brown uniform which meant northern Europe. The orders were pinned up on the barracks wall; we were to take a troop train down to Kent and a holding area there. That was exciting and daunting at the same time. We knew that trying to get horses into a train would not be easy.

My section was made up of good lads. I was lucky in that they were all troopers who worked with horses and had all grown up around Burscough. There were others in the regiment who could ride but mine happened to be the ones who worked and cared for horses. It made life easier. Thus it came about that Major Harrison designated us to be the ones to travel with the horses. The boys complained but secretly they were pleased to have been chosen. It made them seem special. I split the section up so that there were two of three of us with every two horseboxes. It would be an eight-hour journey so we had plenty of water. We also made sure that we had shovels. Horses were messy enough as it was, a rocking railway carriage would do nothing to settle them.

I had the Brown boys with me. I knew them well; they worked on the estate farm next to our cottage. They were dependable. Their conversation left a little to be desired; they were mainly interested in chasing women and girls. They had not had much success but it didn't stop them buying every new hair product which came on to the market. They were convinced that the right combination of oil and perfume smeared on their heads would draw women like moths to a flame. It amused me. The other reason I liked them was that they were good singers and singing kept the horses calm. As we left Burscough Station the horses started to become agitated.

"Come on lads, give us a song. Send them to sleep."

Although they were in different carriages we had the adjoining doors open so that they could hear each other. Doddy hummed the opening and his brother joined in. They chose a lilting Irish melody. Soon every man in my section was singing.

Oh, Danny Boy the pipes are calling
From glen to glen, and down the mountain side,
The summer's gone and all the roses falling,

It's you, it's you must go, and I must bide,
But come ye back when summer's in the meadow,
Or when the valley's hushed and white with snow.
It's I'll be here in sunshine or in shadow,
Oh, Danny Boy, oh Danny Boy, I love you son!

But when ye come, and all the flow'rs are dying,
If I am dead, as dead I well may be,
Ye'll come and fine the place where I am lying,
And kneel and say an A-ve there for me;
And I shall hear though soft you tread above me,
And all my grave will warmer, sweeter be,
For you will bend and tell me that you love me,
And I shall sleep in peace until you come to me!

The effect on the horses was nothing short of miraculous. Soon every horse was chewing happily from their nosebags. The boys all enjoyed the singing. Doddy and Tiny knew many songs and they even sang a couple of the newer songs. Those were sung just by the two of them but, as the others listened and learned the words they joined in too.

Up to mighty London came an Irishman one day,
As the streets are paved with gold, sure ev'ryone was gay;
Singing songs of Piccadilly, Strand and Leicester Square,
Till Paddy got excited, then he shouted to them there:--
"It's a long way to Tipperary,
It's a long way to go;
It's a long way to Tipperary,
To the sweetest girl I know!
Goodbye Picadilly,
Farewell, Leicester Square,
It's a long, long way to Tipperary,
But my heart's right there!"
Paddy wrote a letter to his Irish Molly O',
Saying, "Should you not receive it, write and let me know!
"If I make mistakes in "spelling," Molly dear," said he,
"Remember it's the pen that's bad, don't lay the blame on me"
"It's a long way to Tipperary,
It's a long way to go;
It's a long way to Tipperary,
To the sweetest girl I know!
Goodbye Picadilly,

Farewell, Leicester Square,
It's a long, long way to Tipperary,
But my heart's right there!"
Molly wrote a neat reply to Irish Paddy O',
Saying, "Mike Maloney wants to marry me, and so
Leave the Strand and Piccadilly, or you'll be to blame,
For love has fairly drove me silly--hoping you're the same!"
"It's a long way to Tipperary,
It's a long way to go;
It's a long way to Tipperary,
To the sweetest girl I know!
Goodbye Picadilly,
Farewell, Leicester Square,
It's a long, long way to Tipperary,
But my heart's right there!"

"That's a nice one, lads."

Robbie McGlashan shouted from two carriages up, "Let's have that again. I like that one."

The journey seemed much shorter as they sang their way south. When we stopped at Crewe to change engines, Sergeant Armstrong came down the platform with a bottle of beer for each of us. "Compliments of the major." He winked at me. "He reckons you lads are doing a good job keeping them quiet."

"What is it like in the carriages?"

"The usual. They are all playing cards and most of them are losing. They're mugs. We can hear you singing sometimes when we stop at the points. Your lads are good singers."

"It calms the horses and they enjoy it."

We chose the quieter, country sections of track to clean out the horses. I imagine the farmers were happy to have their fields fertilised but we were happier to have rid ourselves of the smell. It was getting towards dark when we reached the siding close to our new camp. We were not far from the sea; we could smell it. The horses were led down the ramps and each section collected their own. We were the last off the train. I hoped that wouldn't mean we had the worst tents.

I knew that the Quartermaster Sergeant didn't particularly like me. It had been ever since John and Tom had spoiled our Christmas. It seems they had got into a fight in Burscough village and the sergeant's brother had received a black eye. He didn't deliberately go out of his way to make life hard but if he had a choice then we would always get second best.

Luckily for us, Major Harrison had made sure that our tents were on a dry part of the camp. Sergeant Armstrong and the major got on better than the major and some of the officers. In this instance, we were looked after.

I had never spent much time under canvas and it was an interesting experience. I knew that this would be the future. There would be no comfortable billets or barracks. The camp bed was no hardship but I wondered how it would stand up to the rigours of campaigning. We had no idea how long we would have to put up with these conditions. Perhaps peace would break out and this tension would not lead to war. The griffin suggested that this was serious and we wouldn't be going home any time soon.

The next day we received even more equipment. We all had a gas mask or as it soon became known, the *'google-eyed booger with the tit'*. They had a strange rubbery smell and I wondered if we would ever have to use them. When they brought the ones for the horses my heart sank. Even Caesar, a placid and docile horse, baulked when we had to put them on.

"Sarge, if we have to put these on in a hurry then how do we do it?"

I think old Sergeant Armstrong felt the same as we did but he had been obeying orders for years and he shrugged, "The same way as we do anything, practice and more practice."

In the end, we did not have enough time to practise. War was declared on August 4th 1914 and two days later we sailed for France. Our own war had begun. Many of the lads who boarded the boat would never see Blighty again. Even worse, many of the fine animals which we led across the sea to France would fall in a foreign field. To horseman like us, that was even worse; at least, as soldiers, we had had a choice. The horses just followed us and obeyed us. It was sad really.

Chapter 4

I think that the generals thought that we were ready for war. They were wrong. We were as unprepared for war as it was possible to be. We had fired our guns at targets and used live ammunition on a handful of occasions. We had played at war games once or twice but as we had all been wearing either bright red or blue armbands it hardly replicated war. This was not my view but the sergeants and officers like Major Harrison who had been to war themselves. I was lucky with my section; they were sensibly minded and down to earth. They were not expecting a glorious ride to victory over the fleeing Germans but some of those who came from places like Liverpool and Preston were confident that this would be a war won in a few weeks and the Lancashire Yeomanry were just the boys to do it.

We landed at Dunkirk. It was a cold windswept sandy beach. It reminded me of Southport. We unloaded the horses; they were becoming used to being transported. Colonel Mackenzie had gone ahead with the headquarters staff and that left Major Harrison to organise us. We rode east. This time we would have to erect our own tents. The major had the map coordinates but we had no idea what the terrain would be like. As it turned out it was a large farmer's field. I would have expected the farmer to be upset about a regiment of cavalry camping on his land but they were all worried about an army invading them who would not pay for the privilege: the Germans.

This time we had to lay out horse lines, dig latrines as well as erecting our tents too. By the time we had finished the field was a muddy morass which promised to become worse should we get any rain.

Our new officer, replacing Lord Burscough, was Lieutenant Ramsden. He was an affable young chap but terribly keen. He loved to volunteer for anything. We learned that he had been an officer at University and his uncle was Colonel Mackenzie. This was his chance to show what he had learned and we were his guinea pigs.

When the colonel returned from the briefing at the headquarters he held an officers' briefing. The keen lieutenant then called a meeting of his non commissioned officers. We were short of one sergeant and one corporal but as we only had twenty-five troopers in the troop that was not a problem.

The fresh-faced schoolboy rubbed his hands in anticipation. "Well chaps, Major Harrison must like us for he has given us the job of scouting the area to the east. What fun eh?"

Sergeant Armstrong looked at me and gave a slight shake of the head. "Sir, when you say east, can you be more specific?"

The question did not seem to bother the lieutenant. "Just find out what's up the road I expect."

I shifted in my seat, "Sir, do we have any maps?"

If I had spoken in Urdu I might have had the same response. He adopted a puzzled look and then said, "Maps?" His expression seemed to suggest he had never thought of them.

"Yes, sir, maps of the area. It might help. You know to find the roads."

It was as though a penny had actually dropped, "I say, what a capital idea."

Before he could embarrass himself any more Sergeant Armstrong said, "I'll get some from the adjutant sir. There are bound to be some."

"Jolly good. Well, see you tomorrow eh chaps? Reveille, breakfast and then tally ho!"

After he had gone we both burst out laughing. "He means well, William, but you and I will have to steer him in the right direction." I think he meant he would do the steering but I was touched that I was included in the comments.

I went around the men's tents warning them of the planned patrol. "Make sure you have all your equipment with you and that you have spares of anything which needs spares."

"Gas masks as well?" Jack Lynch was a happy go lucky trooper but if there was a line of least resistance then he would take it.

"Everything: full bandoliers of ammunition, swords, the lot. I want to be prepared for whatever we meet. I saw them all exchanging looks. "When we have done this for a week or so then we will have a better idea of what we are likely to meet and we can think about leaving spare equipment in the tents."

It had been easier when I had been one of the lads. They would have just listened to me. Now I was a corporal and a figure of authority. They would push the boundaries as far as they could. The trouble was I didn't know much more than they did. We relied heavily on Sergeant Armstrong.

I was awake and up well before reveille. I wanted to be sure that I was as fully prepared as possible. The gas masks and ammunition made for a heavy load and I was grateful that Caesar was such a big horse. I had cleaned my Lee Enfield the night before and sharpened my sword. I did not think it was likely we would need our swords but it paid to be ready.

I heard a noise behind me and turned to see Sergeant Armstrong yawning. He chuckled, "A good habit to get into William." He tapped his nose, "And it means you get fed first."

After we had saddled our horses we led them to the mess tent. There was a short hitching rail outside and we tied our mounts to it. It could only accommodate five horses and ours were the only ones there.

The mess tent was empty but there was the smell of breakfast in the air. The sergeant cook came from Manchester and was a blunt chap. "What the bloody hell are you two doing up? Have you wet the bed or summat?"

"No, we thought if we came early we might actually get something that was almost edible."

The cook snorted, "Doesn't matter when you get here; the food is always shite. It's what they give us to cook. Tea's up anyroad."

We poured ourselves a mug of hot steaming tea and loaded it heavily with sugar. We sat at one of the trestle tables and Sergeant Armstrong lit his pipe.

"Sarge, do you reckon we will see action today?"

"There's no point worrying about that. We have the hardest of jobs today; we are scouting. That means seeing them before they see you. If there is any action it will be upon you in a minute and over as fast. You have to react faster than the enemy." He shook his head and examined the glowing tobacco in his pipe. "I am too old for this game son. You will need your eyes, ears and wits. I can tell you what to do but I should be at home digging my garden and putting in my taters."

I was surprised at his morose attitude. "I didn't know you had a garden."

"I don't. That is the point. I should have one and I should be retired but I'm not up to the job."

"Then why stay in?"

"Because of you and the young lads. I can pass on what I have learned and some of you might survive. Others did it for me."

"It's ready!"

We wandered over to pick up our plates of hot steaming food. After we had laden the plates with even more food we went back to the table.

"I only know the cavalry. I joined when I was fourteen as a bugler and it's all I know. If I tried to retire and have a garden it would be a toss-up who would die first; me or my spuds!" He began to eat. "And this is a good lesson. Eat when you can; you never know when you will get the chance to eat again." I was learning that you ate when you could; who knew when your rations might dry up? George was a wise old bird.

The food was hot and filling. Despite the cook's comments, it was not bad. It was not like mum's cooking but I had eaten worse during the Yeomanry training sessions. I was hungry and it filled a hole.

Before we stood Sergeant Armstrong tapped out his pipe and said, "Today you ride at the front. Choose the best three men to be with you. Leave the lieutenant to me. I want you to assume there is a German behind every bush. There won't be but we will be safer that way."

"Yes, Sarge."

As reveille sounded we finished our food and we rode back to our tents. "Wakey, wakey rise and shine. Come on you lovely boys, the sun is cracking the flags!"

I smiled at the sergeant's words. Already a thin drizzle was in the air and it felt chilly despite the fact that it was August. The men dragged themselves out of their beds. I had had the luxury of time but they would have to rush to be ready for the patrol. They would have to shave quickly and then wolf down their food. I rode Caesar over to the stables. I needed to be there when my troop prepared their horses. It would need to be my eagle eye which spotted what they might forget.

The bleary-eyed troopers did need me. Between me and the sergeant, we made sure that our troop was equipped and ready to ride.

Lieutenant Ramsden was all polished leather and clean-cut cheeks. His servant, Carson, must have been up all night. "Well done chaps, good turn out." As he turned to face the same way as us he said quietly, to the sergeant, "I think we'll have to have a word about their appearance."

Sergeant Armstrong turned around. We had checked that everything was as it should be. "Why sir, what's wrong?"

"Some of them haven't shaved very well this morning. We have to impress the locals."

Sergeant Armstrong rolled his eyes, "Right sir, I'll have a word with the lads." He proffered two maps, one to me and one to the lieutenant. "I got these from the headquarters. I thought the corporal here could scout out the land ahead of us." I wondered if the lieutenant would argue but Sergeant Armstrong went on, "it will make it easier on us sir. Besides the major thinks the corporal is good at this sort of thing."

"Very well sergeant, but, Corporal Harsker, I want you to report to us the minute you spot anything."

"Yes, sir." I turned to the troopers behind me, McGlashan, Brown and Brown, with me."

I opened the map as I rode along. The sergeant had shown it to me earlier and I knew where we were going. He had wanted the lieutenant to think he was in charge! We had decided to head for Ypres. It was the largest place to the east of us. It was about twenty-seven miles away. Even if we could not reach it the patrol would give Sergeant Armstrong and me a better idea of how far we could travel in a day. We knew that from England but there we knew the roads. Here, everything was new.

I put the map away once I had confirmed that we were heading in the right direction. I turned to the three troopers behind me. "Keep your eyes peeled. We are looking for signs of Germans."

The early drizzle had stopped and the skies began to clear from the west. Within an hour we were feeling the effects of the sun. Caesar snorted and neighed. That was his nose telling him that water was close at hand. I waved the men to the north and we found a stream heading towards the sea. As the horses drank I checked the map. I now knew exactly where we were.

"Doddy, ride back to the lieutenant and tell him where the stream is. Their horses will be as tired and thirsty as ours. Then follow along the road until you catch up with us."

He grinned, "Right Corp."

I knew why he was happy; like me, he enjoyed riding and he enjoyed speed. He would gallop his horse back. We continued along the road. This was an easy duty. The sun was shining, the roads were flat and there were no Germans around. The rest of the day proved as uneventful. We halted at Poperinge for we could see Ypres in the distance.

When the rest of the patrol arrived I could see that the lieutenant was a little more hot and bothered than he had been. I saluted as he rode up, "No sign of any Germans sir. Ypres is probably an hour or so down the road."

The lieutenant took out his pocket watch, "Hm, I think that we will return to camp and make our report. We can ride to Ypres in the morning. Er, well done Corporal Harsker."

I took my four men to the rear of the column and we ate the others' dust on the way back. I had learned much on that first ride but I wished we had seen a German. The war just didn't seem real.

When we reached our camp we saw that it had grown. There was another Yeomanry regiment there, the Cumbrian Hussars. We were now a brigade. The rest of the regiment had had an easy day organising the camp. The lieutenant rushed off to report to the major while we led the men to the horse lines. Unlike the lieutenant, we still had a lot of work to do. Carson took two horses. I was glad that I was not an officer's servant. One horse was enough for me. I never thought, back at Burscough, that I would think that but I had far more to do out here.

That even, in the mess, we discovered that our brigade was out on a limb. The main BEF was many miles away, close to Mons. It was almost a hundred miles south-east of us. Colonel Mackenzie, according to the word around the camp, was not happy to be stuck out on the periphery of the war. We were just guarding an escape route back to Britain. Lieutenant Ramsden had obviously been chewed out when he sought the sergeant and me after we had eaten.

"The colonel wants us to find the Germans tomorrow. He was disappointed we didn't reach Ypres."

"Perhaps if we went south-east we might have more luck, sir?"

"You think so corporal? Well, we will leave earlier and push the men on eh?"

After he had left I wondered what the men would make of it. Another day in the saddle; we all liked riding but few of us had spent eight hours a day on the back of a horse. I smiled, "I'll go and give the lads the good news eh sarge?"

"Aye. Still, they might be better prepared tomorrow." He grinned, "Don't forget to tell them to shave a little better tomorrow eh?"

The men had learned their lesson and we were waiting patiently for the lieutenant to arrive. I noticed that he was not quite as smartly presented: perhaps Carson had been tired too. Like us, Carson had spent all day in the saddle. We pushed hard towards the south-east. An hour into the patrol we heard the unmistakable thunder of guns. Poor Tiny thought it was thunder and he looked at the cloudless sky and said to his big brother, "Thunder?"

"Nay, you dozy bugger. That's guns. We know where the Germans are."

Doddy was right it meant the two armies had collided; the question was where? "Take out your rifles but keep the safety on. We need to be prepared."

There was urgency now to our ride. I did not bother to send a message back to the rest of the patrol. They could hear the same guns we could and would be drawing their own conclusions. I just hoped that the lieutenant would remember to send the message back to the brigade. Failure to do so would result in more than a ticking off. We did not stop for a rest and another hour brought us just past the Belgian town of Heuvelland. The people there were busy packing their belongings into carts. None of them spoke English but they kept pointing to the east and shouting, "Boche! Boche!" We all knew that meant Germans.

"I think we'll wait here for the rest of the troop. Robbie, take the horses and water them. You lads come with me. We'll go to the edge of town."

It was a typical Belgian town. The houses ended and then there were fields. We found a house with a walled garden at the end of the road. It appeared to be deserted. "Get behind the wall and keep your eyes peeled."

I did not need to tell them to listen for the guns were cracking away in the distance. I could now see smoke. The clear blue sky helped. We could now discern the sound of small arms fire. There was a battle going on. The BEF and the Germans had met. Robbie came running up. "I found a river." He pointed ahead. "I worked out it must run over there somewhere."

That could be important. "Are the horses secured?"

"Yes Corp, tied up and eating from their nosebags."

"Good, come with me. You two lads stay here. I am going to see what is ahead." We ran down the road. I had slipped the safety catch off on my rifle. I knew that there was a battle ahead. Anything could happen. There could be a German patrol just like ours. At least our uniforms helped us to blend into the background; we had heard the Germans wore grey.

Robbie had been correct; the river did run to the south-west of the town. The bridge did not look to be in the best condition but soldiers could cross it. "You stay here and I will walk across to see how good it is."

It was a stone bridge but looked old enough to have been built by the Romans. I was concentrating so much on my feet that I didn't look up until I reached the other side. To my horror I saw grey uniformed horsemen; they were a mile away and heading towards me. I just turned and ran. "Robbie, get back! They are German cavalry!"

I know I should have counted and identified them but, to be honest, I was scared witless. I thought I was prepared but I wasn't. I heard their shouts and the thunder of their hooves but I resisted the urge to turn around. That would gain me nothing. I saw the village; it was two hundred yards away. I watched as Robbie hurled himself over the wall. I risked a look around. I turned and saw that they were Uhlans, lancers, and they were two hundred yards away. I lifted my Lee Enfield and fired three shots in rapid succession. Then I turned and ran without waiting to see the result. I honestly expected to hear the thundering hooves get closer and then feel a lance in my back. My three lads began to fire and I dived over the wall. My hat came off but I didn't care. I turned and lined up my rifle. I saw a horse and a German lying on the road. The others had ridden a little way off.

"That was close, Corp!"

"It was. Who got the horse and the rider?"

"You got the horse and Doddy got the rider."

"Well done Doddy!" I counted them. There were just ten of them. We had full bandoliers and they were armed with a lance. "Let's see how good these guns are. Pick your targets. I want accuracy, not just blind firing."

I aimed at someone who was gesticulating a lot. The range was over two hundred yards. I knew that the rifle would have a tendency to buck up and I aimed at the middle of his horse. I squeezed the trigger. There was a puff of smoke and then I saw him pitched from the horse. I don't think he was dead for he struggled to his feet. The other three fired too. I saw one man killed as someone's bullet hit him in the head. They had had enough and they withdrew to the bridge which was well out of range.

"Tiny, go with Robbie and bring up the horses." As they ran off I wondered where the rest of the patrol was. I had expected them before now.

Doddy spat, "How come they have them lances, Corp? Strikes me that they are neither use nor ornament."

"I think they are quite handy if you are charging men who are running away or cavalry armed with swords. They use the Uhlans like we use us; they are scouts, look." I pointed at the rider who had detached himself and was riding south-east from the bridge.

Just then I heard hooves behind us and saw Robbie and Tiny with the rest of the patrol fifty yards behind them.

The lieutenant reined in as I mounted Caesar. His voice seemed unnaturally high, "Report, Corporal Harsker."

"We followed the sound of the guns and found the villagers leaving. We had just found the bridge down there when the Uhlans appeared and they charged us."

"Uhlans? How do you know?"

"The lances sir, that was a bit of a clue."

Someone sniggered and Sergeant Armstrong shouted, "Quiet in the ranks!"

"Well done corporal. Get mounted. Right sergeant. Let's get after them."

"Do you think that is wise sir? Don't you think we ought to get back and report to the colonel?"

"Nonsense. These four have killed or wounded two or three of them and we need prisoners." He stood in his stirrups. "Forward! Sound the charge!"

I saw Sergeant Armstrong shake his head as the bugler sounded the charge. Even I knew that was unnecessary; it merely told the Germans what we intended. We did our duty and we followed the young lieutenant.

The Germans turned and fled. I swear I heard Lieutenant Ramsden shout, "View halloo," as though he was on a fox hunt. Gradually the

Uhlans began to pull away and this was the point at which we should have stopped, but of course, we didn't.

I heard Sergeant Armstrong shout, "Sir, the horses, we need to slow down."

There was no answer at first and then the squeaky voice of our leader shouted, "Trot."

Suddenly there was a ripple of gunfire from the trees ahead. Carson and his horse fell dead and Lieutenant Ramsden and the bugler both clutched their arms. It was lucky for all of us that we had Sergeant Armstrong for he shouted, "Retreat!" He grabbed the lieutenant's reins and pulled the horse back up the road. Jack Lynch did the same for the bugler, Taffy Jones. "Corporal, form a rearguard and give us cover."

"Right sarge! Doddy, Tiny, Robbie, with me. Open fire! Five shots rapid fire!" I chose those three as we had been under attack and we had fired already. We could not see the Germans but knew that they must be in the trees. I just fired my five shots at the tree line. As soon as I counted five shots I shouted, "Fall back!" Bullets were zipping around our heads like angry wasps but they were firing too high. We laid low over our saddles and I prayed we would survive.

When we reached the village Sergeant Armstrong had dismounted the rest of the patrol while he administered first aid to the wounded. "Well done, corporal. Keep an eye on them while I see to these two."

I heard the lieutenant say, "Carson, someone must go back for Carson."

"He's dead sir, forget him."

The sergeant's voice brought the reality of the war home to me. Carson had been alive and shaving his officer that morning and now he lay dead on some obscure Belgium road.

"Right lads make sure you have a full magazine."

Doddy pointed. "It looks like they have stayed where they were."

"Bloody good thing too." Tiny's indignation was matched by our silence.

I heard raised voices behind me. "I tell you, Sergeant Armstrong, I am perfectly capable of carrying on."

"With respect sir, you have lost a lot of blood and I am not a doctor. We need to get you back and looked at."

"I can be the judge of that!"

"And what about our news, Lieutenant Ramsden? We had no idea there were Germans this close to us and now we have infantry and cavalry." Suddenly there was a high pitched noise. "Get down!"

Although the shell exploded a hundred yards away the noise and the concussion deafened me. Dirt and debris showered down on us.

"Everyone, get mounted and get out of here!" No-one thought twice about obeying the sergeant's order.

I had been given the task of rearguard and I waited until the wounded had been helped on their horses and led away before I joined the tail of the patrol. There was another whine and this time the explosion sounded closer. The air was filled with dust and stones. Pieces of debris struck my back too. It felt as though had thrown a handful of pebbles at me. Poor Caesar leapt forward as though I had slapped him. "Steady boy, we are leaving. And not before time too!"

Chapter 5

Sergeant Armstrong sent a rider ahead to the camp. By the time we reached our new home, it was as though someone had upset an ant's nest. The news had alarmed the Brigadier.

Sergeant Armstrong was waiting for me. "You take the lads to the horse lines and I will go and report to the colonel."

"Right sarge."

As I turned to walk away he suddenly said, "Bloody hell! You are wounded!"

"Don't be daft." As I turned to face him I saw that Caesar's rump was flecked with blood.

"You are, son! Get to the doctor. You have been hit by shrapnel. Brown, take Caesar to the vet."

I handed over the reins but I felt a fraud. It was Caesar who was wounded, not me. I obeyed orders and headed for the medical tent. The orderly saw me and smiled, "Come to see how the lieutenant is?"

"No sarge, I have been told I am wounded."

He looked at me and said, "Turn around." I did so. "And they are right. Your back is covered in blood. You have been lucky me old mate. Come in here and we'll get your clothes off."

It was only when he took off my leather webbing and bandoliers that I saw what he meant. The leather had been almost cut through by the tiny pieces of metal but the amount of leather we wore had saved my life. My uniform was shredded as was my shirt.

I heard the doctor sigh, "What a mess but you have been lucky." The orderly swabbed my back down and there was a cool stinging sensation. "This may hurt but I am saving the drugs for slightly more serious cases."

He was right it did hurt as he dug out the tiny fragments of the shell. It hurt even more when the alcohol was used to disinfect it. The orderly handed me a new shirt. "Here you are, a new one. You had better see the quartermaster for the rest of your equipment. And you had better take the ruined uniform and webbing. You know what they are like."

"Thanks."

He shook his head, "I think that we can safely say that our war started today."

"Amen to that."

"And I hear you left one out there?"

"Aye, Carson, the lieutenant's batman."

The orderly shook his head, "I have a feeling it won't be the last."

I think I was lucky in that I was the first to go to the quartermaster for my replacement equipment; he handed it over without any fuss. As the war went on he became increasingly reluctant to part with his new equipment.

I went directly to the vet's and I was relieved that Caesar looked quite happy. The vet was the village vet and I knew him well. "You were both lucky, Billy Boy. Caesar is fine and after a good night's sleep will be fit for duty."

I led my mount to the horse lines. It had been a rude awakening for me. I could have been the second death in the regiment. I was the last to reach the mess and Sergeant Armstrong was waiting for me. "What did the doc say?"

"That I was lucky!"

"And he was right. That dozy young bugger nearly got us all killed. If the Boche had been a bit sharper with that first shell we would all be dead now."

"How is he?"

He gave a derisory snort, "Flesh wound! The way he is going on you would think it was worthy of the V.C.!"

Just then Squadron Sergeant Ritchie burst into the tent. "Right lads eat and run. The Germans have broken through our lines. We are on our own. The colonel wants us ready to move by dawn. We pack everything we can tonight and just drop the tents in the morning." He turned to the cooks, "No hot food in the morning. Get some bully beef on bread."

There was a groan from some of the non commissioned officers but I wondered why we weren't moving straight away.

"If I was the colonel I would be heading south now sarge."

"Aye and so would I but we don't know the roads and it would be too easy to be ambushed." He finished mopping up the last of his gravy with his bread. "This is a fine start eh? Nearly caught with our trousers down and we have only been over here for five minutes."

It was still dark when we broke camp. To be fair to Squadron Sergeant Ritchie, he timed it perfectly. The sun was peering over the horizon as the last tent was put into the wagon and the colonel waved our troop forward. It seems that our zealous Lieutenant Ramsden had persuaded the colonel to let us scout again. In light of the previous day, the sergeant and I thought it was a mistake.

"Corporal Harsker, you did such a fine job yesterday that your section can lead again. I know you won't let me down."

I bit back any retort I might have made. My back was just irritated but it was a reminder of how close death had come. I would be careful but it was not him I was worried about letting down, it was my men. As we trotted down the road I briefed my three companions. "We know a bit more about the Germans now lads. Watch out for ambushes in the trees and keep your rifles ready."

We were all good enough riders to cope with a heavy Lee Enfield in our right hands. It was reassuring. I had been pleased with its performance against the Germans but I knew that we might not be lucky enough to meet lancers again. Our opponents might have rifles too.

The nature of the lands and the road which had appealed so much when we first rode down them now worked against us. The land was flat and you could only see as far as the next bend. I rode at the front next to Robbie. The Brown boys peered towards the sides of the tree-lined roads. We could hear, as we rode along, the crackle of small arms fire. Occasionally there was the unmistakeable stutter of a heavy machine gun. What was missing, thankfully, was the crump of artillery.

This time we were seen before we saw them. There was a crack of rifle fire ahead. Whoever had fired had done so too early and the bullet whizzed harmlessly over our heads. It warned us of the presence of the enemy. We raised our rifles and fired a short burst in the direction of the trees.

"Back to the patrol!"

This time the lieutenant was keeping the patrol closer to us. They heard the firing and met us just two hundred yards from the ambush. Sergeant Armstrong reacted first, "Trooper Smith, ride back to the column and say we have encountered the enemy."

As the trooper rode off the officer gave him an irritated look, "Thank you, sergeant, but perhaps, next time you might wait…"

"Sir, with respect we have an enemy to shift." He turned in the saddle, "Troop, dismount. Skirmish order!"

The lieutenant had a temporary batman in the shape of Trooper Teer. He also took the sergeant's horse.

As Robbie led our horses away I took the Brown boys back down the lane. We kept low as we ran. When we reached the place they had fired on us I waved the lads down and we peered through the bushes. I could see dark shapes in the woods ahead. "Pick your targets boys; we need to know numbers."

I aimed at a grey-black shape and squeezed the trigger. I was rewarded with a yell and a fusillade of fire. As we were lying down and they were aiming for kneeling men the shots whizzed harmlessly overhead. Soon the three of us were firing almost as rapidly as we could work our bolts. The Germans were standing and it made them easier targets, even though they thought they were hidden in the woods.

Sergeant Armstrong and the lieutenant appeared behind me. As bullets hurtled towards us I shouted, "Get down! Sir!"

Sergeant Armstrong threw himself to the road. Lieutenant Ramsden looked as though it was beneath him. The sergeant said, "Sir, you'll get your head blown off this way."

"Thank you, sergeant." He complied with my shout albeit reluctantly.

Sergeant Armstrong said, "Corporal Harsker, can you and your lads work your way down the road and try to flank them?"

"If you can give us covering fire."

He shouted to the nearest troopers, "Crawl here and give rapid-fire at those trees!" He raised his gun and emptied the magazine.

I said to the Brown boys, "Put a fresh magazine in. Then when I shout, run like buggery up the lane. Watch me, when I drop, you drop."

I waited until I heard the rest of the troop open fire and then I shouted, "Run!" I ran as fast as I could. I heard the bullets but they were behind me. There was one cry of pain but I could not afford the time to turn. After a hundred yards I dropped. Doddy crashed next to me and then Tiny. Tiny had lost his hat. He snarled, "The bastards shot me hat, Corp!"

"Are you alright?"

"Aye, it just nicked me head. I've had worse cuts shaving."

"Right let's work our way in the woods and try to flank them."

The hedgerow had hidden us from their view and we slithered under the lower branches and snaked our way towards the enemy we knew were ahead of us. I saw a flash of grey and I tapped Doddy on the shoulder. He dropped as did his brother. I pointed ahead and they both nodded. I raised my rifle as I sighted it on the pickelhaube. I lowered my rifle and fired. There was a cry and the figure pitched forwards. I heard the rifles of my two men as they barked and I sighted on the infantryman who was aiming his gun my direction. The Lee Enfield has a fast action and I fired before he could get his shot off. I was less than fifty yards away and I saw his face explode as the .303 bullet entered his head and smashed through the back of his skull.

Suddenly I heard the terrifying sound of a machine gun as they began firing in our direction. I just lay down and pressed myself into the ground. Bits of branches and leaves cascaded down on my head and my body. I braced myself for the sudden impact of one of the bullets but it never came. When the gun stopped, they needed reloading I suspected, I raised my head and my gun. I saw the gunner a hundred yards away. He was standing to reload the gun and I fired. He fell dead across the gun. Doddy emptied his magazine at the gun and then shouted, "Sod this!" He stood and charged. His brother followed and I had no choice but to join them.

We all roared as we ran. This was no battle cry but it was the adrenalin and emotion of the charge. Miraculously the bullets coming in our direction missed us. I fired from the hip as I ran. We had no bayonets fitted and would have to improvise once we closed with them. I saw an officer level his pistol at me. I dropped to my knees, worked the bolt and fired. The bullet hit him in the chest and he fell backwards.

I heard the bugle sound the charge. The Germans had had enough and they began to stream away east. Doddy and Tiny were swinging their rifles like clubs and looked, for all the world, like some medieval warriors. I ran to the dead officer. He had a surprised look on his face. I took the pistol from his hand. Another second or two and I would be dead. It was my first souvenir. I took his holster and ammunition pouch too.

The rest of the troop appeared and I saw the relief on the sergeant's face. "You are mad buggers! Why did you charge?"

Doddy shrugged, "It was bloody dangerous with that machine gun firing at us sarge."

"That was brave work, I am proud of you."

Just them Major Harrison appeared and took in the scene with the dead bodies. "Well done, sergeant."

It was only then I realised I couldn't see the lieutenant.

"It wasn't me sir, it was Corporal Harsker and the Brown boys. They charged a flaming machine gun."

Major Harrison shook his head. He was still the schoolmaster who couldn't understand the schoolboy prank. "Write me a report, sergeant. By the way, where is Lieutenant Ramsden?"

"With the horses, sir." There was no criticism in the sergeant's voice; it was just matter of fact.

"Very well. Better get your men mounted. Search the officers and sergeants for any maps or papers."

When the sergeant saw the missing gun and holster he grinned, "I see you got yourself a little reminder of this day?"

I blushed a little, "Well I…"

"Look after yourself Billy Boy, you are learning."

We gave the papers to the major. He examined them and Lieutenant Ramsden shuffled up, looking a little shamefaced. "Damned arm! I can't move as fast as I wanted to."

I saw the look exchanged between the major and the sergeant. They were not taken in by the protestations from the young lieutenant.

"From these maps and papers, it seems that these men are from the 1st Army of Von Kluck. It looks like they are trying to sweep around the flanks of our army."

Even I knew what that meant. We had to get through the whole of the 1st Army to reach our own lines. Lieutenant Ramsden was standing next to the major and I saw him pale. "Could we not go back to Dunkirk and get taken home?"

The pitying look given to him by both the old soldiers made him retreat. They did not bother answering him. "I'll tell the colonel." He looked at me. "Are you and your men still happy to be the sharp end, William?"

I smiled, "Yes sir, but I wouldn't mind another couple of lads. If we use a horse holder then there are only three of us."

He nodded at Sergeant Armstrong who said, "Take Lynch and Foster."

The two troopers were quite happy to be selected. At this stage of the war, it was exciting for young lads. It was all still a lark. The dark days had yet to come. I felt happier knowing there were six of us. It was more firepower.

The major waved me over. "We'll try to avoid the Germans by heading due south towards Lys."

We quickly watered and fed our horses; their welfare came first. I gathered the five men I was to lead around me. "If we are attacked we give five volleys. Listen for my orders. Jack, you and Robbie ride close to me. Brian, you and the Brown boys watch the woods. "I grinned, "They are good at that." They nodded proudly. "But Tiny, even though you are a good soldier you are still a big bugger, keep your bleeding head down."

He suddenly flourished a hat, like a conjurer with a rabbit, "I found it, Corp!"

I took it from him and put my finger through the hole. "And that is how close your brother came to having to tell your mam that you were dead!" I could see he hadn't thought it through and he contritely dropped his head. "Right, let's get mounted."

I felt more comfortable now with a trooper on either side of me. Our six eyes could cover more of the ground ahead of us. We were moving faster now. It ran the risk of running into the enemy but it was now a race to see if we could get to our army before the gap was closed.

Suddenly, as we rounded a bend in the road, I saw a machine gun being set up in the road. I had little time to think. The hedgerow was just four feet high and there was a field beyond. "Over the hedge! Now!" To their credit my section obeyed. I knew that Caesar would clear the obstacle and I hoped that the others would too. As I landed I turned, "Foster, get back to the sergeant and warn him about the machine gun. Tell him we will try to deal with it. The rest of you, follow me. And keep low in the saddle."

The field was filled with wheat and was protected by a hedge. I knew that the machine gun would not be able to turn; we just needed to contend with the riflemen accompanying it. There was a lone tree close to the edge of the field. I rode there. "Tie your horses to the branches."

Robbie looked at me, "Bit risky Corp? Suppose they run away?"

"You are right. You can be horse holder."

He shook his head, "No, I was just saying like. You are in charge."

"Good then let's go. Spread out in a skirmish line; the Brown boys to my right. You two to my left. Don't fire until I say."

I heard orders being shouted in German and then the machine gun opened up. It wasn't firing at us and I wondered who was getting the worst of its wicked bite. There was a crack from before us and then smoke from the guns of the hidden Germans.

"Down! Open fire!"

I saw a pair of legs below the hedge and I fired three shots. I heard a scream as their owner fell. I moved my gun up and to the left and fired three more. All I could hear now was the shouts of the Germans and the sound of bullets. I had no idea if we were hitting anyone.

"Forward!" As we ran towards the hedge I thought that a bayonet would come in handy. I had no idea why we had not been issued with them. When we reached the hedge I could see the Germans on the other side. I think they were more surprised to see us. I didn't need to give any orders I emptied my gun. I saw a gun being levelled at me and I remembered the officer's Luger. I pulled it out of my tunic and hoped the safety was off. I pulled the trigger until the gun clicked empty. The remaining Germans held up their hands. We had our first prisoners. We climbed over the hedge, keeping them covered. All of us were grinning. This was easy. Then I heard Doddy say, "Jesus Christ!"

I looked to where he was pointing. In the road were the dead horses and trooper. The machine gun had been slaughtering them.

"You bastard!"

I turned as Tiny swung his rifle at the machine gunner. "Leave it out Brown, he was doing his job. Disarm them and search them for papers." I saw that we had killed their officers and sergeants which explained their surrender. I desperately wanted to see who had been killed but I knew what my duty was.

"Robbie, go and get the horses." I ran down the road to see where the Germans had gone. I could see them, in the distance, fleeing away from us. If it had been cavalry it would have been a different matter.

By the time I reached the scene of devastation and death, Robbie had returned with the horses.

"Here you are, Corp. These are all the papers and maps they had." Doddy grinned as he handed them over. He proudly showed me his Luger. "And a little souvenir for me too."

"Thanks Doddy. We'll have to watch out for ammunition. These are nine millimetres I think." I shoved the papers into my tunic. Mount up. I think we will be finding a different route this time. Move the prisoners along."

We had six prisoners and two were wounded. Doddy glared at them as he shouted, "Move!" It was not German but they understood.

When we reached the rest of the troop I saw that we had lost at least six men and five horses. I watched as Sergeant Armstrong put the fifth out of its misery. The angry looks thrown in Lieutenant Ramsden's direction told me who they blamed.

Colonel Mackenzie rode up and he had an angry red and serious face. "Put the dead in the wagons. Were there any papers amongst the dead?"

"Yes, sir." I handed them over.

He nodded and gave them to Major Harrison, "This the chap you were telling me about?"

"Yes sir, Corporal Harsker."

The colonel pointed down the road. "Your work, Corporal?"

"Yes sir, we flanked them and attacked the gun. I am just sorry we couldn't save the lads sir."

"Not your fault son." He glared at the lieutenant. "Someone panicked. Well Corporal, as of now you are acting sergeant."

"Thank you, sir."

"Don't mention it. You have come out of the last couple of actions with great credit." He turned to Major Harrison, "Well Charles, how do we get out of this dilemma?"

"Head for Calais sir."

"Right. " He turned and shouted, "Someone get these prisoners secured. Sergeant Harsker, do you have the map?"

"Yes, sir."

"Then find us a way to Calais but try to avoid Germans this time eh?" He was smiling as he said it and I felt relieved. I had blamed myself for the machine-gunning of my comrades. I saw now that I was not responsible. As I mounted Caesar I saw Sergeant Armstrong smile and nod. He appeared happy and that pleased me.

Chapter 6

My first task as a sergeant, albeit acting and I completed it, successfully. We reached Calais without further incident and we set up camp east of the port. There was still a great deal of confusion about where the front line was but the presence of the British and French warships in the harbour were reassuring.

Once we had erected the tents and seen to the horses I had time to speak with Sergeant Armstrong. "What happened, sarge?"

He smiled, "We are both sergeants now and it's George."

I nodded, "George then, but it will take some getting used to."

"Mr Ramsden decided that we could charge the gun and reach it before they fired. He ordered the lads to charge." He shook his head. "They never stood a chance. As soon as the first ones fell I shouted to fall back and then you and your boys attacked. That saved us. It was a waste of horses and men."

"But why did he do it? It seems stupid."

He gave me a wry look, "That may be your fault, Bill."

"Mine?" I was mystified. I had been nowhere near him.

"Not directly of course, but everyone was going on, the major, the colonel, everyone, about how gutsy it was of you and the Brown boys to have attacked that emplacement the day before. The difference was he didn't lead. He just ordered the charge."

Quartermaster Sergeant Grimes walked in and saw me, "I hear you are sergeant now?"

"Yes, Quartermaster Sergeant."

"You've done well but just make sure it doesn't go to your head. It's only temporary, remember."

He strode off. George shook his head, "He was always a miserable bugger but he is a good cavalryman."

"It seems daft having two sergeants when the troop is only twenty odd men strong."

"We should have a couple of corporals so you will have to do the work of two men. Mind, those Brown boys look useful."

"They are but they tend to rush into things; a bit like the lieutenant."

George's face became serious, "No, Bill, he just sends others to do his dirty work. I don't think his uncle was impressed."

Over the next two days, we sent out patrols to see where the Germans were. Thankfully they were further east than we were. Orders finally arrived for the brigade to continue its move south to rejoin the BEF which was now digging in around Amiens. Once again we decamped and, once again, it was left to our troop to scout. We had organised the troop so that I had my nine scouts and Sergeant Armstrong led the rest. We had discounted the lieutenant who was a nominal leader at best. He now deferred to George on almost every matter. We would not have to ride the gauntlet of death which our dead comrades had.

Doddy and I had managed to acquire some ammunition for our Lugers. I suspect the colonel would have disapproved but it was handy having a gun which could fire eight shots off even quicker than a rifle. We now had better intelligence than when we had moved south from Dunkirk. The armies of both the French and British were retreating towards Paris and Von Kluck's Corps were ahead of us. We had grown up in the last week and were much more cautious. We checked every bush and hedge to see what lurked behind it. The colonel came to see us as we were preparing to leave.

"The main column will keep to the roads but, Sergeant Harsker, your men can roam at will. You have shown how resourceful you are and the country hereabouts is perfect for cavalry; use it. Find the enemy before he finds us!"

"Yes, sir."

He turned to Lieutenant Ramsden, "And lieutenant, keep in close contact with the rest of the regiment."

"Yes, sir." We could all hear the warning in the colonel's words.

I was happy to have the freedom to ride across the open fields. It meant we were less likely to run into an enemy ambush. I knew that it would be unlikely that they would set up an ambush; they were chasing the French and British towards Paris. Once again we had to find a way through the German Corps.

I had already checked the map out and saw a number of places where we could cut across country where the roads curved. It was an uneventful patrol until early in the afternoon. Doddy suddenly hissed, "There Corp, sorry, Sarge."

I saw where he was pointing. There were lances visible above the hedgerow which lined the road. "Jack, ride back to Sergeant Armstrong and tell him there are lancers on the road ahead. The brigade will have to head further west." I quickly scanned the map. They would be able to take a side road but it would add another five miles to our journey. The colonel had hoped to rejoin the army by nightfall.

I took out my rifle and the rest followed suit. "Let's get a closer look at them. Keep low in the saddle."

Once again our brown uniforms helped us to blend in with the freshly tilled field over which we rode. Soon we could see the grey uniforms riding along the road. I dismounted and handed my reins to Doddy. I whispered, "Keep the men here."

I trotted over to the hedge which was thirty yards away and peered through. I could see down the road and this looked to be the lead regiment. They were Uhlans, much like the ones we had encountered the first day. As I peered left I could see the infantry stretching away to the north. If the sergeant and the regiment had continued on their road they would have run slap-bang into them.

I turned and ran back to Caesar. Suddenly there was the crack of a rifle. I had been spotted. I leapt on Caesar's back. If we rode back to the troop then I would be leading the Germans to the regiment. I had to lay a false trail and that meant heading south. A line of Uhlans emerged through a gap lower down the field.

"Give them five shots and then follow me." I knew that we could not hope to hit many but I wanted them to be wary of us. I aimed at the lead rider and then lowered my gun slightly. I fired five times and then shouted, "Follow me!" We had managed to hit a couple of them but they were now galloping obliquely to cut us off. I put my rifle in its boot and urged Caesar on. I kept glancing over my shoulder. Caesar could outrun anything and I had to keep my patrol together.

I saw a fence looming up and we soared over it. My handpicked men were also good riders and they followed suit. The Uhlans were no slouches when it came to riding but they had lances and they came over slightly slower than we had. A lead began to open. A second fence was cleared and I began to think that we might escape. Suddenly we struck the road and another squadron of Uhlans was hurtling down towards us. They must have taken the road to cut us off.

"Doddy, lead them west. I'll follow." I took out my rifle. I had five shots left in the magazine and I emptied them in the direction of the Germans. A horse and rider fell. I booted my rifle and turned to follow my men. I soon caught up with Robbie who was at the rear. The going was easier but the hedgerows on both sides prevented an easy escape. I glanced over my shoulder and saw that the leading lancers were closing fast. I took out the Luger. As I turned I saw that the lance with its fluttering guidon was barely five feet from Caesar's rump. I opened fire with the gun and saw the horror on the German's face as four shots struck him and his horse. They tumbled to the ground and the others had to slow to clear the dead horse and rider. Once again I had bought us some time but I had emptied my gun. My only weapon now would be my sword and that would be no match for the lances.

I began to overtake my men; Caesar was eating up the ground. I saw a gap in the hedge ahead. "Doddy! Take the gap!" He raised his hand in acknowledgement and the patrol hurtled through. I saw, ahead, a derelict barn. We would have to hold them there. I needed to make sure that the brigade could slip by this German advance.

"Head for the barn. Take cover and then fire at the Uhlans." I was counting on the fact that they might only have handguns. It also meant we would give the horses a breather. This could be a long chase.

The barn had broken doors at each end. We had an escape route if we needed it. As soon as we were through we flung ourselves from our mounts. Doddy and Tiny were already firing even as I tied Caesar to a wooden rail. I drew my rifle and began loading the magazine. As soon as it clicked home I brought the gun up and fired at the grey uniforms heading towards us. The nine rifles spat lead at a prodigious rate. The Uhlans were in a single column and the wall of bullets scythed through the leading riders. The ones at the rear broke away and spread around the barn.

"Doddy, you and Tiny stay here with Robbie. The rest of you come with me."

We ran to the rear doors and reached it just as the lancers wheeled around the side of the barn. We had no time to aim. We just fired at them. Inevitably some of the shots hit horses but we hit enough Uhlans to make them withdraw. I saw Eddie Low holding his leg. "What's up Eddie?"

"Bloody German stuck me with his pig sticker!"

"Robbie, put a dressing on it."

I went to the door and peered out. The Uhlans were heading for the far side of the field. They had us surrounded. "How many Germans are on your side, Doddy?"

"Forty or so!"

"There are only twenty this side. Reload, then mount up and be ready to charge these twenty. Hold your fire until we are on top of them."

Caesar was still not breathing normally but I knew he would cope. I was not so sure about the other horses. "Robbie, keep your eye on Eddie."

"I'm alright sarge. It's just a scratch!"

I kicked Caesar on and the others followed. The Uhlans just charged in a line directly at us. They outnumbered us and they knew how hard it was to fire a gun from the back of a moving horse. I held the Lee Enfield in both hands. I aimed at the leading rider. I waited until the barrel was pointing down and fired. Caesar's movement brought the barrel up and the bullet smashed a hole in the German's horse's head. As the animal fell the Uhlan was pitched forward. There was a sickening crunch as Caesar's hoof shattered his skull. My second shot winged an Uhlan who dropped his lance and then I was through. I reined Caesar around. I saw one Uhlan about to spear Doddy in the back. I fired and the bullet cracked into his leg and he too dropped the lance. The rest were all through although I could see Robbie holding his arm. He had been wounded as well.

We headed through the gate and found a road. The sun was lower in the sky and I led the patrol west to find the regiment. The Germans had had enough. There was no pursuit.

Two miles down the road we halted to apply a field dressing to Robbie's arm. "We were lucky there sarge. If they had had guns then we would have been dead."

"I know Robbie. I am just glad that the cavalry we have met have been lancers."

I had sent Doddy ahead to scout out the land before us. When he returned he shook his head. "No sign of the regiment." He shrugged. "They could be anywhere."

"No, they couldn't. They have to head south and then east to reach the BEF. We will take the next road which goes south and then try to find one that goes south-east." As the patrol mounted I examined the map. We had changed directions so many times that I had no real idea of where we were. My best guess was that we were north of Amiens. If we couldn't find the regiment then I would head there and wait.

We heard guns as we found a road going southeast. From the signs, I knew that it ended up at Amiens. "Keep your eyes peeled for any signs that our lads have passed down this road."

Suddenly we heard the sound of hooves coming along the road behind us. "Sarge, there are riders approaching!" Surely the Germans hadn't picked up our trail again? Fortunately, we had all reloaded and could use our awesome firepower if it was the Uhlans again.

"About face and have your guns ready!"

We wheeled our horses along the road and waited for whoever came thundering down the French road. To our relief, it was Jack Lynch and the rest of the troop.

Sergeant Armstrong had a grin on his face. "We heard the firing in the distance and wondered if it was you." He noticed the bandaged troopers and said, "I see you were lucky again."

"Report, Sergeant Harsker." The lieutenant's whine snapped my head around.

I saluted the lieutenant, "Sir! We ran into some Uhlans and some infantry. I decided not to head back to the brigade and we led them away. After a skirmish, we lost them and made our way here."

He frowned, "If you had led them to the brigade we might have had a great victory."

I saw George roll his eyes as I continued. "The trouble was, sir, that we didn't know how many infantry there were with them. It looked to be the same Uhlans we met the other day and that means they are Von Kluck's Corps."

"Hm, well next time find the exact numbers. That is, after all, what a scout is supposed to do. I will report to the colonel. Carry on Sergeant Armstrong."

As he rode away George said, "What a waste of space he is. He hasn't the first clue. You did the right thing and the major will agree with you."

"The trouble is, when you are out in front you have to make instant decisions. I don't know if they are right or not."

"They are, so don't worry about it." He pointed down the road, "What about Amiens?"

"We were heading there. As the Germans are behind us then perhaps it is still in our hands."

George looked at me, "You and your lads take it easy. The rest of the troop will scout. It's time we shared it around."

"I don't mind, George."

"I know but that doesn't make it right. There are troops behind us who have done nothing but erect tents since we arrived here. Some of them don't even know there is a war on." He turned to his men, "Right then you lazy buggers, let's see how this is done."

It felt strange to ride knowing that we would have warning of any trouble. When Lieutenant Ramsden reached us he asked, "Where is Sergeant Armstrong?"

"Scouting sir. He said we deserved a rest."

"Hm, I think that should have been my decision."

Lieutenant Ramsden sounded so petty as he sulked that it was pathetic. I tried to keep the derision out of my voice when I said, "Well sir, you weren't here so I think he took the decision himself."

I consciously kicked Caesar on and rode next to Robbie. "How's the arm?"

"Just feels numb sarge. It was stupid really I should have leaned out of the way. I could see the lance heading for me. I was sort of frozen. I felt stupid when the blood flowed."

"I know. I had no idea I had been hit by the shrapnel either. I think we are all going to learn to be quick or we'll soon be dead."

As night began to fall I wondered if the colonel would camp for the night. Luckily we reached the outskirts of Amiens before the decision was taken. We found Sergeant Armstrong having a cup of tea with a gun crew. The sergeant saluted, "Looks like we still hold Amiens, sir."

"Jolly good sergeant. Wait here and I'll go and tell the colonel."

The artillery sergeant shook his head. "He looks like an arse-licker to me."

George nodded, "He's always keen to give the colonel any news he can." He pointed to the east. "Seems like we have given the Hun a bloody nose yonder."

"Don't count on any rest, pal. We will be falling back soon. There are thousands of Germans out there and they have much bigger guns than these pea shooters. You, donkey wallopers, are lucky; you can ride faster than their infantry can attack."

As if to emphasise the point there was a sudden screech and scream as a German gun hurled a shell over our heads to explode a mile or so closer to Amiens.

"See what I mean? The bastards do that every so often. I bet they are laughing their heads off."

We waited until the colonel arrived. "Well done you, lads. We have finally managed to reach our lines. I just hope that this is the last time we have to retreat."

Having spoken to the sergeant of artillery I was not too sure but we made our way to Amiens. The Military Police directed us to a field south of the town where we could erect our tents. It was not a perfect site but it was dry. As the war went on then mud began to play an increasing part. But on that last day of August, the ground was dry and the weather was clement.

The colonel went to a briefing with the local commander. The *Griffin* soon followed his return. The rest of the BEF were much further east and we were amongst the only British forces in the middle of the French Sixth Army. Our camp would, perforce, be a temporary one and we prepared to leave early the next day. There was a regiment of French Cuirassiers close to us and they looked to be a throwback to the days of knights. They had breastplates and metal helmets I wondered how they would cope with machine guns. That night we heard that our Cavalry Division, with the best cavalry in the country, had been defeated at Le Cateau. It did not bode well for the future.

We were awoken before dawn by an enemy barrage. We would not have a leisurely ride back to Field Marshal Sir John French. The whole of Von Kluck's Corps was advancing towards Paris and we were in the way. It was fortunate that we had had much practice in taking down tents in a hurry. Once again we were chosen to be the scouts. We now had a nickname: the Forlorn Hope. As the only troop to have suffered casualties we took it as a badge of honour.

We reached Néry on the 31st of August. We were exhausted and our mounts needed serious rest. We were running short of ammunition as well as other vital supplies. We were close enough to the General Headquarters at Dammartin, to be able to see the staff officers as they hurried in and out like so many busy, red-hatted, worker ants. There did not seem to be a lot of order about their movements. To me, they looked like ants when their nest is disturbed.

We had not even had the chance to begin to erect the tents when we heard the fire of small arms. We had no idea where the enemy were but we assumed it was to the north of us. Colonel Mackenzie had had enough of retreating and he ordered the whole brigade north. Suddenly we saw a German Cavalry division; they were hurtling after the retreating British infantry who were trying to avoid the lances and sabres of the grey-clad Germans. The General staff emerged from their building as though it was on fire. They leapt for their cars as the colonel ordered the charge against the Germans.

It was not good country for cavalry but we had no choice, we had to fight where we could. I saw the colonel and many of the officers with their swords out. I turned to my men. "Use your guns! I think these Germans may be better swordsmen than we are."

Doddy and I took out our Lugers and checked they were ready to fire. I know that the rest of my men were all looking for the chance to get a pistol too. They had seen the effect they had.

It was not the meeting of two mighty beasts but rather a chance encounter. We met the enemy piecemeal. I slowed my men down as we approached the Germans. They were too busy trying to sabre the helpless, retreating footsloggers. I aimed my rifle and began to fire at every grey uniform I could see. I was not as accurate as I would have been if stationary but my men and I caused enough disruption for the infantry to escape. When the Huns saw us they changed direction. My rifle empty, I took out the Luger and shot the first two surprised Germans who thought to make a pin cushion out of me.

A rider approached from my left. As his sword swung down I leaned to my right and fired. The bullet smashed his hand and he fell screaming to the ground. My Luger was now empty and I had to, reluctantly, take my sword out. It was sharp and that was about it. I was not confident about its use. I glanced to my left and saw that George and the rest of the troop were also reduced to the use of a blade.

The first German I fought obliged me by coming from my right. I knew I was not skilful but I was strong and I swung the sword overhand with all my might. The smaller German tried to parry but my blow was so hard that he fell backwards from his horse. The second German came at me from my left. I yanked on Caesar's reins. I must have done so too hard for he reared a little and his hooves flailed the air before him. I am a good rider and I managed to shift my weight forward and keep my seat. The Hun was not so lucky. His horse tried to jerk out of the way and, as Caesar landed I slashed down with my blade and caught the German across the back. The blade was sharp and I saw blood on the edge as the rider fled the field.

I heard recall and sighed with relief. This had been my first action in a real battle. As I looked down the line I saw that, although there were many dead Germans there were troopers lying dead and dying amongst them. The Germans had retreated and so we went amongst the dead and dying to offer assistance. Doddy and I took the opportunity of filching more ammunition whilst Tiny, Robbie and Jack manage to acquire guns of their own.

Our troop had only suffered wounds but, as we continued south, towards the Marne we discovered that the rest of the regiment had lost fifteen men. I rode next to George. "Are all cavalry battles like that?"

He shrugged, "That was my first one. In the Boer War, we fought as mounted infantry. The South Africans preferred to hit and run. That is the first time I have had to use my sword."

"Me too and I didn't enjoy it." A thought suddenly struck me, "Where was the lieutenant in all this?"

"Did you not see? His sling miraculously appeared and he stayed with the bugler just behind us."

The lieutenant had shed his sling some days earlier. I am not saying he was a coward but he didn't like to risk his own life. I think that the war games he had played at University had given him a slightly distorted view of what battle would be like. For the ordinary lads, like me, we had no expectation; all we had was the belief that we were fighting for King and Country and that we would do our duty.

Chapter 7

We reached the Marne and finally stopped running. Doddy joked that any further south and we would be in Paris. For us Paris was exotic and filled with ladies who would promise much; it was every soldier's dream to have leave in Paris. It did not materialise and our camp on the Marne was as close as we got. We did use the four-day respite from battle well. We were able to feed, water and groom our mounts and restore them to some semblance of fitness. The Quartermaster acquired more ammunition for us. My scouts were already well stocked with German ammunition. We had learned that you could never have too many magazines nor too much ammunition. Doddy also managed to get us some bayonets. I didn't ask where he got them but he and his brother were masters at scrounging. If the Germans were going to charge us with lances then I wanted something to poke them back with.

On the 5th of September, the colonel came back from his briefing at headquarters. For the first time in a month, he actually looked happy. He saw me and waved me over; I wondered what I had done wrong. "Just thought I'd tell you Harsker, I mentioned you and the two Brown lads in despatches for your action the other day. I also singled you out as a potential candidate for officer training."

"Thank you, sir."

"You deserve it."

When I told George he just nodded. "It's a shame we only have the Victoria Cross. You should have had a medal for what you did. Still, a mention in despatches isn't too bad."

We waited expectantly for the Squadron Sergeant to emerge from his meeting with the colonel. Something was definitely in the air. We waited in the mess tent talking of inconsequential matters. The troopers had all been complaining that they had had no letters from home yet.

"They are all a bit upset, George."

"I can see that Bill but as we have been flitting around like a may fly it's a bit hard to see how they could have found us let alone deliver the letters." I knew he was right but for all of us this was the first time we had been away from home and it was hard.

When Sergeant Ritchie entered he too was happy. He rubbed his hands together. "Well gentlemen, at last, we get a chance to do what we have been trained for. We hit the enemy!" Everyone cheered. "We are acting as a detached brigade and we will be operating to the west of the French Sixth Army and the Cavalry Division. Our job is to probe for weaknesses. We are going to turn the German flank. There will be seventy thousand British soldiers in the attack and a lot more French soldiers. There will be no more retreat. We are going to drive them back to Germany."

Some wag shouted, "Next stop Berlin!"

Everyone laughed and the Squadron Sergeant wagged his finger, "Just one step at a time Jimmy eh?" He unrolled a map and placed it on the blackboard. Using his swagger stick as an improvised pointer he took us through our roles. Each troop was given a sector and we were told to push forward until we met opposition and then send a message to Headquarters. The colonel would have a mobile headquarters and runners would then direct the troops to the weak points.

As George and I checked the routes on the map I ventured. "The problem with this plan is finding where the colonel is."

"I know. We could be left with our arses in the air if we can't find him. Still, we have managed so far and, for a change, it won't be just us who are at the sharp end."

It would be another early start and I briefed my men about what to expect. They were not the rookies they had been a month ago. As I told them I saw them mentally checking off what they would need. We now knew that we needed as many weapons as we could conceivably manage. I even saw Doddy wearing an artilleryman's leather vest below his tunic. When he saw me looking he grinned. "The fit of the uniform is bad so I can get away with it. The Germans are a bit handy with their swords for my liking. Let's see them get through this!"

I suppose the regulations would have frowned upon it but I wanted these men to survive the battle and, as far as I was concerned, they could use every means possible to do so. I checked Caesar before I turned in. He had recovered from the shrapnel and seemed not to have suffered unduly. I just hoped that we could avoid the artillery and machine guns. They cared nought for fine animals and heroic intentions.

It was dark as we headed west. The lieutenant was happier than he had been on the previous patrols. He even rode ahead of us, which was a first. The rest of us were relying on those skills we had acquired since arriving in France. I knew that Caesar would alert me to anything out of the ordinary. His ears would come up and he would slow down. I, too, had learned to trust senses I had barely used in England.

It was still dark as we headed to our allotted patrol. We were not going to use a road, because of our skills, we were going across country. I knew that it would be harder in the dark but, this way, we could close with the enemy under cover of night. The Germans, it seems, were trying to roll up our lines. The colonel had been ordered to strike at their vulnerable flank. It was what the cavalry were designed for. The French cavalry would be joining us and speed would be our best weapon. There would be no artillery barrage, at least not on the left flank of the advance. As we rode along I waited for the crackle of gunfire which would mark the start of the action.

An hour into the patrol and, as dawn was breaking, Lieutenant Ramsden waved me forward and I led my ten men into the first of the fields we would cross. There were cows in this one and they moved out of our way as we silently trotted towards the other side. Suddenly I could smell smoke. I held up my hand and the rest of the men stopped too. I dismounted and led Caesar towards the wall. It was an old wall and a high one. We were hidden from view. I removed my hat and scrambled up the rough stones. I could now hear, in the distance, men's voices. I could also smell coffee and food. As I peered over the top of the wall I saw, in the next field, a German camp. It looked to be infantry.

I slipped back down and led Caesar back to the others. "Jimmy, ride to the lieutenant and tell him we have found a German camp. The colonel will want to know about this one."

As Jimmy rode away I looked for a gate in the field. There was one at the bottom. I mounted Caesar and waved my men forward. I slipped my rifle from its boot. If the Germans were any good then they would have sentries close to the edge of the field. When we reached the gap I tied Caesar to the gate which opened into the field. I waved the men forward and we sheltered beneath the wall of the field where the Hun was camped. They had no tents close to the wall and I assumed that was because there was an entrance on the other side. There were hedges rising above the wall and I used them to hide as I peered through. I could see that they were oblivious to our presence and were busy cooking their breakfast; that was the smell I had noticed earlier. I signalled for Doddy and Tiny to remain on watch and took the rest back to our horses.

The lieutenant and Sergeant Armstrong were there and we held a whispered meeting. "Sir, there is at least a regiment of Germans in the next field. They have a camp there and they are eating breakfast."

I could see, in the half-light of dawn, that he had a dilemma. George gave him the advice that his face sought, "We just need to watch sir until the colonel gets here." He looked at me, "I sent Jimmy to find the colonel."

"Right sergeant, get some horse holders and then you and Sergeant Harsker take the men and form a skirmish line next to the wall. I'll wait with the horses and brief the colonel when he arrives."

Once again it would be us who would be in the firing line and our leader would have a safe way out. We had no time to deliberate and speculate; until the rest of the regiment arrived we would have to hold the Germans. We spread the men out along the wall. It was roughly made and we used the stones at the bottom as an improvised firing step. We leaned our rifles on the top of the wall and used the hedges for cover. The nearest Germans were over a hundred yards away.

It seemed an age as we waited. The sun was now warming the air and the Germans were finishing their breakfast. Jimmy arrived and he whispered to me, "Captain Ashcroft is here. He is talking to the lieutenant but I think the rest of the regiment are going around the far side of the field to attack."

"Thanks, Jimmy.

The lieutenant arrived. His red face told me that he was not happy about his orders. "We are to open fire in precisely fifteen minutes. The regiment will then attack from the other side."

George and I just nodded. It made sense. Of course, we would have to hold the German's attention for long enough to allow the captain to lead his squadron amongst the Germans. If we could time it right then it would be a slaughter.

I did not take out my pocket watch. It was unnecessary for Lieutenant Ramsden looked at his own every few seconds. I sighted my rifle on a group of soldiers sat outside their tent smoking. I heard a sigh and then the lieutenant said, "Open fire!"

The twenty odd rifles all barked at the same time. The soldier I had targeted pitched forwards. I then worked the bolt as fast as I could. The magazine was soon empty. As I reloaded it I saw that the Germans were advancing towards us. The hedges were shredded by their bullets but they were firing blindly. All that they could see was the smoke. I saw Jimmy fall backwards; a bullet hole made him look as though he had three eyes. He was next to the lieutenant who looked shocked.

"We have to pull back now! We have done enough!" He turned and ran to the horses in the other field.

George snapped, "Hold fast! I'll tell you when we go!" To be fair to the men none had followed our officer. The Germans were now much more numerous but we were causing more casualties than they were. The sound of our bugle, signalling the charge was a welcome one. I saw the indecision on the German skirmish line as they glanced over their shoulders.

"Keep pouring it into them!"

The German bugle sounded and the skirmish line about-faced and ran back towards the new threat. I heard the deep rattle of a machine gun and I looked at George. He nodded, "Right lads, over the wall! Let's help the captain and his squadron!"

It was not easy getting through the hedges which had been our friend while the Germans had been firing at us. I rolled over and crashed to the ground. I was up in an instant and I waved forwards my section. I wished that I had fitted my bayonet but that was still on Caesar's saddle along with my sword.

We ran fifty yards and then I held up my hand and shouted, "Halt and fire!" I placed five well-aimed shots in the direction of the Germans. I saw at least one man fall. "Forward." As he moved towards the Germans I could see the horses of our cavalry ahead. We would have to stop soon or risk running into our own men. I was about to order a halt when a German ran from a tent and suddenly bayoneted Tiny in the back. He fell with a scream. Doddy saw his brother and the German. He emptied his magazine at point-blank range into the Hun. The German's head disappeared.

"Bastard!" He dropped to his knees and cradled his brother in his arms. Tiny opened his mouth to speak but all that came out was a trickle of blood. His eyes glazed over and we both knew that he was dead. It had been a quick death.

"Come on Doddy, we'll see to him later." The trooper nodded and, with a determined expression on his face, picked up his gun. "Hold the line here!"

There was a clatter of machine-gun fire and I saw horses and troopers crash to the ground. I saw that the machine gun was a hundred yards away.

"Sergeant Armstrong, I'm going after the machine gun." George waved his acknowledgement. I moved forward. Doddy, Jack and Robbie followed me. I was about to order them to stay when I saw the determination on their faces. "Keep low."

I slung my rifle over my shoulder and took out the Luger. This was where a grenade would have come in handy. The three men operating the machine gun were oblivious to our presence but their comrades were not. I saw a sergeant raise his rifle only to be shot by Robbie. Doddy was like a man possessed. I had never seen anyone fire as fast as he did. Jack raised his gun to fire at the machine gunners but he was shot by three Germans before he could pull the trigger. I shot two of them and Doddy smashed in the head of the third with his rifle. I emptied my magazine at the machine gunners. Two of them fell but they swung the barrel around in our direction as they died. I ran as fast as I could towards them. Doddy and Robbie were right behind me. I reasoned that even if the gunners got me my comrades would be able to finish them off.

I threw myself bodily at the two remaining gunners and the gun. The Luger's barrel collided with the face of one of the men and the machine gun crashed over. The machine gunner's face was bleeding from the Luger and I smashed the butt into his face over and over until he stopped moving. As I stood I saw Doddy pulling a bayonet from the remaining gunner's body. I was about to ask where he had acquired the bayonet when I saw that it was a German rifle. The camp was now filled with the horsemen; I saw the colonel had arrived. The Germans were either surrendering or fleeing. We had won but as I looked around I could see the cost. Not only were my friends Tiny and Jack dead but Captain Ashcroft and many of his squadron lay in a mangled and bloody heap. The Lancashire Yeomanry had come of age.

There was little to celebrate and much to do. Once the prisoners had been disarmed and penned we set to burying our dead. The service was hurried, we still had much to do but we needed to pay our respects to the fallen. The colonel and the chaplain both said words. The colonel then detailed Lieutenant Jackson's troop to escort the prisoners back to the rear while we remounted and headed towards the enemy once more. We had found our gap and now we had to exploit it.

There were now just twenty men left in the troop and that included the less than useful lieutenant. Doddy still looked angry. The funeral of his brother had been perfunctory at best. I remembered that he had promised his widowed mother that he would look after his little brother. "Robbie, keep an eye on the big fellah will you?"

"Right sarge."

We could now hear as we rode north, the sound of the battle all the way along the line. In the distance, we could hear bugles and the stutter of machine guns. They would be our biggest enemy. Our speed would be as nothing compared with the wall of lead they could spit out. A horse will still run, even with a bullet wound but it cannot run if it has been scythed by a machine gun.

George and his section led on this part and it was his scout, Jack Hargreaves, who was shot by the waiting Germans. We turned and rode back to the small stand of trees. This time the whole regiment was close and the colonel took charge.

"Horse holders!" Harry Grimes' voice cracked like thunder.

We formed a skirmish line and the colonel led us forward. He had his Webley in one hand and his sword in the other. There was a look of grim determination on his face. Captain Ashcroft had been a close friend and, like Doddy, he was set on revenge.

The Germans had taken advantage of a fence at the far side of the field. It would be a death trap to try to cross it. As soon as the first troopers tried to run a machine gun opened up and they were scythed down. "Take cover and bring up our machine gun." The regiment only had one machine gun; the regulars had two but the crew were desperate to use it. "The rest of you, independent fire!"

I could see little across the field but I aimed at the smoke. The Germans were doing the same and soon the leaves and branches around my head were being shredded by the enemy bullets. I lay down, which gave me a better platform to shoot. "Lie down lads. It is easier." I saw Doddy still standing and I reached up to tug on his tunic. "Lie down you daft bugger. You getting killed won't bring your brother back will it?"

He glared at me and then nodded. As he lay next to me he said, "How will I tell me mam?"

"I'll do it. I'll write the letter for you. Just calm yourself down a bit eh?"

"Aye sarge. Thanks."

When the machine began to fire all thoughts of conversation disappeared. The leaves on the other side of the field began to disappear as the .303 bullets acted like a mechanical axe.

"B squadron! Begin to work your way across the field. A and C Squadrons give supporting fire."

I watched as Captain Carrick led his men in short runs across the field. I admired their courage. I was not certain if I could run that gauntlet. I saw troopers falling but the German machine gun had stopped. Either it had jammed or the crew had been silenced. Captain Carrick and his men were almost at the other hedge and the colonel shouted, "Lancashire Yeomanry! Charge!"

Doddy and I stood, "Come on lads!" We ran as fast as we could. I still expected the chatter of a machine gun but it was just an occasional desultory shot from a rifle. I saw B Squadron as they disappeared behind the hedgerow and then it was our turn. We all yelled as we burst through but all we found were the dead and the wounded. The Germans had fled. The machine gun lay at a strange angle the crew all dead.

We all grinned at each other. We had thought we would die and yet we had survived. I quickly checked to see if more of my men had died but they had not. We had just lost the three. They would be hard to replace but I still had my section. We had survived again.

Chapter 8

The next two days of the Battle of the Marne followed the same pattern. We rode after the fleeing Germans and, when they stopped, we dismounted and became infantry as we winkled them out of their positions. We found that we were luckier than the real infantry for they were attacking positions which had been prepared. Because we were cavalry we managed to reach them before they had time to prepare themselves. They were just improvising and using whatever was to hand. We still lost men but not in any great numbers. We heard rumours that the infantry were losing thousands of men.

We had not even had time to put up tents at night and we slept where we could. The poor cooks were reduced to adding water to bully beef and serving that as a sort of instant soup. We were so hungry that we wolfed down all that they produced. As we gratefully drank the hot sweet tea I said to George, "Well the sacrifice will be worth it if we can win the war before Christmas."

He shook his head, "This won't end by Christmas. The generals won't be bothered by a few soldiers getting killed. It is land they want. Until we are on the German border and beyond there will be no end to this war."

That brought me up short. I had not thought it through completely but I had assumed that we would all be home by Christmas and I would be back driving Lord Burscough around. I had pictured myself in the Wheatsheaf pub telling the stories of the heroism of people like Doddy and Tiny. Now I felt depressed. This was my future; exhausted, starving and with a uniform which was already showing signs of wear and tear and we hadn't even been here for two months yet.

And then the battle was over and we had won. The Germans were in retreat. Perhaps George was wrong. Looking back I cannot believe how naïve I was. Then we received our next orders. We had been so successful that the cavalry was being sent towards Calais to get around the flank of the German Army. We started what would become known as 'The Race to the Sea'. For us, it became a death race!

For once, we were not the cavalry who were leading this race. That was the role of the 1st Brigade, Cavalry Division. These were the real professionals, the old cavalry regiments. Our job was to support and so we followed in their wake. That meant finding the grass which their mounts had not devoured and travelling along roads which showed the passage of thousands of horses.

Doddy had withdrawn into himself and no matter how many jokes Robbie told him, he did not respond. He had been the big brother. Tiny

had looked up to and admired Doddy. Neither of them ever thought that
the other would die and now the worst had happened. It made me think
of my brothers. We had fallen out but they were still my flesh and blood.
I wondered if they thought of me as they toiled away in their factory. I
knew that Albert would be desperate to be seventeen so that he could join
up. I was not certain if I liked that thought. I had expected the survivors
of the war and the battles to be the better soldiers. That was a mistake.
The machine gun and the artillery barrages were indiscriminate. It was a
lottery and your uniform and gun were your tickets. Tiny had been one of
the best soldiers in the war and yet he had died along with Jack and
Jimmy. I had nearly died when then the artillery shell had burst near to
me. The skill in this war was being able to survive. It was even worse for
the infantry who we had seen walking across fields to their deaths. I
suppose they rationalised that the bullets which came across would strike
others and not them. If they were struck then it was too late to worry.

Of course, the enemy cavalry was trying to outflank us too. That first
day we saw evidence at the side of the road. There were clusters of
bodies. They were lying in the ditches close to the line of retreat and in
fields. There were horses and men, Germans, British and French. Our
advantage was that we had travelled this road when heading south. It was
not much of an advantage but at least we knew where Calais and Dunkirk
were without having to check the maps. Someone had decided to destroy
the road signs. I suspect it was the French cavalry, after all, they knew
the roads but it didn't help our cavalry. We found out we were heading
for a river called the Yser. Perhaps when we reached it we would stop.
We all needed the rest, animals and men alike.

We camped, exhausted in a field which was heavily churned up by
horses and men long before we got there. Everything was covered in a
film of dirt and mud. We were all beginning to smell but at least we all
smelled the same, however disgusting that was. Despite our best efforts
to shave most of us had faces covered in stubble. We were a far cry from
the smartly turned out soldiers who had left England in September.
Lieutenant Ramsden no longer chivvied us about our appearance. This
was a real war and he was no longer playing at soldiers.

We had pickets out each night. It added to the exhaustion of the day.
Our troop took its turn along with the others. Being the scouts gave us no
special privileges. George woke me at 2 a.m. for my section's duty.

"Quiet as the grave." He nodded to the lieutenant's sleeping form.
"His lordship says to wake him at five."

I shook my head. I knew we needed another officer but I suspect he
had not even watched with George. Not only was he a coward he was
lazy too. Lord Burscough had been a much better officer. I wondered

how he was enjoying his new regiment, the Royal Flying Corps. We had seen the occasional aeroplane and it seemed like an insect or bird far away from the horrors of Flanders.

I woke my men. "Doddy, you and Robbie watch the horses. You four come with me." I spread out my remaining men at intervals around the edge of the field. They had done this enough times to be confident. They all found a comfortable place to watch where they were protected from any enemy scouts and the elements. The rain came in waves of showers and that made picket duty a nightmare. Following the showers, then the initial pitter-patter of raindrops made you wonder if it was the sound of an approaching enemy. I walked the line slowly making sure that my lads were all awake. Occasionally I would stop and peer east. The Germans were out there somewhere. I always took Caesar with me on these nightly pickets. I had found I sometimes needed to investigate noises and movements beyond our picket line. So far they had all been false alarms but one night it would be the real thing. Besides that Caesar was like a friend to me. His reassuring presence was like a good luck charm for me and my men.

When I reached Doddy and Robbie I smelled smoke. "Hey you two, put them out. If there are Germans out and about they will smell them and the glow will mark you out as a target."

"Sorry, sarge." They both snuffed out their cigarettes and put them behind their ears for later.

I was about to leave when Caesar's ears pricked up and he began to stamp his foot. It was a warning sign I had learned not to ignore. I slipped the safety off on my rifle and nodded to the other two. The clicks of their safeties sounded loud but I knew it was my imagination. I pointed to my eyes and then to the darkness beyond the hedges. I went to each man in turn and repeated my actions.

I crouched and peered through the hedgerow. The darkness was complete but some of the shadows looked to be darker than others. I raised my rifle and sighted it on one of the darker shadows. The waiting game ended when I heard what sounded like a boot slipping on mud and the shadow I had been following moved. I fired. The flash from my gun showed me grey coated infantry heading towards us. I yelled at the top of my voice, "Stand to!"

The rest of my pickets were now firing. I emptied my magazine and then began firing the Luger. The German infantry were kneeling and firing. I heard cries from my left and right as my troopers were hit. Then I heard the sound of George and the others as they raced to take their places next to us. As they fired I reloaded. I nodded to George and then went to see to Robbie and Doddy. Robbie was lying in a pool of blood.

He had been hit in the left arm. I took off my scarf and tied it tightly around his wound. "Orderly! Wounded man at the horse lines."

Just then I saw three Germans with bayonets hurling themselves at me. I turned and fired from the hip. Two of them fell but the third one stabbed towards my groin with the lethal-looking blade. The butt of Doddy's rifle smashed into the side of his head. He crumpled at my feet, his brains already oozing out. I nodded my thanks and then aimed at the next infantryman.

Then, it became easier as the colonel rushed more men into the line. When our machine gun came into play the Germans fled the field. We stood to until dawn broke and we could see the grey coated bodies lying in small groups in the damp and muddy field. Doddy and I went amongst the bodies searching for ammunition for our Lugers. Then I went back to see my section. Robbie had been taken away to the hospital. We later heard he had been sent back to England. He was alive and that was good. Apart from Doddy only Harry and Danny remained from my section. The rest were dead. Even George's section had not emerged unscathed and our numbers had fallen to less than fifteen troopers.

The German attack had almost succeeded. It was only thanks to Caesar's ears that we had been spared. Because of our losses, the colonel spared us scouting duties the next day. It would have been pointless anyway; we were too few in numbers. Lieutenant Ramsden looked relieved to be at the rear with the wagons. I rode next to Doddy and tried to talk him out of his stupor. It did not work. It was as though half of him had died along with his brother.

"Thanks for last night, Doddy, you saved my life."

"I saw the bayonet coming at you and thought of Tiny. Perhaps if I had been more careful and alert I could have saved him too."

"You can't change the past and Tiny wouldn't want you like this. You know that."

George had been listening and he nudged his horse next to Doddy's. I saw the angry look on the lieutenant's face. It spoiled his symmetry but neither George nor I were bothered.

"You know, Doddy, I lost a cousin in the Boer War so I know what you are going through."

Doddy respected the old solider and he asked, "How did you get through it then?"

"By trying to be as good a soldier as he was and by never forgetting him. All the lads who have died in the last month need to be remembered. They died for their country." He shrugged, "I am lucky to have lived this long and I know it. Make the most of every day that God lets you live and remember that there may well be a bullet or a shell with your name on it. It was Tiny's time and he died well."

That speech, which was one of the longest I had ever heard George give, seemed to have the right effect and Doddy brightened more than he had. I could see him digesting what the old soldier had said.

We were just twenty miles from where we had landed, Dunkirk, when the battle began. I say 'battle' but it was a series of skirmishes as our cavalry clashed with the German cavalry. We could hear the small arms fire and, as the colonel ordered us forwards, we heard the clash of sword on sword. As we approached we could see that the Dragoon Guards were heavily involved in a fierce fight with Uhlans. The Germans were pushing forward and had not seen the approach of our brigade. This was the colonel's chance and he ordered the charge.

I took out my sword but checked that my Luger was secure. We would be travelling too fast to use my rifle effectively but I knew how good German cavalry were with swords. For once we were riding boot to boot across the flat and obstacle-free field. We were on the plain of the Yser. We crashed into the side of the Uhlans. The tip of my sword entered the eye of an unsuspecting German who did not see our oblique approach and he fell beneath the hooves of our horses. Caesar barrelled through them and horses fell. He was a big and powerful horse. He was made for such work. I slashed with my sword and felt it bite into the arm of another cavalryman. He wheeled away and we ploughed through them. We had struck when they least expected it and they fell in their droves.

The pressure was too much for the Germans who were now being attacked from two sides and they turned to flee. I heard their bugle and saw them as they all turned to flee east and the safety of their own lines. The colonel did not relent and we hurtled after them. I think, on reflection, that he thought we might make a breakthrough which would shorten the war. There was no line and no order. It was every man for himself. Caesar's legs opened and he began to eat up the ground. I sheathed my sword and took out my Luger. I fired at four Germans. They were so close to me that I could not miss and a couple of them dropped from their saddles. I holstered my pistol for I was wasting bullets.

I kept expecting the colonel to sound recall but, as I looked down the line I saw that the whole brigade was charging east. Before me, all that I could see was the backs of the fleeing Germans. I saw that they were heading for a small wood. It made sense; they could regroup there and perhaps fire back at us. The colonel saw it too and we angled towards it. It would suit us as we could dismount and fight with our rifles. We had picked off all those who were close to us and the survivors had made it into the woods.

I began to slow Caesar down; he was breathing heavily. There was little point in charging into the woods; he might stumble. Suddenly, when we were less than a hundred and fifty yards from the wood, the German infantry hidden within began to open fire with machine guns and rifles. The troopers who were in front of me seemed to disappear as the rifles and machine guns found solid targets. The horses tumbled and screamed and men were hurled from the backs of their dead and dying mounts. As they struggled to rise they, too, were ripped apart from the bullets of the ruthless machine guns. It was a slaughter.

I had started to wheel Caesar around to seek safety when the machine guns ripped a line of holes in the side and chest of my brave horse and I felt him stumble. I could not see the damage and he kept on running. I thought I had escaped unscathed but I felt a sudden pain in my leg as though I had been kicked hard by a horse. I knew that I had been struck by the deadly bullets. Caesar continued to wheel and I found myself heading back through the regiment. All of those following were trying to stop and I saw riders pitched from their horses. Those at the rear, the Cumbrian Hussars, were already retreating. They were not waiting for the recall. I could see the death and destruction all around me. There were bodies of men and horses everywhere. Caesar managed another ten yards before his mighty heart finally gave out and the noble beast collapsed to the ground. I rolled clear and winced at the pain in my leg. I crawled over to Caesar. As I held his head he gave a slight whinny and then the life left his eyes. My horse was dead. The horse I had seen born was gone. He had done his best to save me but he would run no more on the sands at Formby. I closed my eyes as I stroked his head. I wished then I had left him at home; there he would have been safe. He had died for no good purpose but he had saved my life. It was then that I heard the retreat sounded. I had lost my rifle and my sword but I still had my Luger.

I struggled to my feet and began to limp slowly west. The battle seemed to be far away or perhaps I was hallucinating. The sound of the guns was muffled and the horizon seemed to be hazy and moving. I could hear someone calling my name but it appeared to be coming from the skies. Perhaps I was dying and God was talking to me. I know that sounds stupid now but then, having seen so many of my comrades die, it seemed plausible. My wounded left leg finally gave up supporting me and I fell in a heap in the muddy field. As I looked up I saw George. He dismounted, "Why didn't you stop, you daft bugger, I have been shouting you." I struggled to answer but no words would come.

He dismounted and put his arms under me. He began to lift me. His horse just stood calmly waiting. "Put your good leg in the stirrup."

I tried to focus on the stirrup but my leg would not cooperate. I gave him a weak smile. "Sorry George I…." Suddenly it all went black.

Chapter 9

I could hear moans before I opened my eyes. Where was I? The last thing I remembered was trying to climb on to George's horse and failing. I awoke and it was night. There were dim oil lamps lighting the tent and I saw that I was in a hospital. There were nurses leaning over patients and I could smell ether and antiseptic. At least I wasn't dead. I saw my uniform next to the bed. I looked beneath the covers. I was in pyjamas. Someone had undressed me. It sounds silly in hindsight but that was the thing which shocked me. It was only then I remembered my wound. We had heard horror stories from George about men having legs and arms amputated because of bullet wounds. I lifted the covers again and saw, to my relief, that my leg was still attached.

My mouth felt dry and I looked for water. There was none. The nurses all seemed to be busy and I did not want to disturb them. I tentatively moved my left leg. It tingled but I thought that I could move it. I threw back the covers and tried to sit up. It was a mistake and I suddenly felt dizzy. A sense of annoyance with my body washed over me. Why could I not stand? I was a soldier. I tried to force myself up but my arm had no strength in it and I fell backwards. As I did so my other arm caught my webbing and it crashed noisily to the floor.

One of the nurses turned around and glared at me. "Where do you think you are going?" She strode over to me.

I said, weakly, "I was thirsty and I needed a drink... sorry."

The glare turned to a grin and she shook her head. "You men! Why didn't you ask?"

"You all looked busy."

She turned to a table in the middle of the tent and poured a tin mug of water. "We aren't too busy to get you a drink of water." As she handed it to me she said, "We wondered when you would come out of it."

I swallowed the whole mug and she refilled it. I sipped half of the second mug. "How long since I was wounded?"

"This is the second day."

Two whole days; I had never been in bed for one whole day before now. "My leg?"

"You were lucky. The bullets passed through the fleshy part of your thigh and missed everything that was vital. It was the same with your arm."

"I was wounded in the arm?" No wonder I couldn't support myself.

"Oh, you were a right mess when that old sergeant brought you in. There was so much blood we all thought that you had bought it. Still, you will be out of the war for a while now. You are to be sent back to Blighty on a hospital ship. Now get some rest and I'll bring you something to eat. The doctor will want to talk with you." She gestured with her head. "He was doing his rounds when one of your cavalrymen took a turn for the worse."

It was when she left me that I remembered the battle. I saw Caesar, dead and the others lying riddled with bullet holes. She was right I had been lucky. I closed my eyes. I was not sleepy but I did not want to see the hospital tent. It was too much a reminder of the horror. Could I go back to riding a horse? I had only ever ridden Caesar. Would I be able to ride another? Would I want to ride another? There was just Doddy left alive from those who had set sail from England. Doddy and George Armstrong were the last ones. I didn't count Lieutenant Ramsden. He would have survived. He was the surviving kind.

"Are you in pain? Would you like something to take the edge off it?"

I opened my eyes and saw a doctor. He looked to be older than George. I smiled, "No sir. I was just resting like the nurse told me to. I don't want to be a bother."

"And you are not." He turned to the nurse. It was the one who had spoken with me earlier. "Nurse, roll back the covers so that I can check the dressing."

"How is the soldier you were attending?"

The nurse looked sad and shook her head. The doctor said, "Trooper Brown? I'm sorry he was too far gone. It was a miracle he had lasted as long as he did."

"Doddy?"

"You knew him? A giant of a man?"

I nodded, "I was his sergeant. His brother died the other day."

The nurse put her hand on mine, "I am so sorry. I didn't know."

It had been many years since I had cried. I don't know if it was just the thought of Doddy's death or everything combining: the death of Caesar and the slaughter of my whole section. I had let them all down. Whatever the reason I began to cry and sob. I felt like a baby. The nurse put her arm around me and I cried into her apron. When I finally stopped she handed me a handkerchief.

"It is over for him now, sergeant. You'll just have to remember him as he was."

The doctor had finished examining me. Tactfully he had ignored my tears. I suspected that he might have seen it before. "The wound is healing nicely. He can go aboard the hospital ship tomorrow, nurse. We need the beds."

I was left alone with my thoughts. I would have to write a letter to Mrs Brown, telling her of her loss. By rights, it should have been the lieutenant but he did not know them and so I would do it. Then there were the others. Most of them had come from within ten miles of the estate and I had known almost all of them for my whole life. I resolved there and then that I did not want the responsibility of other's lives again. There were other troop sergeants in the regiment who had not lost most of their men and that was down to me. Nurse Simpson, I had learned her name by now, badgered me until I ate something. Even as I was eating they were removing Doddy's body and another patient was taking his place. It was like a plough going over a field. New bodies were turned and old ones removed.

I dozed off after the food and was awoken by a tap on the arm. It was George. He had a bandage on his hand. I shook my head, "And I thought that you were untouchable."

He laughed, "Aye well it's not a wound as will get me home that's for certain but I reckon the regiment will have to go back home anyway."

"Why is that?"

"We lost too many men and horses. I heard that those who wish to, can transfer to a regular regiment."

"It was that bad?"

"Aye. It was an ambush of sorts. We should have stopped sooner but, well, when the blood is up."

"Did many survive from our troop?"

"Just me, Danny Graham and the lieutenant." He pointed at me, "And you, of course."

"Doddy died this afternoon."

"I know. I don't know how he survived. He should get a medal. He fought like a maniac." He shook his head. "I have never seen owt like it."

"It didn't do us much good did it?"

He became serious, "I told you once before that any soldier who expects him and all his mates to survive a war is missing a few screws up top. It was bad enough in the old days but with these machine guns and the German guns, well, we stand no chance." I could see that he was right. "What will you do, Bill?"

"They are sending me to a hospital and then... well, home I suppose."

"And then what?"

I had not thought that far ahead. "I think I will just get home first. I'll have to see Mrs Brown and tell her about her lads. She will be all alone now. Will you go back home?"

"I suppose I will. The colonel asked me to be caretaker for the barracks. They won't be needing it for a while and… well, it will keep me occupied."

"I take it the colonel is going to transfer?"

"He is, although what young Mr Ramsden will do is anybody's guess."

"Just so long as they keep him out of the front line. Too many men lost their lives because of his mistakes."

George suddenly looked furtive. He rummaged around in his knapsack. "Here, they didn't like the idea of you having this but I thought you might want it." He slipped me my Luger, holster and ammunition. "I'll put them in your knapsack. You never know, if you do join up again then you might need it."

Nurse Simpson came along, "He needs his sleep now, sergeant."

George smiled, "I know love. Can I see him in the morning before he goes on the hospital ship?"

"You'll need to be here early they will be leaving for the ship at dawn, but, yes, of course, you can."

"You take care, Bill. I don't know how you survived but you did and I think you have a job to do. You are a good sergeant and a good soldier. Don't waste those talents."

After he had gone Nurse Simpson tucked me in, "It's a shame old men like him having to fight."

"You think it should be the young eh?"

She seemed taken aback, "Well, no, but he is old enough to be my grandfather."

"George has no kids and no family. His life was the army. Being inactive will be as bad for him as getting a wound."

"That sounds a bit wise for someone so young."

"Over there," I gestured with my good hand towards what I assumed was the front line, "you grow up fast or you don't grow up at all."

"Well, you get some sleep. You will be out of it all for a while at least."

George was there as soon as I woke up. "I had to say, goodbye son. I am not sure I will be seeing you again but when you do get home then come to the barracks and look me up. We are leaving next week so I should be there before you."

"I think I will see you again George but on the off chance, I don't then it has been an honour to serve with you. I know Doddy and the other lads thought so too. Without you, we wouldn't have lasted a week." I saluted and he stood to attention.

"Be seeing you, Bill." I could hear the emotion as he spoke and I noticed that he seemed older somehow, more bent over. He only had a flesh wound but the war had hurt him more deeply than that.

Nurse Simpson insisted on helping me to dress. She laughed when I complained, "You silly goose! Who do you think undressed you? You men!"

To my chagrin, they would not let me walk. The doctor and the bossy Nurse Simpson were adamant that my leg needed rest. The doctor shook his head. "It might be weeks before you walk again."

I gave him a grim stare. "I'll be walking in a week and then it's home for me."

"Rest as much as you can Sergeant Harsker, this war will last a long time even a girl like me can see that."

Perhaps Nurse Simpson was right; the war was not over by Christmas as the papers had predicted.

The hospital ship was far cleaner than the tent I had spent the last couple of days in but I missed Nurse Simpson and I missed George. I found myself withdrawn and I just wrote. I wrote letters to my mother and to Mrs Brown. I had no idea when I would send them but it gave me something to do and helped me to get some sort of perspective.

Dear Mrs Brown,

I am Sergeant William Harsker and I had the honour of commanding your two boys.

They both died bravely and they did their duty. Your son Doddy has been recommended for a medal. I know that I owe my life to him. Both boys were very popular with the rest of the troop and I cannot speak highly enough of them.

I am heading back home to convalesce and I will call in to see you.

Hoping this finds you well,

Sergeant William Harsker

As soon as we landed I gave the letters to an orderly and asked him to post them. We then spent a day in Grange Hospital at Deal before we were all sent to hospitals closer to home. There were twenty of us from the regiment who were carted, like so much sick livestock, aboard the train north to Lord Derby's War Hospital at Winwick. I was not looking forward to the journey until I found that Robbie McGlashan was on board the train too. He had had to have his left arm amputated. As he said, "I am right-handed. I'll learn to cope. Poor Doddy and Tiny would give their right arms to be where we are now." He shook his head. "I never thought so many would buy it."

It gave me pause for thought. He was right and I knew I had to stop moping around. The journey passed quickly as I told him of the race to the sea and told him how the others had died. Like George, he was dismissive of the lieutenant. "I agree with you sarge, he will get a cushy little number somewhere safe."

The hospital in Winwick was huge. There were over three thousand beds but, in those early days of the war, there were less than two hundred of us occupying them. As time went on the beds filled up but for that first week, it was, virtually, just our regiment. The staff knew their business and Robbie showed great progress. The doctor told him he could have a false hand. Of course, Robbie couldn't resist the jokes, "I've got to hand it to you doc... that'll come in handy."

The doctor smiled when I groaned; I was in the next bed. "It's very healthy, sergeant. Better to look on the glass half full rather than half empty." He was right. You needed a positive attitude or you would want to end it all.

My arm healed really quickly but my leg would not bear my weight at first. One of the male orderlies, who was a huge man himself, had a suggestion. "Let's try to exercise the muscle. He rigged up a weight and a pulley. I was able to use my injured leg to pull up the weight. As the leg did not have to bear my weight the muscle was able to work better. "You keep working at that sarge and we'll have you up and about in a couple of days."

My life suddenly got better as I was able to do something constructive for myself. I worked as much as I could. The pain from the exercise also helped, in a strange way. I lifted the weights until I could lift no more. Life began to get back to normal. The final joy came when we received our back mail then it was even better.

I had a letter from mum which was the first I had received since the war had started.

2nd September 1914
Dear Son,

I hope you are safe. We read that there were many young men killed and wounded in August. I hope the war is over soon.

Your sister is getting married next month. She and her young man have decided that they cannot wait until after the war. It's a shame you'll miss it but it will just be a quiet affair. Lord Burscough has said we can use the chapel at the big house. The estate is almost deserted. Most of the young lads are in the army. Young Lord Burscough has joined the Royal Flying Corps! Can you imagine it? You wouldn't get me up in one of those contraptions. He was kind enough to call round to see us last time he was home on leave.

Bert loves driving Lord Burscough around but he misses you. All he wants is to become a soldier just like you. I hope to get a letter from you soon. I know it might be hard to get to a post box but do try.

Your loving mother

xxx

I felt better knowing that my sister was getting married and they were safe. It had been kind of Lord Burscough to visit them. I had always liked the young Lord Burscough. I wondered if things would have been different if he had not left the regiment.

It spurred me on to get better. I spent every waking minute working on my leg. When the nurse made me stop I wrote a letter to mum and told her I had been wounded. I knew she would have had a telegram but she would imagine the worst, I knew that. The next morning Robbie came to say goodbye. His false hand would be ready in a month and he was going home until then.

"Tell mum I am not badly hurt will you?"

"Of course I will."

"And one more thing, could you help me to my feet. I want to try walking."

He glanced over his shoulder to see if the nurses were watching. "You'll get me shot."

I laughed, "Why what can they do? Stop your hand?"

He laughed. "All right but remember I only have one arm."

I put my good leg on the floor and he held out his arm. I put my left arm on his and then used my right to push me up. I slowly lowered my left leg to the floor. It was a strange sensation as all the blood rushed to my foot. My leg felt as though it was on fire. When my bare foot touched the cold tiles I put my right arm on Robbie's shoulder. As I put my weight on my left leg it felt as though someone was jabbing red hot needles into it. But it did not collapse.

"Let's try walking. You go backwards."

He did so and I picked up my left leg and it moved forward. The hard part was when I put all my weight on to the injured limb. It hurt so much that I thought I would cry but then it held.

Before I could take a second step the nurse had raced over. "Sergeant Harsker! You could injure Trooper McGlashan. I will help you when you are ready."

Although there was anger in her voice there was none in her face and she smiled. "Now off you go, Trooper McGlashan, and we'll see you here in a month and you, Sergeant Harsker, back in bed. You'll need something on your feet and a stick before you can attempt to walk."

They were good nurses at the hospital but it still took me over three weeks to master walking again. Every time I thought I could do it unaided I would trip or burst my wound. My prediction of a week was off by some measure. By the 18th of October, when I left, the hospital was filling up. It would fill up, even more, a few days later in the aftermath of the Battle of Ypres. I only read about that horror but I could imagine it all too vividly.

Chapter 10

I went home.

The ambulance took me to Warrington station. The commanding officer had given me a railway warrant and a pass to travel home. The railway warrant was for 2nd Class; the army treated me better than his lordship had. The colonel had addressed me more like a father than a soldier as he had handed them to me. "Your regiment no longer exists and you are free to continue your life if you wish, Sergeant Harsker. However, I have to say that your comrades who are here speak very highly of you. This country needs warriors such as you. I know that you have suffered but we must all make sacrifices if this country and her Empire are to survive."

I had thanked him and his words filled my head all the way to Burscough Station. I could not ride a horse into battle again; I had nightmares still of Caesar's dying eyes. What was the alternative? Could I face the Germans as an infantryman? I had been considered a good shot but the reason I had joined the Yeomanry was because of the speed of the horse and the swiftness of battle. I had seen the infantry, well nicknamed, the footsloggers as they trudged to war. I had watched them walk across a field into the machine guns which harvested them like wheat. I shuddered as I walked across the platform at Lime Street Station where I had to change to catch my last train. I could not do that. I lacked that kind of courage. A woman looked over and gave me a sympathetic look. She must have thought it was a war wound which made me shudder; it was a memory and they were slow to heal. The pass in my knapsack was freedom. I did not need to be a soldier.

On the train to Burscough, I found myself in a carriage with a husband and wife returning from a Saturday shopping trip to the busy city. He looked prosperous and his hands showed that he did not do manual labour. His neatly trimmed and waxed moustache spoke of many hours in front of a mirror and his clothes were tailored. A professional man I guessed or perhaps someone with an income. I estimated them to be in their late twenties.

"On leave, sergeant?"

"Yes sir, I am."

"Were you in France?"

"I was, sir."

"Well, when you return you must urge your fellows to show true British spirit. It's all very well for the French to retreat but we are British! We do not want another debacle like Mons."

I clenched and unclenched my fists. My friends had all died and this man thought it was not enough.

His wife put her hand on his, "I am sure they did their best, my dear, besides there weren't that many of them according to the paper."

He nodded, "You may be right. Well, there are thousands volunteering now and it won't be long before the Hun are driven back. We'll show them who rules Europe!"

I closed my eyes. I just wanted to get out of the train. It would do no good to punch this idiot. His wife asked, "Are you in pain, sergeant? Were you wounded?"

I opened my eyes and saw real concern in the woman's eyes. "I was wounded but there is no pain." I looked at the man. "The men I left in Flanders feel no pain either; for they are all dead. They died for this country."

I think the man realised then that I disliked his words and he brought up the newspaper to hide behind. His wife flashed him an angry look. "Did you lose many of your friends?"

I nodded, "There were just two who survived. All the rest gave their life for the King. I just hope the people at home recognise the sacrifice."

She nodded. "They will, believe me, they will."

As I limped from the station at Burscough I realised that I was being harsh on the man. I had read the newspapers whilst in hospital and they were full of disappointment that we were not thrashing the Germans. They were making it sound like a test match at cricket. All we needed to do was play with a straight bat and we would win. There was a belief that we were British, we ruled the waves and victory would inevitably follow. Everyone was being blamed as though we had a divine right to win on the battlefield. In my time in France, I had never seen a newspaperman. I suspect they got their news from the War Office. They would be speaking to staff versions of Lieutenant Ramsden; the kind who are never close to either fighting or danger. I shook my head to clear it. I was home now and my priority was my family. I had missed them. When I was back in the cottage then life would make sense, once again.

It is strange but the fields at home looked greener. It was autumn but many of the fields in Flanders had been churned up by boots and hooves. Here they were green and the leaves, undamaged by bullets, were still on the trees. This was a different world from France and Flanders. It was as though I had crossed a continent and not just the English Channel. The journey to the cottage took longer than it should have as everyone on the estate and in the village wanted to speak with me. They had all seen Robbie and had been anticipating my return. I had no idea what stories my friend had been telling but they all looked at me with something approaching awe.

"Your mam will be glad to see you!"

"They must feed you well in the army or you are still growing!"

"You showed them Huns what a lad from Lancashire can do!"

And so it went on until I became weary. I just wanted to enter the cottage and close the door. Mum was waiting for me with our Alice. I worked out that the others would still be working, even though it was Saturday afternoon. Mum threw her arms around me and began sobbing. She kept saying, over and over, "Our Bill, eeh, our Bill!" I felt Alice stroking my back, much as one might do with a sick child. It was comforting but I felt foolish. I was now healed.

Eventually, I disentangled myself and said, "Let's go in mum. I am dying to be inside the cottage again."

"Of course, Alice, make a pot of tea for your brother."

I knew the kettle would have been on. It was always on the fire just waiting for such a command. The cottage seemed tiny now that I had been away for some time. I wondered how we had all fitted in such a cramped space. I went to sit on the stool by the fire but mum pointed to dad's seat. "No, you sit there."

I was shocked. No one sat in dad's seat. "But that is dad's place!"

"He won't mind son." She stood back and looked at me. "Well, you look well. Where did they wound you? Young Robert told us."

I pointed to my left arm, "In the arm and here." I pointed to the top of my leg.

"Are you all better now son? Are you out of the army?"

I avoided the second question. "The doctors passed me fit. They say another two weeks of convalescence and then I will be fit for anything." Alice handed me my tea and a piece of parkin. "My favourite!"

My mother and sister looked happy and I certainly was. This was normality and it felt wonderful.

Alice put some bread on the toasting fork, "I'll make you some toast too."

The thought of hot toast cooked by the fire, dripping with butter made my mouth water. I sipped the tea and bit into the moist and spicy parkin; it took me back to the days before the war when everything was much simpler.

Alice went to take my knapsack. "No, Alice, I'll look after that." By way of apology, I said, "It has my travel documents in there and I need to keep them safe." I didn't want my sister seeing the Luger which still nestled in the bottom of my bag beneath my gas mask. It would be a harsh reminder of the war.

The door burst open and Albert stood there. He looked taller somehow. "I ran all the way when I heard you were back. Dad, Sarah and Kath are coming. Show me your wounds!"

Mother was shocked, "Albert Harsker! You get yourself washed up and stop bothering your brother! I've never heard the like."

I winked at his crestfallen face and whispered, "I'll show you later."

Dad came through the door next and I saw his eyes filling. He didn't say anything but threw his arms around me and just held me.

"I'm glad to be home, dad."

His voice, heavy with emotion whispered, "I'm bloody glad to see you, too, son." He never swore and was a mark of his feelings.

I heard Sarah say, "Come on you two. Let me see the hero."

Dad stepped aside and Sarah embraced me. "Congratulations our Sarah. When is the big day?"

"You timed it well our Bill. Next Saturday. It will be good to have you there."

Our Kath threw her arms around me and planted a huge kiss on my cheek. I thought she was going to crush me. "My big brother, the hero! I'm right proud of you, our Bill."

"Right Bill, get your bag upstairs and then we'll have tea. I've made a nice cow heel stew and potato cakes."

I almost leapt upstairs. They were my two favourite things and we never had them together. It was a treat just for me. They were spoiling me. Once in the old room, I had shared with my brothers I put the knapsack on the shelf above my bed. My old clothes were still there. I decided to get out of my uniform.

I had just taken my trousers off when Albert burst into the room. I was slightly embarrassed and annoyed. "Have you never heard of knocking?"

The shout was a sergeant's shout which I regretted the minute it left my mouth. He looked as though I had slapped him. He turned to leave, "Sorry Bill. I…"

"Come in you daft bugger! I didn't mean owt. This is your room after all. You just took me by surprise. I thought it was our Alice."

He shut the door and stared at the scar on my thigh. It was no longer angry but it was a big scar. He moved his hand towards it as though to touch and then thought better of it. "Did it hurt?"

"That's a daft question; what do you think?"

I had taken my jacket off and he saw the wound on my arm. It was less dramatic but the scar was still there. I tried to change the subject. "How is the driving going?"

"Robbie McGlashan told us that Caesar was killed." He meant nothing by it but I had hidden that memory and suddenly it was there again. I relived the moment that brave beast had stumbled to his death. I felt the tears spring into my eyes and saw the shock on Albert's face. "Eeh I am sorry Bill. I know how much you loved that horse."

His words gave me the chance to recover my composure and begin to dress myself. "Aye, he was a grand horse."

"When do you go back?"

I shook my head and laughed, "Do you mind if I come home first?"

"Sorry." He sat on his own bed. "As soon as I am old enough I am enlisting. Our Tom and John have both joined up. They are in a Pals Battalion."

I was surprised. The last time I had seen them they had seemed to hate the idea of a ruling class and the British Empire and yet here they were volunteering. I had heard of these battalions in Lord Derby's hospital. They were a clever way of getting men to volunteer. You fought with your workmates or friends. I had just left Flanders and they would be heading for that charnel house. Could I sit at home while they fought?

We went down to tea. Everyone crowded around the tiny table, I wondered how we had managed when we all lived at home. Despite the cramped conditions, it was joyous. I cannot remember us all laughing quite as much. The subjects we did not cover were the war and my brothers. I learned all about the estate and how Lord Burscough was learning to drive. Albert was pleased with his lordship's progress. I knew why- as soon as his lordship could drive it would free up Albert to join up. I said nothing. I could not blame the boy. I, too, had been eager enough to serve. I was not quite as keen to return now.

Dad took me, for the first time in my life, to the Wheatsheaf, the village pub. I had been there, of course, but never with dad. As we strolled to the pub he told me of an Act of Parliament which would restrict the opening hours of the pubs. It was not yet law but it would be in the next month or so.

"Daft, if you ask me. Some lads who drive horses and carts call in at five in the morning for a nip to keep the cold out. And what about those shift workers who finish after the pub has shut? It's not fair. I don't often agree with your brothers but on this I do. Those politicians in London won't go short of a drink but the working lads do. It's about time they stopped trying to make us live the way they think we ought to."

This, in itself, was unusual, dad never had political views. "You know dad, this will be the first drink I have had since I left home."

"I thought they all drank wine in France."

I shrugged, "They might do but we were never near any towns. So I shall enjoy my first pint with my dad." I put my arm around his shoulder and noticed, for the first time, that I was now much bigger than my dad. When I had been growing up I couldn't wait to be the same size as my dad and it had happened without me noticing.

There was a cheer when we entered the fuggy, smoke filled crowded pub. The smell was of tobacco, stale ale and sweaty working men. Returning soldiers were a rarity and everyone wanted to buy me a drink. My dad slammed his hand on the bar. "It's my son and I shall buy him his first pint. After that, we are both happy to allow you all to buy us our ale!"

I was questioned all night about the lads I had left the village with. Each death was toasted and a silence for the trooper. I found it quite moving. They were not forgotten and that was how it should be. I saw one of Doddy's old neighbours, "How is Mrs Brown coping?"

He shook his head, "It's a bloody shame. She hears about Tiny and then five minutes later Doddy buys it." He looked at me. "She appreciated your letter. I think she is keen to see you."

At that time a respectable woman would not be seen near a pub. I would see her in the morning. It promised to be a traumatic and trying experience.

I was a little drunk as dad helped me home. I was not used to drinking and they had all been desperate to buy me ale. When we reached home I was ready for bed. I saw a slightly disapproving look from my mother but our Sarah said, "Mum, after what he has been through I think he deserves it eh?" Mum nodded and Sarah and Alice helped me up the stairs.

There was a light under the door. Albert was still up. When I reached the door I disentangled myself. "I think, ladies, that I can manage the next part all by myself." They giggled, each planted a kiss on my cheek and trotted down the stairs.

When I went in I saw Albert hurriedly stuffing the Luger back into my knapsack. It sobered me up rapidly. I was glad that I had unloaded it and taken out the magazine or there could have been a tragic accident. I shook my head as I took the knapsack from him. "I thought better of you Bert."

"Sorry Bill, but I just thought you might have brought back some souvenirs. I never thought you would have a German's gun."

"Aye well, you mind you don't tell mother about it. Understand?"

"I swear down."

After I had undressed and I had turned out the light I lay in the bed feeling quite comfortable. Then I heard Bert's voice, "Tell me how you got the gun, Bill."

"In the morning, I am tired now. I promise you I will but not tonight eh?"

Chapter 11

As I was eating my breakfast mum asked, "Well our Bill, what will you be getting up to today?" She had noticed that I was wearing my uniform and I could see a worried look on her face. We were alone in the cottage. The rest were all at church. Albert had woken me so that I could tell him how I got the pistol and then I fell back asleep to rid myself of the hangover. Mum had waited for me and she would go to the services at Evensong.

I put down my knife and fork. "I have to go and see Mrs Brown. I promised Doddy I would."

"That poor woman. She loses her husband and then her two lads who should look after her in her old age are both killed. It's not right." I could see, in her eyes, that she was thinking of a similar scenario for herself if the worst happened.

I stood and kissed her on her forehead, "Don't worry! We will all survive. It's not as bad as you might think out there." That was a lie and it is a sad thing when you have to lie to your mother but it was better than the alternative. Mum was a worrier and I would save her from as much worry as I could. I walked the long way around to her cottage for I needed time to think and I needed to give Mrs Brown the time to get back from church.

The Brown's house had closed curtains. It did not mean she was abed; in Burscough, they did things the old fashioned way. The curtains would remain closed until she had finished mourning her boys. When she opened the door she was exactly as I had expected. She was dressed from head to toe in black.

As soon as she saw me she burst into tears and threw her arms around me. "I'm right glad that you are safe. My boys always thought the world of you. Come in, I'll put the kettle on."

I knew there was no point in saying I was not thirsty; there was a protocol to this. There would also be a cake and it would be the best china. This was my world now and I knew where I was and the rituals involved. After she had poured the tea and given me my slice of fruit cake she engaged in small talk about my mum and the girls. She was excited about the wedding; the whole village would be attending.

Then I made the mistake of complimenting her on the cake. She burst into tears again. "It was to be for Christmas. Donald, especially, liked it but there'll be just me." Donald had been Doddy's given name. It sounded strange to hear it.

The fruit cake suddenly turned to sawdust in my mouth. After she had dried her eyes she took a worn letter from the drawer of her table.

"Donald sent this when his brother died." She proffered the letter as
though I needed to read it. I took it and opened it. I recognised Doddy's
scrawl. "He said that you promised to tell me what happened to his
brother. He thought highly of you did our Donald. He said the boys
would follow you anywhere. He said you looked after them." She
reached over and touched my hand, "Thank you for trying to take care of
my lads."

I scanned the letter but I could not take it in. I had not known he had
written the letter. I looked at the envelope and recognised George's
handwriting. He must have found the letter amongst Doddy's things. I
saw, for the first time, the slightly pink tinge to the letter. It was Doddy's
blood. I took a deep breath, "Well Mrs Brown I promised Dod... Donald,
that I would tell about your boys and I am a man of my word."

I spent the next hour telling her, without any of the graphic detail,
how her sons had performed in Flanders. I did not have to make anything
up. They were both fine soldiers. I told her of Doddy and Tiny's heroism
and how Doddy had saved my life. I ended by telling her of his final act
of valour. "He should get a medal for what he did."

As she folded the letter and put it away she said, "But it won't bring
them back, will it?" The ticking of the grandfather clock in the corner
was the only sound. There was nothing I could say; she was right.

I left the cottage with a heavy heart. As I walked home I wondered if
I could have done anything more to stop their deaths and I knew I could
not. It was tragic and unnecessary but, given that we were in battle, it
was inevitable. At least Robbie and George had survived.

When I reached home I took off my uniform and changed into my
civilian clothes. They were my best clothes for it was Sunday and that
was the most important day of the week. Dad and the rest had not got
back from church. Mum told me that they had gone to speak with Lord
Burscough about the wedding.

When they returned they were all bubbling, even my dad. "Lord
Burscough drove us in his motor car to the hall from church!"

You would have thought it ranked alongside a knighthood. Sarah
nodded, "Mum you should have seen the faces of the others they were
green with envy."

Albert turned to me, "Lord Burscough asked after you Bill."

"He wondered why I wasn't in church more likely." The looks on
their faces confirmed my thoughts. I was not certain I was ready for
church. Any God who could condone the slaughter I had seen was a
strange god of love and peace.

Kath said, "Ooh and young Lord Burscough will be here on Friday.
He's coming for the wedding."

That brightened me up. It would be good to see him again. He was a reminder of life before the war. Sunday was a lovely lazy day. After lunch, the men dozed while the women cleaned up and prepared high tea. It was the day in the week when the best china came out and we all perched precarious plates on our knees and tried to get huge fingers into tiny cup handles.

Dad went back to church with mum for the evening service. I knew they wanted me to go but they never said a word. After they had gone Kath and Sarah came to talk with me as I wandered around the garden.

"I am glad that you are home for my wedding. It wouldn't have been the same without you."

"Aye well if it wasn't for this wound I wouldn't be. For that reason, I am glad about the wound. It means I can see my sister get married. Is Cedric worried about having to fight?"

"No, Lord Burscough says he is more valuable working in the big house."

"Good. I am pleased."

"Of course he gets some snide comments and funny looks. He has stopped going down to the Wheatsheaf."

I wondered why I had not seen him there. "Well next Saturday night, I'll take him there for a pint and we'll see if he gets any comments."

Kath giggled and Sarah laughed, "You will not."

I was taken aback. It was not like our Sarah to back away from a fight, "I won't cause trouble."

"No, you goose, it's my wedding night. I hope that my husband will be too busy to go out with his new brother in law."

I laughed too. It was good to be back in a normal world.

I spent the next day digging in the garden. The potatoes needed harvesting and then the plot needed turning over. It was good physical exercise and was just what I needed. There is something satisfying about a garden; it is producing something. Even the dead from the garden bring forth new life.

The exercise did me good. That evening, at tea, I said, "I think I will go to the barracks tomorrow."

It was as though I had dropped the best china. Everyone stopped eating and their cutlery clattered on to their plates.

"Whatever for son?"

I could not understand their reaction. "Well our Sarah wants me in my dress uniform for the wedding and it is at the barracks." The relief was palpable. "What? Did you think I was going back to the war?"

Dad shrugged, "We didn't know son. You've said nowt about it yet."

"Well, the regiment has been disbanded. I shall have to transfer if I want to go back to the war."

Mother brightened but Albert looked disappointed. "You'd think about not going back then Bill?"

"I haven't made my mind up, Bert. Besides I need to talk to George Armstrong. He works there now. I am still making my mind up. I still have some time before my pass runs out."

I could have borrowed a horse from the stables but I chose to walk. I needed to exercise my leg and walking helped me to think. I was also uncertain how I would feel riding a horse again. Mum insisted on giving me a packed lunch and I put it in my knapsack. I felt happier knowing that the Luger was away from Albert. He might be tempted again.

The barracks looked the same and yet, as with the cottage, somehow smaller. The regiment had rarely had to sleep there but even so it had been the home for a couple of hundred men. It was tidy but looked forlorn and empty. I walked into the silent yard and thought about those men who would not be returning.

"You made it then? You are walking better that is for sure." I turned to see a smartly turned out George. I strode up to him and shook his hand. He waved a hand around the square, "Welcome to my world." He leaned in, "It is a bit quiet, mind. Come on, I have a little bottle in my office and we can celebrate."

Once in his very neat and immaculately organised office, he produced a bottle of cognac. "Compliments of the French. Most of the lads got something when we boarded the boat for home. I made sure I got something decent."

"I notice none of them came home. Did they all re-enlist or transfer?"

"Aye. I think it was you and the others that made them do that. The colonel made a lovely speech about how our troop had made all these sacrifices and given the regiment a good reputation. He made it sound like they would be letting you and the others down if they didn't re-enlist."

"That's not right, George."

"Son, if we don't fight then the Germans will win and they won't be happy with just ruling the French and the Belgians, they will look over here. Now I don't know about you but I don't want shells falling on our womenfolk and the bairns. We shouldn't have to fight but so long as there are people like the Germans who want to take everything we have then we'll have to fight. We are fighting for a British way of life and I think it is worth fighting for." He suddenly looked embarrassed. "Sorry about that Bill, I'll get down off my high horse now. You make up your own mind. That is just the view of an old man who is now the caretaker of this edifice."

We talked about the hospital and Robbie. I told him about my family and the wedding. He seemed genuinely pleased. "It's almost as though you were meant to get wounded so that you could get home." He grinned and stood up. "You'll be wanting your dress uniform then?"

"I will. I hope it hasn't been attacked by moths. I didn't mothball it."

"It's in perfect condition. The first thing I did after I tidied my office was to make sure they were safe. Come on. I'll take you there."

Not only was it in perfect condition, George had even put his stripes on to it."George, you shouldn't have."

"I won't need them. I didn't know you were going to a wedding but I am glad that I did it now. You'll be a credit to the Lancashire Yeomanry."

When I left, in the late afternoon, I had much to think on. George was a wise old bird and what he had said had struck a chord. I needed time to think.

They were all quite worried when I entered the cottage as it was after dark. "Where have you been, our Bill? Anything could have happened to you."

"Why, have criminals suddenly moved in? The last trouble we had in the village was ten years ago when those gypsies tried to steal his Lordship's horse."

"Well, sit down and get your tea. It'll be stone-cold now." They were worried about me still, even when I was home.

I spent the rest of the week getting fit again. I worked in the garden and did all the lifting and carrying mum normally did by herself. I knew she was pleased for washing day was normally a hard one as she had to fill the huge boilers with boiling water and then work the posser. I quite enjoyed the labour. I made short work of the wringer and we finished by noon. All in all the week was just what I needed. On Friday I was working in the garden again when there was a roar from the road as the Singer 10 crunched around the gravel and screeched to a halt. My mother came to the kitchen door, "Mercy me! What on earth is that?"

Lord Burscough leapt from the car and said, "Sorry about that Mrs Harsker. I forgot you hadn't seen one."

She bobbed a curtsy, "Sorry my lord. It is good to see you."

He was wearing a flying helmet and goggles. When he took them off I could see that he had grown a large moustache. He ostentatiously twirled the end. "And you William, a war hero and a sergeant to boot." He shook my hand vigorously. "Good show! Good show!"

"Would you care for tea my lord?"

The look on his face showed that he had no desire for tea. "Sorry, Mrs Harsker. I just came to take William for a spin if that is all right with you?"

I smiled to myself. Of course, it was all right with my mother. Nothing that Burscough family did could be considered in any way wrong.

"Of course, my lord. Will you be back for tea William?"

"Will I?"

Lord Burscough had a mischievous look on his face, "Probably not! Don't wait up for him Mrs Harsker. He's in safe hands with me." He replaced the helmet. "Right, hop in old chap and let's see what she'll do eh?"

I had only driven the car around the estate and I was not prepared for the speed when we hit the A6 north. We leapt forward with such a burst of speed that I thought my head was going to fly off. I found myself gripping the door and the seat. I could see why his lordship wore goggles. My eyes were watering just ten miles up the road. Conversation was impossible and, once I became used to the speed, I just enjoyed the views as we headed north. I had no idea where we were going but it did not matter. I loved the way the car skidded around the bends and then leapt forward when his lordship jammed down on the accelerator.

When I saw the hills rise ahead of us I knew that we were going to the Lake District. It was sixty miles from home and yet we had done it in just less than an hour. It was unbelievable. Of course, we only saw another couple of motors as we headed north and they were staid and slow cars driven by serious-looking men. His Lordship drove like a maniac.

We screeched to a halt outside a huge hotel. I was still excited by the ride and I did not even notice its name. The destination was not the most important thing, it was the journey. His lordship didn't say a word until we were in the hotel. "Table for two and send over a bottle of your finest claret." He turned to me, "Well, what did you think of the ride?"

"It was beyond words, my lord. It was the most fantastic experience I have ever had."

The head waiter directed us to a table and took his lordships coat helmet and goggles. I had not even noticed the cold but now we were in the hotel I felt the warmth.

"I knew you would like it! Now I am starving." The waiter brought over the claret, "Ah spot on. That will do nicely. Do you still do the game pie?"

"Yes my lord."

He leaned over to me, "I had it last year too but this is the best season for game pie." He looked back at the waiter. "We'll have that and bring us some oxtail soup to start. My friend here needs warming up."

He laughed but I was listening to his words. He had called me, 'my friend'! He poured me a glass of wine. I had never drunk wine before, not even in France but it would have been churlish to refuse. I raised my glass, "Cheers sir, and here's to the boys who didn't come back."

He suddenly became serious, "Well said, William. Here's to our fallen comrades." I drank the wine it felt warm but it had a slightly bitter taste. It was not unpleasant but I couldn't drink a pint of it. "Tell me about it, William. I have read the reports but I didn't see any of the chaps. I hear Captain Ashcroft bought it?"

I nodded and then told him the story. He got the truth, including Lieutenant Ramsden. The food came, as did the second bottle of wine. He nodded and made appropriate comments.

"I think the day of the horse and the cavalry are over. Poor Caesar should have ended his days on the estate. I am sorry that you both had to suffer like that. I feel guilty for I was the one who got you to join."

"No, my lord, I wanted to go. The fact that I didn't find it as glorious as I thought is my fault." He nodded and we both withdrew into our own thoughts.

The waiter returned and his lordship ordered two glasses of port and asked for the bill. He paid and said, "Let's go on the terrace and watch the lake. It is lovely at this time of year." I had had port before, or ruby wine at least and I liked it but I knew enough just to sip it.

The view was magnificent with the hills and sky reflected in the huge lake that was Windermere. "And how is the Royal Flying Corps sir?"

He clapped me on the back. "Capital, absolutely capital! That is the main reason I called for you today." He swallowed the port, "Look we have known each other a long time and there is no point in beating about the bush. I'd like you to transfer to the RFC and be my observer."

It was a bombshell, quite literally. I had never even seen an aeroplane let alone thought about flying in one. "Why me sir? I am just an ordinary chap who is a bit useful around horses."

"I think you are doing yourself a disservice. I happen to know that you are a crack shot and a fine leader of men. I also know that you are one of the best scouts the regiment ever had. That is what you will need to be, a scout and a crack shot. I have been flying single-seater aircraft but we are changing over to the Vickers Gunbus and I need an observer who can fire the Lewis gun. What do you say? If you liked the speed of the old Singer you will love the bus. We go much faster and we are as free as a bird."

"It is an attractive offer sir but I need time to think about it."

He nodded and rained his glass. "Come on then, let's get you back before your mother begins to worry." He nodded to the head waiter as we left, "I went to the barracks, you know, and saw Sergeant Armstrong. We had a long chat. It was him who told me how good you were and he told me of your worries." We climbed into the car. "You know they will bring conscription in and you will have to fight again. The question you need to ask yourself is will that be in the air or in the mud?" He held up his hand. "Think about it on the way back and give me your answer there eh?" He put his foot on the accelerator and we roared away south: the silence of the lakes shattered by the Singer's throaty roar.

My thoughts were filled with his ideas rather than the car and the scenery. That told me all that I needed to know. He had spoken to George and George had recommended me. I could not go back to the war as an infantryman. It had killed all but one of my friends. At least in the air, I would not have to think of others, I would just have to do what his Lordship asked.

Chapter 12

As we pulled up outside the cottage, a little bit slower this time, I had made up my mind. He turned to look at me. He raised his goggles and said, "Well?"

"Yes, Captain Burscough I would like to join you."

He grinned and pumped my hand, "Well done Sergeant Harsker. You will not regret it."

"I am still a sergeant?"

"Of course. Mind you there are very few in our squadron who aren't officers but that will come when you learn to fly."

"Learn to fly? I thought I would just be an observer."

"Well yes but we all tinker with engines and we all need to know how to fly. Don't worry William. It's a piece of cake. You will be a whizz at it." I got out of the car. "Well, I shall see you tomorrow for the wedding and then we leave on Sunday bright and early."

He floored the car and with it me. I had less than two days left with my family. My dilemma was, did I tell them tonight and risk spoiling the wedding or leave it until after the wedding? I had to do it now or else Sarah would not be able to say goodbye. Besides which I was certain that his lordship would say something on the wedding day. I braced myself. This would be as daunting as a cavalry charge!

The drive back had cleared my head a little and I braced myself. My mother's face was a picture as she opened the door. It was a mixture of anger and relief. As I had been with his lordship she could not criticise but I saw it in her eyes.

"Did you have a nice time?" There was a heartbeat of a pause and then she said, "Your dinner will be all dried up now."

I hugged her, "It will still taste delicious." I would have to eat it or upset her even more.

She placed the plate on the table, "Mind now, it'll be hot. Your dad bought a bottle of brown ale for you to have with it."

I forced the smile, "Thanks dad, that'll be just the job eh?"

I was full but this was a small sacrifice to make. I think I saw the hint of a grin on my dad's face as he looked up from his paper. He knew me better than anyone. I might be fooling my mum but not him. He could see that there was something on my mind. The beer helped the food to go down. I told the story of the car journey which also gave me a breathing space.

Dad shook his head, "I cannot believe you got to the Lake District and back in less than a day. Why when I took his lordship up there we left at dawn and didn't reach the lodge until after dark."

"That's the motor car for you, dad. I am afraid that the day of the horse is over. It will soon be something people use for hunting and that is all. That car could go sixty miles an hour. That's faster than the train to Liverpool."

He angrily tapped his pipe out on the fire, "Why things have to change I don't know. It was bad enough when they got those noisy steam engines and we got rid of those beautiful Clydesdales. Do you remember them, Bill?"

"Aye, they were lovely. Watching them plough was a real pleasure."

"Exactly! What pleasure do you get watching a noisy steam engine belch fumes all over you!"

Albert had remained silent. "But they get the job done quicker dad."

"No they don't, not in the long run. It takes longer to set them up than it does a horse and plough."

"It's cheaper."

"Don't talk nonsense young Albert. A horse eats hay and grass. Those steam engines eat coal."

"Well, you don't need as many men, do you?"

I think dad had been waiting for that point. He jabbed his pipe triumphantly at Albert, "Precisely and that's the real reason they use them smelly, noisy beasts. It's cheaper. You mark my words, Albert, within ten years all the men will be in the big cities with Tom and John."

Mum was rocking in her chair and knitting. She shook her head sadly, "The ones that are still here." She nodded towards dad's paper. "There's a battle in France and they say there are thousands of casualties."

I pushed my finished plate away, "That doesn't mean they are dead. I was a casualty and I am fine aren't I?"

She glanced down at my leg but continued knitting. "And I am glad that you are out of the war now."

Sarah was also sewing, probably something for the wedding as it was blue. I caught her eye and then quickly looked away. I drank some more of the beer.

A quiet descended and the only sounds which could be heard were the ticking clock, the clicking of the needles and the swish of turning pages. I sipped my beer wondering how to bring up my imminent departure.

Sarah finished her sewing and held it up to admire. She said, "I think our Bill has something to tell us but he doesn't know how to start. Am I right our Bill?"

Dad put down his paper and mum stopped knitting. "What is it, son? You can tell us." He began filling his pipe. He used that as a way of listening while keeping his hands busy. It meant he didn't have to look at you. I think he did that to make it easier. He had done the same thing when John had told him he was going to work in a factory.

"Well, his lordship has asked me to go with him on Sunday."

Mother's eyes widened like a startled deer. "Sunday? Where to?"

I hesitated and Sarah, who knew me well, gave a slight nod of her head, "To join the Royal Flying Corps as an observer."

This time it was a stunned silence. Albert looked delighted, Sarah gave me a sad smile and mother looked as though I had told her I had been sentenced to death. Dad had his pipe halfway to his mouth and he said, "You mean in an aeroplane? Up in the air?"

I nodded, "I would have to join up again anyway. You said yourself dad, in the pub the other night, that they need every man they can get."

"But you have done your bit."

"No mum, I have done a bit but the job isn't done yet. You didn't raise me to give up did you?"

Dad lit his pipe and nodded his agreement. Mum started knitting again. The needles click-clacking furiously, "No, but you nearly died and there are others who could go."

"You mean married men, fathers? Think about it mum, I am single; we are the ones who have the least to lose. I have been thinking about it over the last few days; if we think this country is worth fighting for then we shouldn't shirk our duty."

"He's right mother." Dad looked at me and I think there was pride in his eyes. "So you'll be away Sunday then?"

"Yes," I grabbed Sarah's hand. "But I shall be here for the wedding."

She stood and hugged me, "I should think so and we will make it a real family celebration." She whispered in my ear, "Mum will be all right but give her a cuddle. You were always her favourite." She turned to Alice and Kath. "Come on you pair we have dresses to get ready for tomorrow."

I knelt next to mum and I saw the tears trickling down her rosy cheeks. I saw that her hair now had more flecks of grey than I remembered and I wondered if that was down to me. I took her hand in mine. "I have to go, mum, but I promise you, I swear, that I will not take risks. If I was in the infantry then I would be in greater danger but with aeroplanes we just observe. There will be little chance of me coming to harm." I think that was a lie but I didn't know for certain and I excused myself.

"What if they crash? Albert has had to repair Lord Burscough's car more than enough. If it breaks down in the air it will crash."

"And that is another reason his lordship wants me. He knows I am good with engines. I'll make sure we don't crash. In a way, I'm looking after Lord Burscough too." I could see that I had nearly persuaded her. I took my leave. "I had best get to bed. Tomorrow will be a big day for us all."

Albert followed me to bed, "You are lucky, Bill. I would love to fly an aeroplane. When I am old enough then I will join you."

I felt depressed to think that my little brother might have to endure the horrors of Flanders. "You never know, it may be over by then."

His voice sounded sad in the dark. "I hope not."

Perhaps because of my impending departure, the wedding day flew by. It was a lovely wedding, well at least all the women thought so. Lady Burscough had decorated the chapel beautifully and my sister looked gorgeous. Her husband Cedric Rogers was a quiet, unassuming man. I had been at school with him and he would make her a good husband. I wondered if my little sisters would make such good matches. I noticed that there were few young men at the wedding. The war was already having an effect.

Young Lord Burscough sought me out during the day. "We shall have to leave at five a.m. I am afraid. We have a long drive down to Kent. Make sure you pack all the warm clothes you can."

That puzzled me, "Why sir?"

"It gets damned cold up in an aeroplane. You will need gloves, scarves and a thick coat."

I wish I had known. Mother could have knitted me some gloves, a scarf and I could have bought a decent and thick coat.

Everyone in the cottage was normally up early but that Sunday I am not sure my mother had even been to bed. She was red-eyed and fretful when Albert and I went downstairs before the crack of dawn. She had pushed the boat out and there was a hearty breakfast of porridge and then a fry up. I saw her dab her eyes when she saw me in my uniform again. It was a visible sign that I was returning to war. Until that moment I could have been going off for another drive with his lordship. The uniform was the last nail.

"This is lovely, mum, you shouldn't have."

"Well, at least I'll know you'll have one decent meal in you."

"Don't worry Mary, I can't imagine that his lordship will go hungry." Having had time to sleep on it Dad was much more philosophical about the whole thing.

Mother shook her head and sat down with her cup of tea. Mum ate when everyone else had finished and if that meant no food for her then she was pleased for her family had been fed. "Now is there anything that you might need?"

"His lordship said it might be cold up there so a scarf might be…"

She leapt up from the table like a scalded cat. I looked at dad who smiled and shrugged. She came down beaming from ear to ear. In her hands, she held an assortment of woollen goods. "Here's a scarf, a balaclava, a pair of gloves and a pair of fingerless gloves."

I jumped up and hugged her. "You are a marvel! How did you know?"

She sat down flushed and pleased, "I didn't but Mary Burns told me that her son was in Flanders and he had written to say how cold and wet it was. She was knitting for him. I thought Tom or John might need them but I can make more for them."

I had just put them in my old holdall when we heard the roar and screech of the Singer. Dad shook his head, "Does he never drive at a normal speed?"

"I'd better go. He said we have a long way to drive today."

I had said farewell to Sarah the night before but Alice and Kathleen came on either side of me and kissed me. Kath whispered, "And write this time! Start a letter today! She misses you terribly, our Bill."

"I will and you two keep an eye on them both eh? They're not spring chickens anymore." I punched Albert playfully in the arm. "And you take care- don't rush into anything eh?" I gave him a look which I knew he would understand and he nodded.

Dad shook hands, "Just do your duty son but come back safe."

"I will dad." Mother said nothing for she was in floods of tears. He body was wracked by sobs. I hugged her and felt myself filling up. "I love you, mum." I felt her nod beneath my arm.

The door opened and Lord Burscough stood there, "Come on old chap. We have the open road ahead of us."He suddenly saw my mother's face and flushed, "Don't worry Mrs Harsker, I'll make sure nothing happens to him."

She gave a slight bob and dabbed her eyes, "Make sure you look after both of you Lord Burscough."

I threw my bag into the space behind my seat and sat down. Impulsively I put on the balaclava. My sisters laughed and Lord Burscough smiled, "Just the ticket! Off we go then!"

There was no long goodbye we just hurtled off down the dark road and I was grateful that we couldn't speak for I wanted that picture of my family etched into my mind. We left the quiet English village and as we zoomed away in the dark, I knew that this was what we were fighting for.

Not the Belgians, or the Serbs and certainly not the politicians. We were fighting for our families and a way of life.

Chapter 13

Joyce Green Airfield at Dartford in Kent was really a holding Aerodrome. When we stopped for lunch close to Wolverhampton at a little place called Codsall his Lordship told me all about the squadron.

"We have been flying little trainers called the Avro 504K. We are now moving to the F.E. 2b. Much better bus. They have a machine gun at the front. Jolly stable little aeroplane. We'll be flying them over to France to a place called Vert Galand close to Amiens. We will just be in Blighty overnight and then we hop over the Channel. Most of the chaps will be flying today. The C.O. gave me permission to be late because of your sister's wedding. Bit of luck that. It means the others get to do the donkey work around the new airfield. The squadron Commander is a nice chap, Major Brack. A damned good flier. It was he who suggested that I get an observer gunner who knew engines. If we are lucky the Quartermaster won't have gone yet and we can get you kitted out."

He was right about being a holding aerodrome. There were the remnants of about four squadrons there and all of them were headed for France.

The Major, when I was introduced to him, looked remarkably young. I had thought that his lordship was young to be a captain but the major looked to be even younger.

He had a young face but an old man's handshake. It was very firm. Dad had always set great store by a firm handshake. He said it told you everything you needed to know about a man. "Welcome, Flight Sergeant Harsker. Could I see your papers please?" I handed them to him and he scanned them. "Good, they appear to be in order." He shouted through the door, "Flight Sergeant Lowery take these papers to Lieutenant Marshall tell him our new Flight Sergeant is here."

An older man came through the door, gave me a cursory glance and then left with my papers. "Marshall is the adjutant and deals with all the paperwork. We'll have you signed up in a jiffy. Now I'll be rude and talk to the captain here."

I felt embarrassed, "That's fine sir. I can wait outside if…"

He flapped a hand before me, "No need to do that old chap." He addressed his lordship. "Now then James you will be leading three aircraft tomorrow. Lieutenant Devries will be in one of the new buses and Lieutenant Dundas will take the old Avro."

I saw his lordship's face fall. "That will slow us down."

"Can't be helped." He suddenly turned to me. "By the by can you read a map? James said you were a scout in the cavalry."

"Yes sir, I can read a map."

"Excellent. Then that is settled. You better go and get your chap's equipment before the damned quartermaster sells it all!"

His lordship was laughing as we left. "Don't repeat that to Quartermaster Doyle. The C.O. was just joking. Mr Doyle is very conscientious."

We arrived at a newly erected building which was empty save for a sergeant. "Ah, Sergeant Doyle. This is Flight Sergeant Harsker. We'll be toddling over to France tomorrow in one of the new buses and we will need some equipment."

Sergeant Doyle was almost completely bald and seemed to be perpetually grinning. He was from Liverpool, not far from Burscough and had what is known as a Scouse accent. He was the antithesis of Quartermaster Grimes. I liked him from the off.

He looked at me from head to toe as though sizing me up. "Right then Flight, let's see you'll need a flying helmet." As he named each item he scurried to a shelf to get one. "Goggles, two pairs. Heavy-duty gloves. Great coat, I think it is your size. Just try it on." I did so and it seemed a little large. "Perfect. One holster and belt, Mess tins, two. Mess kit, one. RFC badge, one. Fur-lined boots. What size?"

"Nine."

"Fur-lined boots size nine, one pair. And finally," he took down a canvas wrap around bag which looked very heavy. "One tool kit, Flight Sergeants for the use of." The happy Liverpudlian grinned and looked at his almost empty shelves. "Anything else will have to wait until France. I'm going over at the end of the week with one of the new trucks they are giving us and a bowser." He flourished a piece of paper before me. "Sign here and we are done." He saw me looking at the holster. "See the armourer for your pistol and ammo."

He went whistling back to work and I carried the equipment he had given me. Once outside I was taken to the armourer who gave me a .45 Webley and fifty rounds of ammunition, which I had to sign for.

His lordship laughed, "It's just like the army. You sign for everything. Let's go back to the Singer and get your stuff. When I have shown you your tent I'll give you a quick shufti around the old bus." There were a row of tents. "Pick an empty one. These belonged to the lads who left this morning. Just bring your coat and flying helmet; the rest we can leave here."

He already had his own flying helmet on and he almost ran to get to his aircraft. I had never seen an aeroplane before. At least I hadn't seen one close up. We had heard them in France but they had been high up and sounded like angry insects. This one was what is called a pusher. It meant that the propeller pushed the aircraft from behind, rather than pulling from the front. There was a Lewis gun in the front cockpit. What worried me was that there did not seem to be any protection for the gunner. I would be the gunner!

He stood back admiringly. "Well, what do you think?"

"If I am to be honest, sir, I am terrified."

"Don't worry, you will love it." He looked up at the sky. "We have an hour of daylight left. We'll take her for a quick spin to get you used to it and then its maps for you young William."

I put my helmet and coat on. His lordship climbed into the cockpit. I went to climb in the forward cockpit with the gun when he said, "Not yet. You have to start it for me. Go and stand by the propeller."

When I reached it the propeller looked huge. The captain was hidden by the engine and propeller but I heard his voice. "When I shout, 'contact', then you spin the propeller and get out of the way."

It seemed a little dangerous to me but it looked as though I would need to learn how to do this sooner rather than later. I made sure that I could spring back out of the way and then held the propeller. He hadn't told me which way to spin it but I had seen the flywheels on the cars I had serviced and had an idea that it would be clockwise. It seemed to me quite similar to starting a car with a starting handle.

"Contact!"

I flung the propeller around and there was a bang, some smoke and then it stopped. There were two sergeants working on the aeroplane next to me and they came over. One of them stubbed his cigarette out and said, "Are you the new bloke?"

I grinned, "Does it show?"

He laughed, "Just a bit. Stand back and I'll show you how it is done. Ready, Captain Burscough!"

"Contact!"

The sergeant threw his whole body weight behind his action and then jumped backwards. There was a bang and a black plume of smoke but the engine caught. After a couple of coughs, it began to roar.

"Thanks, sergeant."

"That's flight and you are welcome but it's the only lesson you get. You have to be a fast learner in the RFC!" He pointed to the cockpit. "I should get on board if I were you."

"Come on Harsker, get on board!"

I ran round to the front and clambered up. It was not easy, especially in the greatcoat. I saw the two sergeants smiling. There was a lot to learn here. I managed to get myself into the seat and I held on to the sides with both hands. I could barely hear the captain but I did manage to hear. "Fasten your seat belt." I raised my hand to show I had heard and I fastened the belt over my lap. It looked to me like this was the only safety equipment I had. I saw the captain wave both his hands and Ted pulled something from below the wheels. I later found they were called chocks. We began to trundle along the grassy field.

Suddenly I head the engine speed increase and we were moving quicker over the grass. It was very bumpy. There was no warning that we were about to go aloft; the nose, and me, rose steeply into the air. His lordship was correct. This was unlike anything I had ever experienced and already I loved it. I was glad I had the goggles. The wind was rushing into my face and was quite painful. I could hear the captain shouting but I couldn't hear any of his words. Besides I was too busy watching the city of London unfold beneath me. In the distance, I could see the Houses of Parliament and the Thames which snaked west. I saw that the captain was flying along the river. I suppose it made sense. That way you knew where you were. The aeroplane began to climb and then he banked it. I could now see the aerodrome in the distance with the river close by. He shouted again and I turned to try to see. He pointed down. We were landing.

If I thought the take off was exciting then it was nothing compared with the landing; the ground rushed towards us and the tents seemed to be within touching distance. We bumped and went up in the air and then settled down again. His lordship swung the tail of the aeroplane round so that it was facing in the opposite direction and then the propeller stopped. It was silent.

He was out of the aircraft before me and stood there like an eager child, "Well?"

"You were right sir. It is wonderful."

He clapped his arm around my shoulder. "It is isn't it? Sorry about the bumpy landing. I am not used to the bus yet. But I'll get better." He took off his helmet. He pointed to a rubber tube which was attached to the ear. "I forgot to show you how to attach this to the rubber pipe. It enables us to speak with each other." He shook his head. "That's my fault. I am too impetuous. I should have given you a good briefing before we tried that. Still, it should be easier in the morning." We heard a bell. "That's the bell for the mess tent."

One of the cooks came out and yelled, "Jippo!"

He pointed at the tent to which the sergeants were running. "Go and get fed. I'll drop the maps off tomorrow. If you could study them tonight then we might not end up paddling across the channel eh?" He strode off whistling; the RFC worked for him; he was as happy as I had ever seen him.

I dumped my helmet and my coat and picked up my mess kit. The first visit to a mess was always an ordeal. I knew that from our Yeomanry mess. When we had new men you could see the nervousness. Where should they sit? Who were the ones they shouldn't offend? What protocols and written rules were there? I knew I would make a mistake or two and I resolved to make the best of it.

The tent was almost deserted. I saw the armourer and quartermaster sergeants in one corner. The two Flight Sergeants I had spoken to were just sitting down when I went in. I collected my food and asked, "Mind if I sit here, lads?"

The one who had given me the advice said, "Free country pal."

"Thanks and thanks for the advice."

"No problem. Us Flights have to stick together don't we?"

I nodded in a non-committal manner. "Tell me, how did you know I was new?"

They both grinned at each other. "The coat."

"The coat? I thought it was standard issue."

"It is but it is bloody useless. It isn't warm enough and when it gets wet it makes the front end of the aeroplane heavy and almost impossible to fly."

The other one said, "That's why you need either a leather coat or a fur coat or a combination of both. Your officer, he has a coat from America, like the cowboys wear, a duster. It is made of hide and underneath it, he wears a fur waistcoat. He's warm and dry."

"And your gloves. They are useless too. They keep your hands warm but you can't pull the triggers on the Lewis and you can't change the magazine easily."

"What you need is some fingerless gloves to wear underneath and you tie a string on the gloves and pass it through the arms of your coat so when you drop them to fire the gun you don't lose them." He chewed his meat and pulled a piece of gristle from it. "Get yourself a balaclava and wear it under the helmet; otherwise your ears will freeze."

"Thanks, lads." I held out my hand, "I am Sergeant Bill Harsker."

The first one shook mine and said, "No you're not, you are Flight Sergeant Bill Harsker. The flight part gets you more pay." He tapped the side of his nose, "I am Gordon Hewitt, call me Gordy and this miserable looking bugger is Ted Thomas." He leaned back and lit a cigarette. "Someone told me you've already been over there," he gestured with his thumb, "in France."

"Aye, I was in the cavalry. I was invalided out."

They leaned forward both interested now. "We both changed to the RFC before the BEF left for France. Tell us what was it like?"

How could I begin to describe it? I put my palms flat on the table and leaned back. "There were thirty blokes in my troop. Twenty-nine good 'uns and an officer, who was about as much use as a one-legged man in an arse-kicking contest." They looked at each other and smiled; that type of officer was a common bird. There are four survivors: me, a cracking old sergeant now retired, my mate Robbie who lost his left hand and..."

I let Gordy finish the sentence off, "The useless bastard." They both nodded.

"You've got it. No, it was no fun. The day of cavalry is over. Horses weren't made to charge machine guns but this is the future."

"It is but don't think it will be easy."

"I thought you hadn't been in combat."

"We haven't but unlike some of the chinless wonders who fly us, we know the limitations of our aircraft. That's why you need to learn how to fly as soon as you can. Our old trainers had dual controls. If the pilot bought it you could land it if you could fly. If not then you are already in your wooden box."

Ted chuckled, "Except these only get cremated."

"Now these new ones have a major flaw." I looked at him expectantly. "The Hun can come from behind. You cannot turn the gun to cover the back and so Herr Fritz will keep firing until either your pilot is dead or he hits the engine block. Either way, you are dead."

Ted nodded, "And in our case, because we have the most experience we have been given the new Loots. We need every trick we can lay our hands on."

"What can you do?"

"Did you shoot when you were in the cavalry?"

"Aye, I was quite a good shot."

"Good, then get yourself a rifle and keep it in the front cockpit. That way you make Fritz need a quick change of trousers. You can stand up and fire behind you when he thinks he has you by the short and curlies."

"I'm glad I spoke to you two."

"Don't mention it, Bill. As I said, we need to stick together. All the pilots do is get us over the enemy. It is our job to observe and fire the guns."

When I got to my tent I found the maps and an oil lamp. I lit the lamp. Its light illuminated my balaclava, scarf and gloves. "Thanks, mum; you've saved my life if you did but know it."

I was up bright and early the next day. In the mess tent, I saw the armourer. He was alone and I felt happy about approaching him, "Flight?"

He looked up from his fried bread and bacon. He looked as though he was trying to recognise me. Enlightenment dawned. "You're the new bloke. What can I do you for?"

"I need a rifle and some .303 ammo."

He laughed, "I see you've been talking to Ted and Gordy. Come to the tent after breakfast and I'll sort you." He rubbed his fingers together.

I went for my own food. I assumed that it was the same in the RFC as the Yeomanry. You had to pay for little extras. You did not use money. You had a ration of tobacco each week. I didn't smoke and so I had given most of it to my dad. I still had a few ounces of the stuff and I knew the armourer was a smoker. It would be worth it to keep me and his lordship safe.

He left before me and then Gordy and Ted came in to join me. "Wet the bed or something?"

I laughed, "No, I just needed to see the armourer. He is getting me a rifle."

They began eating. Ted said, between mouthfuls, "I hear you are navigating today?" I nodded. "Ever done that before?"

"From the air? No. But I was the one who led the regiment around northern France reading a map. I travelled through the area around Amiens before."

"It's different from the air you know."

I nodded. I had studied the maps and thought this through. "I know, it should be easier. You can see features like rivers and towns easier from the air. You want to try it on the back of a horse with hedges all around you."

Gordy grinned and lit a cigarette, "He's right, Ted." He gestured at his morose friend. "I told you before, Ted is a miserable half empty sort of bloke. It's bad enough flying with a couple of virgins but Ted thought you didn't know one end of a map from another."

Ted looked indignant, "Now don't put words in my mouth. I can offend people easy enough all on my own." He gave what passed as a smile, "You learn to look out for yourself so no offence intended."

"And none taken. I'd be just as curious if you two had joined the cavalry. At least with a horse, the front end is where you expect it to be."

Gordy laughed, "You mean the pusher? It works well enough and it means you can fire forward. The Avro meant you had to fire up all the time."

Ted shook his head, "And guess which unlucky bugger is flying in an Avro today?" He pointed at himself. "Muggins!"

"We shouldn't meet anything should we?"

Gordy shrugged. "We could do. Make sure you check your Lewis and have your rifle ready."

I exchanged the tobacco. The armourer charged me more than he should have but I didn't smoke and I would soon make up the loss. As I took the rifle to the aeroplane I wondered if it had been cleaned and degreased. I would have to wait until we landed in France for that particular task. Having spoken to Gordy and Ted I knew that I had to pack the aircraft well. Luckily I did not have too much gear to take. I draped the coat over the wing; I would not need that until airborne. However, I did wear the fur lined boots. I placed the Luger and rifle in the bottom of the cockpit. I still had the bandoliers from my days in the cavalry and I packed the ammunition in those.

I clambered into the cockpit to stow all the gear. My two new friends had impressed upon me the need for balance. "Keep everything in the middle and don't put anything in the nose. That Lewis gun is heavy enough as it is."

With everything stowed I checked the Lewis gun. I had fired one before and knew the action. I had one magazine fitted and a spare one. I had less than a hundred bullets in the two magazines. I did not fancy trying to reload the magazine in the air. It appeared to function correctly but I would strip it and clean it along with the rifle once we had landed.

Dawn broke and there was still no sign of his lordship. I saw Ted and Gordy working on their aeroplanes. I strolled to the engine. In theory, it worked the same as the Lanchester and the Singer although it was driving a two-bladed propeller. I knew how to check the oil and fuel. I did so and they appeared to be full. I knew that lines could wear and, although this was a new aircraft, I checked that all the lines had neither kink nor crack. I saw Gordy checking the cables and struts on the wing of his F.E.2b. I walked over to him.

"What are you checking for?"

"Just make sure that the cables are tight and that there is no damage to the struts. That landing yesterday might have shaken them loose. Just tighten them." He nodded over to Ted. "Poor Ted has a harder job. That is our oldest aircraft and every bugger has bumped that down at one time or another."

I nodded, "Where do you stow the tool kit. I imagine it is too heavy for the front."

"There's a compartment behind the roundel. It goes under your seat." He laughed cynically, "It is armour for your arse!"

My struts, wires and cables were all sound and so I stowed the tool kit and donned my balaclava, greatcoat and checked the maps while I waited for the officers. It seemed straight forward. I would fly along the river and then the coast until I reached Dover. I knew that you could see Calais from Dover so that short hop over the Channel wouldn't be a problem. Once there we could fly down the coast and follow the river up to Amiens and the aerodrome. It might not be the quickest route but it would be both the most reliable and the safest.

The three officers finally strolled out. Four privates strolled behind them with equipment which they loaded into the cockpits. I hoped they loaded it well. "Ah good morning, Flight Sergeant Harsker. Everything ready?"

"Yes, sir."

"Route all planned?"

"Yes, sir."

"Jolly good. Well, let's hope we see France and not Belgium eh?" The two young lieutenants who looked to be about fourteen years old both laughed. He turned to them. "You two keep on my tail. If you have a problem get your observer to fire his Lewis in the air to attract my attention." He grinned, "Not that I will be able to do much about it but at least I can write your people a nice letter eh?"

Their faces fell at the prospect. When we reached our aeroplane the captain showed me how to attach the rubber tubes which enabled us to speak with each other.

"Right then. I'll go and get ready."

It did not take him long and I heard, "Contact!"

This time I knew what to do and I put all my weight behind it. There was a cloud of smoke and then the engine coughed into life. I waited until it achieved a steady rhythm and then ran to the front. I clambered in and then attached the tubes into my flying helmet which I then donned. I saw one of the privates waiting with the chocks. In my ear, I heard a muffled voice say. "Everything good there Harsker?"

"Yes, sir!"

He must have waved his hands for we started to move forward. I was about to fly to war. My life had changed, forever.

Chapter 14

The aeroplane seemed slower to climb but then I realised we now had a full load of fuel and our baggage. "Well Flight, have you our route all ready?"

"Yes, sir. Straight down the river and turn south at the coast and then a hop over to Calais."

"Good. I don't fancy having to climb over the hills and waste fuel. This way we can keep low."

We did keep low. To me we appeared to be skimming over the rooftops but, later when we landed, I was told we were four hundred feet in the air. The warm boots certainly helped as did the balaclava. It was cold and overcast. I was pleased that we were flying low.

I had the map folded so that I could trace our course. I kept checking for the different landmarks and I told the captain time we passed one. "You are doing a fine job. Could you stand and check that the others are still following?"

I couldn't refuse an order but I was petrified. I undid the seat belt and then held on to the two sides as I stood. I tried to crane my neck around but I could see nothing. I turned myself in the cockpit. I was terrified. The sides barely came to my knee. I could be tipped out at any time. Eventually, I faced the rear. I could see the grin on the captain's face. "Scary eh William?"

"Yes, sir. I'm just glad that the uniform trousers are brown." I heard him laugh. I could see the two planes. They were echeloned back from our port wing. The Avro was slightly lower than the F.E. 2b. "They are both there sir!"

"Right then face the front and tell me when to turn."

The journey was uneventful until we struck the coast and then flew over Dover. "Dover sir. We need to head due east."

"Right Flight. Cock and arm the Lewis."

"Sir?" I could not keep the incredulity from my voice. This was the English Channel.

"Intelligence has it that there are a couple of Huns around. They sometimes fly over Dover. Keep an eye out eh?"

I knew that I would never be able to discriminate a German from a British plane. I had to unfasten my seatbelt to stand and to cock the gun. I quickly sat down and fastened my seatbelt again. I pulled out my rifle and loaded it. It may sound cowardly but I worked out I could fire the rifle from a seated position. I was not ready to fight quite yet!

The water looked grey and cold from our lofty position. I stirred myself. I was supposed to be watching for the enemy. I was happy when I saw the old Medieval Tower of Calais appear ahead.

"Calais, Captain Burscough. Turn south and follow the coast." I knew that I would need a compass to give him more precise directions in future. So far we appeared to be on course and, I think, making good time. I knew that we were faster than the Avro and so the captain could go faster if he had to.

We reached the river and I told the captain to head south-east. We were almost there. I saw what looked like a bird in the distance. The hairs on the back of my neck told me it wasn't and I took no chances, better to appear a fool than be killed the first day on the job.

"Sir, I think there is an aeroplane ahead." I took off my belt and stood. I pointed directly ahead. Putting both hands on the Lewis gun I braced my knees against the side of the cockpit.

"I see it." There was a pause. "I can't tell yet whose it is. Signal to the others."

I half turned and waved at Gordy. I saw him stand and wave back. He waved to Ted. I looked ahead again and saw that the single bird had become two and they were closing with us. They were biplanes but I could not see any markings as they were head-on.

"Keep an eye on them, Flight. If they are the Hun then they will try to climb and drop down on us."

I looked at the map and saw that we had less than twenty miles to go to the airfield. How could the Germans operate this close to our lines?"

Then I saw them begin to climb and as they did I saw the black crosses on their wings. They were Germans. "They are the Hun sir."

"I can see. Don't fire until we are much closer and only use short bursts."

"Sir!"

Even though they were some way away I tracked them with my gun. I knew you had to lead a target but these aeroplanes could travel at almost a hundred miles an hour. That was faster than any target I had fired upon. My only consolation was that there were three of us. We outnumbered them.

"What kind are they sir?"

"Albatrosses I think. I am not sure if they are armed but if they are climbing to attack then they must think they can."

Suddenly the climb stopped and I saw them swoop down towards us. They were heading for Gordy's aeroplane and they were in one line. I aimed ahead of the screaming German. I heard Gordy fire and so I did too. The bullets missed the tail of the first aircraft. I tried a second burst with the second aircraft and this time I saw a couple of pieces of fabric detach themselves from the tail.

The gun jammed. I took off the magazine to clear the blockage and the captain banked the aeroplane at the same time. If I had not been holding on to the Lewis gun I would have been over the side. I cleared the blockage and replaced the magazine. I looked for the Germans but could not see them. I heard the captain's voice in my ear. "The cunning blighter's are going overhead where the Lewis can't fire."

I sat down and brought out the Lee Enfield; my rifle could. I felt much more comfortable seated and I raised the gun. I could hear the Albatros' engine as it moved above us less than fifty feet away. I wondered why they hadn't fired on us. As soon as I saw the engine and propeller in my sights I emptied the magazine and then reached down for the Luger. As I looked up I saw two things: the pilot aiming a rifle at me and then smoke and oil coming from the engine. I aimed the Luger and emptied the magazine at the pilot. I didn't hit him but as he had been flying at the same speed as us, I had managed to hit his aeroplane and I saw the holes appear just behind him. The pilot banked and headed north, away from us. The second one followed the damaged leader.

"Good show William! You are a bag filled with surprises. And just in the nick of time too. It looks like our airfield is right ahead."

I risked a look to the left and saw that both aeroplanes were still there although the Avro had an oil trail coming from its engine. As we came in I noticed that there were clusters of aeroplanes around the field. It looked to be the base for a number of squadrons.

The second landing was much smoother than the first and we rolled to a halt close to the other aeroplanes from the squadron. When the engine stopped I closed my eyes and said a quick prayer of thanks. We had been lucky. I was only a novice airman but I knew that the day could have ended badly for us. If Gordy had not advised me about the gun then it might have gone ill for us.

I clambered out of the cockpit and I have to admit I was shaking. It had been both exhilarating and terrifying.

Lord Burscough slapped me on the back. "I say, well done. I didn't know you had a Luger."

"A souvenir from Flanders but at least it made him shift."

"It did indeed."

We turned as the Avro limped in. "Looks like Lieutenant Devries had a few problems there."

I looked around. There were tents laid out and a mess tent. I could only one wooden building. It was in the far corner of the field and looked to have nothing to do with the aircraft parked on the grass. It was back to life in the cavalry. I knew I would cope. If I ever felt sorry for myself I would think of Doddy and Tiny; they would happily change places with me.

Two privates ran over with chocks. They saluted both of us. I returned the salute but I was not used to it. We had been much more informal in the Yeomanry.

"Right, I'll go and report. Bring my stuff to the main tent and I will see where we are billeted."

I realised then that I was a servant still. "Sir."

I took out my gear first and then found the bags the captain had brought on board. When I had collected them all Gordy and Ted wandered over.

"Nice shooting. Those Huns can climb better than we can. You did well."

I turned to Ted, "Did you get hit?"

"Nah, it was just a seal which went. It looked worse than it was but I will have to strip it down tomorrow."

Gordy nodded with his head. "Come on let's go and get our tents sorted. We can service the aircraft later."

I was surprised. "We have to service them as well as fly them?"

Ted grimaced, "Technically, no. But the blokes they have servicing them don't have to fly them so we do it. They can refuel them and do the magazines."

Gordy held his hand up, "I do that myself." He looked at me. "Your Lewis jammed?"

"It did. "

"Strip it down, clean it and reload the magazines yourself. That way you know it is done right."

"The mechanics have an easy time then?"

Red chuckled, "We make them spin the propellers. It's about all they are good for and it saves us struggling into the front."

We found three tents together and we dumped our gear. I was glad to take off my warm weather gear now that we were on the ground. I dropped the captain's bags at the main tent. I saw him inside with the two lieutenants talking to another captain.

I returned to the aeroplane. There were a couple of bullet holes in the wing. I would need to get them repaired. I took the magazines from the Lewis and laid them on the ground. I then stripped and cleaned the Lewis gun. It was still filled with the factory grease. The ground crew had done nothing but fit it. I became angry. That could have cost the lives of a valuable pilot, an aeroplane and me! When it was fixed I went to the engine and checked everything that could be checked. I heard

"Jippo!" yelled. They obviously had no bell here yet. I went to my tent to get my mess tins and nipped into the latrines to wash down a little. I was hungry. Fear did that to me.

Ted and Gordy had saved a place for me. It was a much more crowded sergeant's mess than the one we had left in England. I sat opposite the two of them.

"Looks like there are three squadrons here." Gordy leaned over and spoke more quietly, "Better watch your stuff. Our lads are all right but these others are thieving bastards!"

I smiled. It was the same in the cavalry. No one trusted another regiment. After we had eaten, Ted and Gordy lit up and I leaned back. "What happens next then?"

"The next couple of days should be easy until the C.O. and the rest of the lads arrive and then all hell will break loose." Ted nodded at me. "Get his lordship to give you a lesson in the Avro."

"Hang on Gordy. The bloody thing is knackered as it is."

"You'll get a new one soon enough. The sooner it is wrecked the sooner they get you a new aeroplane."

Ted almost brightened, "I hadn't thought of that. It'll be right by tomorrow, son."

"Do you think I am ready?"

"Listen Bill, the only way we will survive this war is if we become officers. That means becoming a pilot. Ted and I will soon be ready to fly and when someone pops his clogs then we will be made up. It is cheaper than training a fresh-faced young toff in England."

"You are right, Ted, and those two Beer Boys will not last a week over here. I thought they were going to fill their pants when those two Huns arrived."

I wondered what they would think of me. I had been as a scared as anyone. I had been lucky no one had noticed.

The next day was strange. I heard reveille and, after my wash and shave, took my mess tins for breakfast. The only people in the mess were our squadron. I sat next to Gordy and Ted again. "Where is everyone?"

"On patrol. That's why we make the most of this quiet time. The C.O. won't be here for a couple of days. Make hay while the sun shines."

After I had checked the aeroplane again I sought out Captain Burscough. He smiled at me. "It will be quiet for a couple of days. It'll give you the chance to get to know people."

"Thank you, sir, but I was wondering if I could have a flying lesson." He gave me a strange look. "Flight Sergeant Hewitt thought it might be a good idea." I thought he might say no and so I made something up. "If I knew how to fly then it might help me to work the gun better as I would know what you were going to do."

He smiled and I was relieved, "Good idea but the Avro is Kaput at the moment."

"No sir, Ted, er Flight Sergeant Thomas said it would be fixed." That was an outright lie but I hoped that Ted would have made the crate airworthy.

He paused and then a smile split his face, "Very well. It will give me a chance to get the lie of the land."

Ted had, by the look on his face, only just got the aeroplane ready. "Well done, Flight Sergeant Thomas."

"No problem sir, it's what we do." Ted rubbed his thumb and first finger together. I knew what that meant- I would have to pay him in tobacco for his work. I nodded. "I even reloaded the guns, sir. If you like I'll start her for you."

"Good fellow."

They had the same rubber pipe system in the aeroplane and when I had connected it up I heard his lordship's voice in my ear. Before he starts it up I'll take you through the controls. You have a joystick in front of you. Push it forward to go down and pull it back to go up. On the floor in front of you are a couple of pedals: right banks you starboard and left banks you port. That is about it. I'll take us up and then I'll let you have a bash eh?"

"How do I make it go faster?"

I heard a guffaw from behind me. "Let's just see if you can keep us in the air first eh?"

"Yes, sir."

"Contact!"

I saw Ted spin the propeller and it caught. This was different for a start. I had a propeller in front of me. The F.E. 2 had been open. Captain Burscough took off smoothly enough and headed west towards the sea. I could see that I had dials in front of me and I had some idea of the height of the aeroplane. It took him some time to get to a height where he was happy but eventually I heard his voice. "Get hold of the stick. Forget the pedals for the moment. Let's just try to fly straight. Just tell me when you are about to do something eh?"

"Right sir. I have the stick."

"You have the aeroplane."

There was no difference. We kept on heading west. This was easy. After a few minutes, I heard the tone of the engine change. It sounded as though it was struggling.

"Flight, you are climbing. Look at your gauges. You are about to stall the aeroplane. Put the nose down a touch."

I panicked and pushed forward on the stick. Suddenly we were heading down in a dive and going much faster.

I heard a chuckle. "A bit too much stick. Try to keep it in the middle eh?"

I pulled back slowly and, gradually, our speed slowed until the engine sounded better. I checked our height and we had dropped about two hundred feet.

"That's better. Now fly straight until I tell you to turn. Have your feet ready on the pedals."

I saw that there were clouds, seemingly just above my head, and the grey sea looked too close for comfort, but I was flying. "Jolly good, now right pedal and, ever so slightly to the right with the stick." I had learned my lesson and did everything slowly. I must have pleased the captain. "Excellent. Now centre the stick and foot off the pedal. Look ahead and you'll see France. We are going to take her down to the airfield. Fly straight until I tell you otherwise."

I began to recognise the land. I saw the river and knew where we were.

"Start to drop the nose a little." I did so and saw the altimeter register the fact that we were descending. "Can you see the airfield? Look for the windsock."

I peered ahead and saw, in the distance the tents and the green field. "Yes, sir."

"We are coming in the right way and you will be landing into the wind. Keep watching the windsock."

"Landing?"

"Why not? You are doing quite well. I will adjust the engine speed for you. All you have to do is to take it down slowly and keep the nose up."

I hoped he knew what he was doing. The voice kept telling me when to go lower. The ground seemed to rush up at me far too quickly. "Use the pedals, you are too far to port."

I corrected and then I heard the noise of the engine change and Captain Burscough shouted, "Nose up a little and get ready for the bump."

I moved the stick a tiny amount and we hit the ground and then came up again. "Nose down a fraction and we are there."

This time we bumped but stayed down. We rolled forward and then the engine stopped. I saw Ted and Gordy run over. We were not in the perfect place. In fact, we were in the middle of the runway. They began to push us towards the other aeroplanes. I disconnected the tubes and, when we stopped, leapt from the aeroplane.

Gordy grinned and said, "Not bad. You just had the one bump."

Ted sniffed, "Of course I'll have to check everything now." I threw him my pouch of tobacco. He grinned. "Thanks, Bill."

Captain Burscough descended and clapped me on the back. "You are a natural, Flight Sergeant. We'll have another go tomorrow eh? You had better check our aircraft. When the C.O. arrives we'll have to be ready to fly at a moment's notice."

Gordy and Ted took me through the basics of servicing our aircraft. It seemed straightforward but I knew that it was not like servicing a car. If I got this wrong then we could fall from the sky.

"So the mechanics don't do anything at all?"

"The officers who fly the single-seater jobs, they don't service their own aeroplanes."

"They don't want to get their hands dirty. The mechanics look after them."

I could see that, for the captain and myself, it was better if I looked after our F.E. 2.

Chapter 15

It was in the late afternoon when a red-faced and angry Captain Burscough strode over to us. I had stripped and cleaned the Lewis and my Lee Enfield. I had hand-loaded both magazines and the aeroplane was purring like a kitten. I was feeling pleased with myself.

"Can I see you for a moment in private, Flight?"

"Certainly sir." We walked away from the line of aeroplanes.

"I've just had my ears chewed out by the Aerodrome commander, Colonel Pemberton-Smythe. Apparently, I am not qualified to teach you to fly and it is not necessary for you to fly."

"But Ted and Gordy both told me it is common practice."

"It is in our squadron but the colonel, who doesn't fly, by the way, wants things done the way they were in his cavalry regiment. We have to do things by the book! Sorry. The lessons will need to stop until the C.O. gets here. He can argue the case. I am merely a captain."

"That's all right sir. I wouldn't want you to get into trouble. Besides, I found the lesson very useful. The things I learned will help me to be a better observer. Now I know what you are going to be doing and why." I smiled.

"You are a good egg you know. I would have been dreadfully miffed if this had happened to me."

"I suppose I have been lucky with the officers I have known but I know there are some stiff-necked officers out there who are still fighting the Battle of Waterloo."

"And that is true."

The colonel, it seems had more rules for us to obey than I had imagined. That evening, as we went for our evening meal, we were stopped from entering by the Colonel and a Sergeant Major who looked older than George had been. The colonel did not speak but he glowered at us while his wishes were transmitted by his sergeant.

"You men need to change for dinner."

Even the normally affable Gordy was shocked. "But we never dress for dinner unless it is a special occasion."

"That may have been true before but now you obey the camp rules and you need to change."

Ted shook his head. "We don't have formal clothes, sergeant. We only have a change of uniform."

The colonel could not help himself and he spluttered, "That is a disgrace!"

Gordy chose his moment well, "And as the spare uniform is still dirty from the flight over then a change of clothes would not make us any smarter... sir."

The sergeant-major leaned in to Gordy, "Watch your mouth Flight Sergeant or you will be on a fizzer!"

"Sorry, sir."

The colonel was on the horns of a dilemma. "Very well, you may go in this evening but tomorrow I want clean uniforms and, as soon as it is possible, formal dress for the mess."

We all saluted smartly and snapped a, "Sir!"

As we sat eating, feeling like poor relations, I told them what had happened to the captain. Gordy shook his head and waved a fork around at the other diners. "Look at them. The other squadrons are all dressed in their number ones. Our lot look like they have been kitted out by the Salvation Army. The wrong people are running this war."

Ted nodded his agreement, "And that's the truth, brother!"

Gordy winked at me. "Don't worry about the flying lessons. Me and Ted can teach you. We might not be as good as his lordship but we can fly and we know the planes. We'll just say we are taking it up to check instruments. He's a cavalryman and won't have the first clue. When the C.O. gets here, then watch out for fireworks."

I was not so sure, "He seemed a little young to me."

"He might look young but he has a fearsome temper and he has more than enough influence."

They were as good as their word. The next day, after we had washed our uniforms Ted took me up and gave me a second lesson. I didn't stall it and I learned to regulate the speed. I still bumped the landing but Ted was impressed. As we went into the evening meal, smartly dressed this time, the colonel and the Sergeant Major were waiting for us. He put his hand up and tapped Ted in the chest. Ted's eyes narrowed, "What were you doing taking this Flight Sergeant up in your Avro this afternoon?"

Ted moved the hand away and said, in a monotone as though rehearsed, "Flight Sergeant Harsker is new to the squadron having just transferred from the cavalry and I took him up to familiarise him with the Avro, Sergeant Major."

I could see that the N.C.O. was not convinced but he could not argue with the motives. The colonel looked at me, "What regiment?"

"The Lancashire Yeomanry, sir."

I saw recognition in his eyes at the name. "A damned fine regiment and they performed heroically in Flanders. A shame they had to be disbanded." He looked at me with fresh eyes, "Why didn't you transfer to the cavalry then, sergeant?"

I looked him directly in the eye, "Sir, did you ever charge machine guns when you were in the cavalry?"

I felt the Sergeant Major bristle at my impertinence but the colonel held up his hand and said, "No, sergeant, I don't believe I ever did."

"When we did I lost the horse I had ridden for ten years and twenty-seven of my troop, sir. I don't want to witness that again, sir."

He looked thoughtful, "I see, carry on."

As he turned away the Sergeant Major said quietly, "You want to watch yourself, my son."

I turned to him, "And you want to watch who you put your hands on Sergeant Major. If you put your hands on me like you did on Flight Sergeant Thomas then I shall have you on a charge as it is against King's Regulations to lay hands on a junior officer. I know King's Regulations." I didn't flinch from his belligerent stare. He turned away with an angry snap of his heels.

Gordy shook his head, "Have you got a death wish or what?"

"He's just a bully and you stand up to bullies. He was out of order and he knew it. I knew some decent N.C.O.s. They taught me the rules and how to use them. He doesn't worry me."

That evening marked a change in my relationship with my friends. I think until then they thought that I was young and naïve. They learned I was not. George and my time in Flanders had put a steel rod in my backbone. I had faced death and survived. I was not afraid of a man who had not seen modern combat and had no concept of the horrors that went with it.

The rest of the squadron arrived the next day. The C.O. flew in first and then the rest arrived by noon. I had only met the major briefly but he seemed like a decent sort. I felt sorry for him when the officers descended upon him like seagulls for a scrap of food. Gordy and Ted wiped their hands free of grease and wandered over. "I have never seen that lot so excited."

Ted gave his usual sniff, "Too used to getting their own way they are."

Gordy shook his head, "I'm with them on this. I don't mind rules but only when they are for a purpose. The dress code and the ban on flying lessons do nothing to help us win this war."

He was correct, of course. I had seen the mistakes made in the early days of the war; British soldiers had died when they shouldn't have done. If our brigade had stayed at Dunkirk then we would not have needed to race to the sea.

We did not discover what the outcome of the deputation was. At least not right away. The C.O. was keen for us to get as many hours in as we could before the weather and the shorter days curtailed our flying. He had the best British aeroplane and he wanted to use that advantage.

We were all gathered in the mess tent, both observers and pilots, to be briefed. "Right chaps. I know that things have not gone well here. Perhaps that is my fault, I don't know. We will sort these matters out later. They are not important. Winning the war is! And we start to win that war at dawn tomorrow." There was a cheer and the pilots all banged the table. I thought that the colonel would frown on such actions. "We are going to divide into four flights of three. We will each patrol the front line from Bapaume to Peronne. Observers we need to know where the German trenches are and what artillery they have there. Our brave lads paid a heavy price up at Ypres and we are going to do something about that. There is a French Corps at Albert. With the right intelligence then they can break through and relieve the pressure on Ypres. Do not let me down."

The major was the kind of passionate man you believed in. We would do as he said.

Lieutenant Marshall, the adjutant, stood, "We have detailed maps for the observers. You need to be aware that the Germans have begun to use more aeroplanes in this sector. You will have to watch out for them." He grinned and suddenly looked a lot younger than his grey hair suggested. "Of course they haven't met the F.E. 2b yet. They may be in for a surprise."

I collected my maps and the captain and I found a quiet corner to examine them. "I take it the bus is in top condition?"

"Yes sir, two magazines, my rifle and Luger and the engine is tuned to perfection." His lordship slapped my back and I felt guilty. "The other Flight Sergeants helped me, sir."

"I know but you are settling in well. I am pleased."

We were up long before dawn. The mechanics all stood next to the propellers. I would not have to start her today. It was not raining but I knew that, when it did rain, my greatcoat would be a handicap and not a help. We were to wait for the first rays of dawn's light to launch and take off when the Very Light was fired. I was nervous. I had my map and I knew our target. The major had left our three aeroplanes together which gave me some comfort. I had flown the Avro and knew that Ted had a machine gun too. His was facing towards the rear. We would have protection should anyone try a stern attack.

When the Very light was fired we took off three abreast. Each flight would assemble above the field. As we were first it gave me the chance to orientate myself. The moment we were airborne I cocked and armed the Lewis. We were close to the front and the Germans would have patrols up too. We circled as we waited for our two companions to reach our altitude. The target was to the east of Albert. I could see, in the distance, balloons. Their job would be to spot for artillery. If they were slow to retrieve them, then one task would be to destroy them. Some of the Flight Sergeants from the other squadrons had told us that it was not as easy as it seemed.

Once we were all airborne the captain took us east. We were flying at over six hundred feet but that still seemed remarkably close to the ground. We passed over the British artillery, secure behind sandbags. Then I saw black lines in the earth. They zig-zagged east. These were the trenches messengers would use to reach the front line.

"Get ready Harsker. We are coming up on their lines. You need to keep your eyes peeled for the Hun and the artillery." If I hadn't had a go at flying an aeroplane I would have been resentful but I knew how hard it was. My job was easy by comparison.

I saw that three of the barrage balloons were already halfway down but the last one was not moving. Either the winch was stuck or they were asleep. I would be ready. "Sir, the balloon looks like a good target."

"Right Ho! Have a pop at him. I'll fly as straight as I can and then bank left." I waited until I was less than a hundred and fifty yards away I gave a couple of short bursts. I could not miss; it was an enormous target. I expected an explosion but instead, it just seemed to collapse on itself and then crumple slowly down to the ground. I saw the crew as they jumped out. They were brave men. They would be falling to their death but I assumed they hoped that they might survive.

Suddenly there was the crack of small arms fire and machine guns. I saw two holes appear in the wing as the captain banked us left and over the German trenches. "I'm going to climb. Keep your eye on the ground."

I could see the flashes from the guns but no more holes appeared. As we levelled out I saw the huge guns in the distance. I gave the coordinates to the captain and the F.E.2 headed for them. The other two pilots had to just follow us. There was no way for us to talk aeroplane to aeroplane in the air. I took out my pencil and, using my compass, marked the position of the guns. I also saw a column of men marching west. I marked that down too.

"I'll fly along the line of guns so that you can mark them all. Identify each individual gun."

"Sir."

The fire from below was becoming more intense. Luckily for us, the rear of the aircraft was largely air and they missed hitting anything vital.

More holes appeared in the wings and I noticed that Captain Burscough was having a harder time keeping it straight.

I could hear the tension in his voice as he said, "I think we have chanced our arm enough. Let's go home."

He banked the aircraft and we headed west. We were not out of the woods yet. We had to cross two lines of trenches before we could return to our field. Suddenly I heard the chatter of a Lewis gun. I took off my seatbelt and turned around. I saw that Ted's Avro was being attacked by three Albatros aeroplanes.

"Sir. Germans attacking the Avro."

The limitations of our aeroplane were now obvious to me. We had no way to defend from an attack to the rear. We needed a rear-mounted Lewis on the wing. But that was the future.

"How is Lieutenant Devries coping?"

"Hard to say, sir." Then I saw smoke appear. "Sir, he has been hit."

"Right, I will climb. Use your Lee Enfield until I can turn us around."

I reached down and took out my rifle. I braced my legs against the sides of the cockpit and rested the end of the rifle on the upper wing. The fact that we were climbing helped. I sighted on the Albatros closest to the Avro and fired slowly. I fired at the engine block and worked backwards. I had fired six shots and three of them had hit. The pilot must have been worried for he began to bank. The second Hun began firing. I emptied the magazine at him without success.

I turned around, replaced the rifle and cocked the front Lewis. Lieutenant Dundas had followed us and was now abreast of us. I saw Gordy with his hands on the Lewis. We had gained height and now the captain dived down to rescue our beleaguered comrade. I held my fire until we were a hundred yards away and then, as we dived from above, I watched my bullets stitch a line along the wing and strike the gunner. Then the bus suddenly swerved. I changed my target to the next Albatros, the one I had fired on with my rifle. I finished the magazine and saw his tail sprout holes. I reached down to change the magazine and heard the captain shout, "That's sorted them. They are heading for home."

I saw the three planes, two of them with holes and the third trailing smoke, as they headed east. The captain turned us around and we took up a position above the damaged Avro. I was not sure she would make it home but we, at least, would stop any more attacks from above and behind.

We did make it home and I almost kissed the ground after I had leapt from the cockpit. Gordy and I ran over to Ted. "Anyone hurt?"

He shook his head. "No, but they nearly had us." He pointed to Captain Burscough. "That was a nice manoeuvre, to get above them, and you two lads were handy with those guns, thanks."

Gordy put his arm around Ted's shoulder. "If you hadn't alerted us they would have had three of us dead to rights."

The captain came over to us, "Give me your reports and I'll take them to the major." He pointed to our aeroplane. "Better get the holes fixed, Flight. It looks like the mice have been at it."

He was right. Still, it was only a few holes and they would soon be repaired. Poor Ted had holes and a damaged engine to deal with. I doubted that he would be flying on the morrow. When we had finished I went to the armourer.

"Flight Sergeant Richardson, any chance of a second Lewis?"

I could see that he was intrigued, "Whatever for?"

"If we fixed it to the wing we could fire behind us."

He nodded. He knew his guns. "That would work but we have no spares at the moment. As soon as we do I'll let you have one." He gave a rueful smile, "Of course the minute I do, every bugger will want one."

I gave an innocent look, "I'll just keep quiet about it then."

When we went up the next day there were just two of us and we had a different role. We were to patrol above the flight led by Major Brack. He had been worried by the appearance of the Albatros. We climbed until we were a thousand feet up. There were some low clouds below us but we knew where the major was headed and trusted to our instruments. Out of nowhere we suddenly saw three German aeroplanes. They were below us and were heading towards the major.

"Flight, signal the other aeroplane."

I waved my arms until Gordy looked around and then pointed down. I saw him nod. I cocked the Lewis as Captain Burscough dived down towards the Germans. Our maximum speed was supposed to be ninety miles an hour but diving down I am sure we exceeded that. The problem was you only had the enemy in your sights for the shortest time. You had to be accurate. The captain had discussed our tactics with me and we headed for the rearmost aeroplane first. Lieutenant Dundas would follow us.

At fifty yards I opened fire and gave him a twenty shot burst. His tail disappeared and the bus became unstable. I had no time to see the effects of my shooting for the second aeroplane was in my sights. I was slow to fire and I hit his engine. Nothing appeared to happen. I only had ten shots left and I fired them all at the leading German Albatros. I was lucky and I saw pieces of wood fly from the propeller.

I quickly changed the magazine as the captain climbed once more. He banked and I saw that the three Germans were heading home. I wondered if we would do the same and then I heard in my ears. "I think we can bag one of these. Let's get after the one with the damaged tail."

The one I had struck first was finding it hard to fly in a straight line. The observer had a rear-facing machine gun and he began to fire at us. I realised how exposed I was. Perhaps that gave me an incentive to be accurate. I gave a short burst at the tail and then fired along the fuselage towards the gunner. I saw the gunner slump in his cockpit. They were at our mercy. I watched as the pilot turned and saw his imminent death. He began to descend. I shredded his tail but his wild movements stopped me from finishing him off and I saw him land close to the German trenches. Land is probably a generous term for his wheels broke and he shattered his propeller. We headed home. It was not a kill but we had forced one down and it would not fly soon; if at all.

Because of our foray east, we were the last to land and we had a welcome party. The major pumped his lordship's hand. "Well done my dear fellow. Did you get any of them?"

"We forced one down. Harsker here got the gunner and he pranged his kite."

"Well done both of you. That is our first victory. We'll celebrate tonight!"

Gordy was effusive in his praise. "You have an eye for this young, William. That was fine shooting."

For the first time, I felt a success. No one had died and I had not risked anyone's life. This was better than charging machine guns with horses.

Major Brack's sergeant came over to the three of us in the mess. He slipped us a bottle of rum, "With the compliments of the major. Well done you lads."

Ted said morosely, "It was his kill!"

I laughed, "Listen we are the three musketeers. All for one and one for all." I turned to the major's sergeant, "Care to join us?"

"A generous offer, but no thanks. We are up again tomorrow. You lads get to stand down."

That was even better news. I poured us all a generous slug. "This could be my best night in France, ever!"

We did not finish the bottle but we were all more than a little tipsy as we made our way back to our tents. The next day we were woken by the sound of the major's patrol taking off and we had the luxury of a leisurely breakfast and then repairs on our aeroplanes.

Our elation only lasted until the three planes returned. They had all been damaged but the one which led them in was pouring smoke from its engine. We dropped what we were doing and raced to the runway. The damaged aeroplane landed and then did a cartwheel. We saw the gunner cartwheel from this cockpit and land with a sickening and lethal sounding crack. The aircraft was upside down. The pilot was restrained only by his belt and already flames were flickering and licking around the engine. I ran to the stricken aeroplane and leapt towards Captain Dixon. I had no knife and I tore at his seat belt. It must have been damaged in the crash for, to my relief it ripped. I grabbed him and we fell out of the cockpit. I felt Gordy and Ted grab us and we ran away. Suddenly there was a mighty crump and we were thrown to the ground as it exploded.

I was dazed but alive. I turned over the pilot, Captain Dixon. His hands were burned but his eyes opened. "Good show Flight Sergeant. I thought I was going west for a moment."

Major Brack ran up and looked at the captain. "That was damned close, George."

"It certainly was."

He turned to me. "Thank you, Flight Sergeant, that was brave, not to say foolhardy. I'm damned glad that James brought you along as his observer."

I nodded and just stared at the inferno that had been a serviceable aeroplane. The only parts which remained were the engine block, the wheel hubs and the Lewis gun. Captain Dixon wandered over the body of his observer. It was obvious he was dead. He was our first casualty. As I looked Gordy put his arm on my shoulder. "It was quick, at least. If you hadn't got the pilot out imagine him being burned to death." He looked at me in all seriousness. "If I am ever in that situation Bill, shoot me. I don't want to burn to death."

It was a horrible thought but I knew he was right I nodded slowly and Ted tutted, "And you call me the miserable bugger!"

There was nothing more we could do and we returned to our own aeroplanes. Even though we were certain that they had been serviced well we had to check. The fire which was dying behind us was a reminder of how close to death we could come flying in fire traps made of wood and canvas.

After the evening meal, I returned to the wreck. It was still warm but you could approach it. To my amazement, the Lewis gun was still largely intact. The magazine had disappeared but otherwise, it looked repairable. I pulled it from the wreck. It was not too hot to touch and I took it back to my tent. I was not certain what I ought to do. Then I remembered what a stickler the colonel was for rules and regulations. I went to the mess tent where the sergeants were playing cards and chatting. I sought out the armourer. He was watching a game of dominoes.

"Percy, can I have a word please?"

"Certainly. That took bottle, today son. Well done. What can I do for you? I still haven't got a spare Lewis."

I smiled, "No, but I have."

"Where the hell did you get one from? You haven't nicked one have you?"

"No, I took it from the wreck. I reckon I can repair it."

That satisfied him. "Well, you are resourceful. If you can repair it then you can have it. I had written it off the books anyway."

"Will it be all right with the colonel?"

"Good question. I'll tell you what I'll officially scrap it and send a copy of the report to the adjutant. How's that?"

"You'll do for me."

I returned to my tent where I began to strip the gun into its component parts. I knew that Percy would have spare parts if I needed them. I just wanted to see if it would still work. An hour's work bore fruit. I just needed a couple of screws and a new magazine and it would work. As I lay down for sleep I went through the problems I might have rigging it up in the aircraft. I always found answers that way and so it proved. I would attach a pole behind my seat and slight offset so that the captain could still see and I could fire behind him. I just had to convince him that it was a good idea.

The next day we were all grounded as it was a wet and stormy day. There would have been little point in going up. That was one benefit of the R.F.C. Unlike the footsloggers, rain did stop play. The poor sods in the trenches would be up to their necks in mud and still fighting. I approached the captain and outlined my idea. I think that my actions the previous day had pleased him more than anyone. "If you think you can do it then have a go." He paused, "By the way the major is putting you forward for a medal for what you did yesterday."

"But I was just doing what anyone would have done."

He laughed, "You are priceless. Everyone else was watching but you just dived in there. Of course, it is worthy of a medal."

I still didn't see what all the fuss was about. In the Yeomanry, we had all put our lives on the line for our comrades. I took my tool kit. I rigged an old piece of canvas so that I was a little drier as I worked on the mounting. I was the only one working in the middle of the aerodrome. I found it quite challenging and yet relaxing at the same time. I used a wooden pole to fix the gun and allow it to swivel; that saved weight. I had salvaged the mounting from the wreck and I used that. By the time I had rigged it up, it was almost time for the evening meal. I was filthy and, bearing in mind the colonel's views, I headed for the wash tent. When I emerged I found the colonel waiting for me.

I saluted.

"Flight Sergeant Harsker, what you did yesterday was extremely brave and just wanted to say you are a credit to your squadron."

It sounded awkward but I could see from his face that he was sincere. "Just doing what I had to, sir."

He nodded, "I took the trouble of reading your service record. It seems you have been mentioned in despatches and were recommended for a medal after the Yser."

There was little I could say to that. It was still a bitter memory for me. "I always try to do my duty sir."

The answer seemed to please him. "Good, then, er carry on, Flight Sergeant."

In my head, I heard an unspoken apology for his initial reaction to me. It had no effect on me; I always did my best. If I fell short of someone else's standards then that was their problem and not mine.

Chapter 16

We did not fly much for the next two or three weeks. The bad weather continued. When we did go up we managed to avoid contact with any German aeroplanes. While that was in many ways a good thing, we did not have the chance to try out our new gun. We flew a couple of patrols but we saw nothing. The captain was pleased that the new gun did not adversely affect the balance of the aeroplane.

Ted was the one who spotted the flaw in my plan. "How do you fire it then?"

We were on the ground and I demonstrated. I stood with my feet on the seat and held the Lewis gun. "Just like this."

He shook his head, "There's nowt to hold you in, lad. If the aeroplane moves to port or starboard, how do you stay on board?"

I jumped down, "I keep my balance and hang on to the gun."

Even Gordy was not optimistic about that happening. "He's right Bill. You would need great balance."

I shook my head. I knew I could balance."If I had a horse here I could show you. Have either of you ever ridden?"

"No."

"I have been riding since I could walk. I can ride a horse using just my knees and I can fire a rifle at the same time. I can jump a six feet high fence even when the horse is turning. Trust me, I will be able to stay on board."

I knew I had not convinced them but I was convinced that, when we ran into the Germans again, I would be able to do so. However, before we could do so we were moved. The situation around Ypres had dramatically deteriorated and German aeroplanes were ruling the sky. We were ordered to an area east of St.Omer. We would be less than thirty miles from Ypres. As we had the newest aircraft we were sent north. We did not have far to go and the vehicles made almost as good time as the aeroplanes.

This time we had a field all to ourselves. That was the good news. The bad news was that we would not have all the resources of the larger base we had just left. There was a windsock and three large tents and that was it. As we flew in Captain Burscough said, "Keep your eye out for any sort of building close by. I don't fancy freezing in a tent over winter."

I spied a large barn just half a mile from the airfield. I could not tell if it was occupied or not. What I did notice, however, was some familiar roads. We were not far from the Yser where so many of my regiment had fallen. That wound would not heal.

The weather, as well as the situation, had deteriorated and it was very cold when we were erecting our tents. We managed to get ours up quickly and the three of us were sent by Captain Burscough to scout out the barn. We could see it from the large tents and we crossed the airfield to reach it. There were a pair of huge wooden doors but, when we examined them, we saw that they had not been opened for some time. The metal hinges were rusted. Before we attempted to break in we looked for a farmhouse but we could not see one.

When we opened the door the smell which reached us was horrible. There had been two cows in the building and they had died. The half ravaged carcasses lay in their stalls.

"I wonder what happened here?"

"I've no idea but this will need cleaning out before we can use it."

Ted turned and left. Over his shoulder, he said, "And I think there are some privates back at the airfield who are perfect for that job."

For once I agreed with my morose companion. The major happily ordered the mechanics to make the barn habitable for us and we checked our aeroplanes again. We would be having our first patrol over Ypres the next morning. Our first foray in this new sector would be the dawn patrol and this time we would be expecting stiffer opposition.

The captain briefed the pilots and observers of his flight. Our task was to go in after the balloons which were directing their fire on the British trenches. The rest of the squadron would be waiting above us in case a German Jasta tried to interfere. As we went back to our tents, Ted, the permanent pessimist, moaned, "Why us?"

"I think we can blame you, because you have the Avro and our young hero here has fitted a rear-firing Lewis gun. We are the flight which has the best chance to fight off enemy planes."

"Oh."

"Sorry, Ted. Look on the bright side, at least balloons don't fire back."

We took off as dawn broke. We flew east. It was low cloud but there was no rain. It was just freezing cold. I still had not acquired a leather greatcoat and I was suffering from the wet conditions. I had to put that thought from my mind as we skimmed just four hundred feet above the trenches. We saw the British Tommies waving at us as we roared above them. We knew when we were over the German trenches as their rifles pop popped at us. I knew from experience that they would have to be extremely lucky to do any damage but it was nerve-wracking nonetheless. We saw the balloons just behind the German lines. As usual, they were trying to get down quickly which was why we had gone in at a lower altitude than normal.

I opened fire and saw my bullets strike the first balloon. They had machine guns aimed up at us and the air was filled with the hot lead, sounding like a swarm of hornets. As the captain swept through I heard Gordy firing and I turned as I heard a crump. He had somehow managed to blow one up. I saw the observer flung into the air. I could only hope he was dead already. Ted also managed to destroy one. This was our most successful mission so far. The other four balloons had made it to the ground. I heard, in my ears, "Let's try to get them on the ground. They should be easier. They aren't moving!"

I knew that the others would follow us but it would be a daunting experience. We were much lower and every German in their trenches would be desperate to bring down a British aeroplane. One advantage we had was our speed. We were approaching almost a hundred miles an hour as we dived. The captain flew along the length of the four balloons and I held down the trigger and emptied the magazine. I changed it as we climbed to escape the ground fire. As I glanced over my shoulder to see how the others had fared I saw twelve bird-like shapes hurrying from the east.

"Sir, Huns to the east."

"Righto, when the others have fired I will turn west. You had better get ready to try your new contraption."

We had already decided that Gordy's bus would go ahead of us to allow us to protect him. When he tucked in behind us I pointed to the Germans and he nodded. As his lordship slowed us down he flew in front of us.

It was a Jasta of Albatrosses. They had machine guns on the top wing which the observer could fire. Annoyingly they had two of them which gave them twice as much chance of hitting us. I just hoped that they would not have noticed our modification. I turned and clambered into position. I had had to disconnect my rubber tube but my face was just four feet from the captain's and I would be able to shout to him.

"Here they come, sir." We were flying next to Lieutenant Devries and Ted and I would be able to concentrate our fire on the leading aeroplane. I saw that it was aiming for me because they thought we had no defence. They were in for a shock.

Ted opened fire first when they were a hundred yards away and they were also firing at us. I waited; I could not change a magazine easily and I wanted all forty-seven bullets to count. I saw the bullets as they left the German guns but I didn't hear anything. They must have missed. Half of the F.E.2 is just air. When the first Albatros was fifty yards away I opened fire. I saw the bullets clang into the engine and saw a plume of smoke. The pilot jerked his aeroplane away and Ted's bullets stitched a line along the fuselage. I saw the observer slump in his seat and the aeroplane gave a wobble as though the pilot had been struck. I had no time for self-congratulation as the next German loomed into my sights. As the second aeroplane fired so did I. I could not hear Ted's gun and I assumed he was reloading. This time chunks of our tail flew off and we banked alarmingly to one side until his lordship regained control. I flexed my knees and gripped the gun even harder. I would have a problem if I had to try to reload and so I stopped firing. The second Albatros flew off. Behind it, I saw the major and the rest of the squadron engaging the Jasta. The third aeroplane swooped down and this time I heard Ted's gun. I finished off my magazine and shouted to the captain, "That's it, sir. We are out of ammo."

He nodded and pointed to the ground. As the third Albatros flew by us I took out my Luger and emptied the magazine. The enemy was only forty yards from our wing and I managed to strike the pilot. The aeroplane banked to port and I wondered if they would be able to recover. The Albatros almost reached the trenches before the pilot regained control and it limped east over the trenches.

The last aeroplane had seen what had happened to the others and he did not even fire. He must have thought I still had loaded guns. As I sat back in the cockpit I breathed a sigh of relief. We had survived.

We were the first to land. Gordy jumped from his bus and chocked it. By the time we had rolled to a halt, he had joined us. He slapped me on the back. That looks like half an Albatros each for you and Ted."

"Did it crash?"

He mimed with his hands, "Kaboom!"

I had not heard the explosion but I had been concentrating on the other aeroplanes. Captain Burscough was delighted. "That gun was a godsend, Harsker."

"Yes sir but I need to be able to reload; especially if we are to be bait again."

He nodded and pointed to our shredded tail. "And we nearly came a cropper when the Hun hit us. Still, a couple of balloons aren't too bad."

Gordy shouted, "No sir, he and Ted shot down that first Hun. I saw him crash!"

"Well done Flight Sergeant."

We turned as we saw the other aeroplanes cough and splutter across the field. It was Ted, lighting a cigarette, who spotted the missing planes. "There are two short." That dampened our enthusiasm. It had not all gone our way. What had happened to the others?

We found out that one of the aeroplanes had been shot down behind the enemy lines but the second had crash-landed on our side. The major had his first kill and so we have broken even. The other Flight Sergeants were all convinced that at least two of the aeroplanes must have crashed and so we had won but, without confirmation, we had to settle for half each and our balloons.

The snow and the ice put an end to operations and the last two weeks of December 1914 were peaceful. Three things happened the week before Christmas which made our chilly lives more bearable: the barn was made habitable and became our mess. We received a present of a tin from Princess Mary and a card from King George and the most important event was that we finally got our back mail.

The tin was a nice memento. Even though I was a non-smoker I was given the one intended for smokers. It had a pipe, pipe tobacco, tinder lighter, cigarettes and a photograph of the young Princess Mary. I didn't mind. I would give dad the pipe and tobacco when I was granted leave and the cigarettes I could trade. The photograph I would send to mother as a Christmas present. The letters were the most important Christmas present we received. I waited until I could read them in the lighted barn drinking my rum ration. I wanted to savour every word.

I read mum's first.

October 31ˢᵗ 1914
Dearest William,

I pray that you are safe. This war is an evil visited on us by wicked foreigners.

I have some bad news to give you. Your brothers Jack and Tom were both killed in the Battle of Ypres. Their commanding officer said that they were both brave soldiers and had saved the lives of many others. I wish someone had saved their life. We never had the chance to speak with them after that terrible night. I hope that they can hear me now as I tell them I wish we had not parted on such bad terms.

Your father has taken the news particularly badly. He blames himself and says he should have forgiven them before they went to France.

Your brother Albert is desperate to join up. He is old enough to do so next month. I hope the war is over by then but I do not believe it will be.

Kathleen is walking out just now with a fine young man. He is the new curate in the church. I am just grateful that they cannot take him to war. Sarah's husband is also safe. Now I worry each night that you will be taken from me. Please, my dearest son, take care of yourself for you are precious to us now. Keep this letter and, when you read it, remember your mother and your father for we think of you constantly. Each night we talk of you and wonder how you are doing.

Pray God he spares you.

Your loving Mother
xxx

I could not believe it; my older brothers were both dead. They had lasted, in the army, barely two months. I had flown over the site of their end and I had never known it. I raised my glass and sipped my rum. "To you John and Tom, I am sorry we fell out."

I saw Ted and Gordy looking at me curiously but there was an unwritten rule that a man's letters from home were private.

I opened Sarah's letter.

20th November 1914
Dear Bill,

I suppose you have received Mother's letter about John and Tom. It is heartbreaking to see the two of them now. They both blame themselves for the argument but I know it was drink that did it. John and Tom would never have said what they did if they had been sober. The whole estate is shocked. Dad is a shadow of his former self. Even Lord Burscough is worried. He brought round some flowers for mother and spent the longest time talking to them. He does care.

I have tried to talk Bert out of joining up but he is adamant. He wants to be just like you. Please write to him and tell him not to join. He will listen to you. Mother could not bear to lose another son.

Kathleen has a young man now. I am not keen on him but she is besotted and Mother likes him. He is pompous and full of himself. He believes we have a God-given right to fight. That is all very well but he will be safe.

We do worry about you and read in the newspapers about the Royal Flying Corps and their endeavours. We are proud of what you are doing but we can't help being afraid for you. Promise me that you will take care of yourself.

I would not be doing my duty as a sister if I didn't chastise you. Where are the letters you promised? Poor Mother waits for the postman each day and when there is no letter she then waits for the boy with the telegram to say you are dead. I know you mean no harm but it is killing Mother slowly and our Father too.

I pray to God that he keeps you safe,
Your loving sister
Sarah xxx

That was worse than the first letter and I felt so guilty. I felt tears springing into my eyes. Why was I such a heartless bastard? I had promised that I would write and I had not. I swallowed my rum and hurried from the barn. I had letters to write.

It took me several hours but I wrote letters to my mother, Sarah and Albert. I put everything in my heart into those letters. I suppose I was saying to them what I had not said to Tom and John. Now it was too late. I would not make that mistake with my family. I put the photograph in mother's letter. I made a parcel of the pipe and the pipe tobacco and addressed that to my dad. I did not write a letter but I put in a note which I hoped would tell him how I felt. The men in our family did not go in for shows of emotion. It was late when I had finished but I felt that a weight had been lifted from my shoulders. I now had even more responsibility; I was the hope and dreams of my whole family. That was far more important than a Government and even a King and Queen.

The next day I was asked by the captain what was wrong and I told him. Even though he was a different class and an officer, he understood far better than either Gordy or Ted. He had known Tom and John. A day or so later he took me to Armentières, a small town not far from Ypres. They had met recently at a bar behind the front. A chum of his was an officer at the front. The man looked like a skeleton and even the captain was shocked. He told us of the Battle of Ypres. It seemed the battle had raged for many days. In fact, the battle of the Yser had been the preliminary engagement and I had been in hospital at Winwick when my brothers had died. The young major knew of my brothers' regiment. They had fought with the Dragoon Guards and the London Scottish regiments. Outnumbered by twelve to one they had allowed the rest of the army to stabilise the line and foil the enemy attack. It was when he described the conditions: the weather and the mud that I realised how hopeless it had been for my brothers. They must have known it was hopeless and yet they continued to fight. They had redeemed themselves. I would not commit this to a letter home; the censors would not allow it through but I vowed to tell my family of the bravery of my brothers.

Chapter 17

After Christmas, we endured freezing temperatures when it was impossible to fly. It was all that we could do to keep the engine warm. We wrapped blankets and tarpaulins around each engine. Every morning we struggled to start them and run them for fifteen minutes to stop them from freezing completely. We, at least, were not having to fight off enemy attacks and we had somewhere warm to go each evening. I could not get the picture of Tom and John struggling through mud with frozen fingers and limited ammunition out of my mind. It made me more determined than ever to do the best job that I could and that job meant killing Germans. I would do that with a passion.

As soon as the weather improved we were able to fly. We did not fly every day and, when we did not patrol, then I badgered anyone I could for more flying lessons. I knew that as a pilot, I could hurt the Germans more than as a mere observer and gunner. I could be the one making the decisions about who to shoot.

It was early in February and we were patrolling north of Ypres. We no longer flew the whole squadron; we just flew in flights of three. Once again we were after balloons. The balloons could spot for the German artillery. British soldiers were dying because of the German balloons. We found six of them tethered along a long section of the front. By now the pilots had mastered the technique of flying just a couple of hundred feet above the ground, sometimes even lower. We had discovered that the ground fire could not react quickly enough to hit us and we were, ironically, safer. It also meant that the balloons could not get down in time. As we roared, in line abreast, towards them the winch crew desperately tried to bring down to ground level and safety. This time I aimed at the observer rather than the balloon. I waited until we were eighty yards from the target and gave a ten shot burst. The observer's head disappeared in a red explosion. I fired five more shots at forty yards and the balloon collapsed. As Captain Burscough banked I repeated my action with the next balloon in line and had the same success. By waiting until I was so close and by using fewer bullets I could kill more Germans. It was simple arithmetic. The last balloon was struck by both Gordy and myself.

"Captain, let's machine gun the winches. I still have a full magazine." Even as I was speaking I was reloading.

"Righto!"

We screamed down to one hundred feet and I sprayed the winches and the men operating them. All forty-seven .303 bullets struck something, either man or machine. The other two aeroplanes had not been as frugal with their bullets and it was we alone who inflicted the damage.

That evening, in the mess, Gordy looked at me quite seriously. Normally this was the time for laughing and joking but Gordy looked deadly serious. "That was good shooting today, Bill, but it seemed to me you were going for the men and not the balloon."

I nodded, "Damned right I was."

"They are just doing their job the same as we are."

"I know but this war will be over a lot quicker if we kill them faster than they kill us. They can make more balloons but a trained observer or winchman is harder to replace."

"It won't bring your brothers back."

I clenched my fists and then unclenched them. "I know that; I am not stupid but I can make the Germans pay." I stood. "When you have lost two brothers then feel free to come and lecture me about the morals of war until then keep your nose out of my business."

I stormed off. Even as I went I felt guilty. I should not have spoken to Gordy that way; he meant well. My brothers' deaths had affected me more than I cared to admit but blood is thicker than water. We had parted on bad terms and that thought haunted me.

We received replacement aeroplanes later that week and more equipment. They fitted another Lewis gun for the captain to operate. It was fixed and would just fire in the direction we were flying but it doubled our firepower. My seat was moved slightly so that I would not get my head blown off and the captain could not fire it when I used the rear Lewis but it meant we could still fire when I changed the magazine. Ted was delighted to be flying in a brand new F.E.2. The Avro was reserved for flying lessons and I became quite competent as a pilot. I had no doubt that, if we ever flew in a dual-control aeroplane, I would be able to fly it should the captain become incapacitated.

The new pilots looked remarkably young. The major gave one of them, Lieutenant Shaw to us. The other two had been promoted to captain and were no longer the novices who terrified Gordy and Ted. The Flight Sergeant was also young. I remembered how kind Gordy and Ted had been to me and I determined to do the same for young Stan. He took in every word I said.

On our first patrol with our new guns, we ran into some of the new Albatros aeroplanes. We were flying high for it was more of an initiation into life on the Western Front. Lieutenant Shaw needed to know how to fly with other aeroplanes. Ted saw them and he attracted my attention.

I recognised the shape of the aeroplane and told the captain. "Sir, three Albatros aeroplanes directly below us to the east."

It looked like they were heading back from a patrol. "Good. This might be an opportunity to try out the new kit eh?"

He banked the aeroplane and set it into a shallow dive. It was the most efficient way to pick up speed. We were a couple of hundred feet above the Germans when they spotted us and by then it was too late to do anything about it. The captain had targeted the last aeroplane and we would be able to hit multiple targets as they were still, largely, in one line.

"I shall fire too, Flight. Just to see what it is like."

"Sir."

I have to say that I was more than intrigued about the effect. The captain fired too early and the Albatros veered to the right. It gave me the chance to fire at the pilot when he came into my sights. I began firing when I saw the propeller and used half a magazine. Smoke came from the engine and then I hit the pilot. As he fell forward the aeroplane went into a vertical dive. We were so close to the ground that I saw the whole aircraft burst into flames as it hit the earth and we all felt the concussion of the explosion.

When we climbed into the sky we saw the other two aeroplanes limping east. Both were damaged. The new arrangement worked. "I can see I need to time my shots a little better, eh Bill?"

"It worked sir. It gave me an easier shot but yes, I like to wait until we are closer."

The war in the air was changing. We were now needed more to observe enemy movements in the rear of their lines and report back. That meant we had smaller patrols but ranged further behind the enemy lines. Captain Dundas and Lieutenant Shaw were paired up and we worked with Captain Devries. I felt that we had the advantage over the other three aeroplanes of our flight as we had the rear-firing machine gun. It slowed us down but not by much.

The third week in February the weather improved. We were sent beyond Ypres to see what reserves there were available to the German Army. The British Army had lost many men and it was hard to replace the Old Contemptibles who had died slowing down the enemy advance. They were doggedly defending the trenches around Ypres and anything we could do would alleviate the pressure a little. We travelled with ten miles between the two halves of the flight. We flew very high until we had passed the enemy lines. We did not want to be jumped by a Jasta of Albatrosses.

We used the airspeed and a watch to estimate where we were. "I think that is far enough, sir. We could go down for a look-see."

"Righto."

The captain signalled the other aeroplane and we gently swooped to a lower altitude. As soon as we cleared the cloud cover I looked at the map and identified where we were. Some of the other squadrons had been fitted with cameras but we were still doing it the old fashioned way. I would have to identify what we saw. I saw a train heading west and it was laden with heavy artillery. They looked to me to be the 42cm howitzers. The road which ran parallel with the railway line was thronged with a column of German infantry. As our engines whined they all took cover and one or two fired hopeful shots at us. We could have strafed them but our task was to observe. We flew down the length of the column. I estimated it to be at least four regiments. An attack was coming.

"Seen enough, Flight?"

"Yes sir, let's go home."

We had just climbed to five hundred feet when they jumped us. There were three of them. There were two Aviatiks and an Albatros. Their firepower was less than ours but they had superior numbers. I saw Ted take out his rifle as I stood on my seat and faced to the rear. They swooped down on us and fired their machine guns. They had to fire over their propellers which made aiming difficult. Of course, once they had passed us then the observer could fire the rear gun. I used short bursts to discourage them. They had height advantage and they used it to gain speed. As they sped by us I felt the hail of bullets as the captain dived towards the earth. The barrel of my Lewis gun was pointed at the sky as I clung on for dear life. As we banked left an Aviatik was suddenly in the captain's sights and he fired a burst. It was a frightening experience as the Lewis spat bullets just inches from my legs. I heard a crack and, as we completed our turn I saw the German aeroplane tumbling from the sky. The captain had his first kill! The other two Germans headed east again as we turned west for home.

All four of us were excited beyond words. It had been an outstanding kill for the captain. He had had a very short window of opportunity but he had taken it well. It might have been an old German aeroplane but the pilot would have died in the crash. We were hurting the enemy.

Out elation was short-lived as Gordy's aeroplane arrived alone. We met them as they descended.

Captain Burscough said, "Lieutenant Shaw?"

Captain Devries shook his head, "He was forced down behind their lines. He is alive but they have captured him and his observer. Lieutenant Shaw's war is over."

We were like a balloon suddenly deflated of air. He had been a likeable chap and now he would be a prisoner of war. His only hope would be that we could capture one of their pilots and exchange them. For Stan, the Flight Sergeant, the prospects were a little bleaker. It was only officers who were exchanged. It would be a prisoner of war camp for him.

The major sent us alone the next day and the other two aeroplanes were dispatched to patrol the same sector where Lieutenant Shaw had come to grief. In many ways, it was easier being on your own. You had to be more alert but you didn't need to worry about the other aeroplane. We went further north. Our report had pleased the major but Intelligence needed to know about the left flank of our lines. This was new territory for us. We flew high for safety and then swept down. There was no railway line but the road had a column of cavalry on it. I would not be firing on the column. I could not inflict on horses what our regiment had endured.

We turned and headed south. "We'll come back along the railway line and see if there are more troops using it."

"Right sir."

It was a cold day but there was neither rain nor snow and my boots, scarf and balaclava kept me warm. The fingerless gloves had proved to be a godsend and I had asked my mother for another couple of pairs. I wore my gloves as I scanned the map. When we reached the railway line there was a goods train heading towards the front. We could not see what it carried and so the captain dived for a closer look. To our horror, they had a flat car fitted with multiple machine guns. They opened up and a cone of fire headed towards us. The captain yanked hard on the stick and the engine screamed as we tried to climb. I thought we had escaped until I saw the smoke coming from the engine.

"Sir, we have been hit. Better get lower."

"Right. Keep your eyes peeled for a field." The engine was really struggling and I saw the smoke getting thicker.

"Sir, we need to land before we fall out of the sky."

"Keep watch for one."

I looked up to see if there were any German aeroplanes and I flicked my eyes to the ground. We needed a flat field. The weather worked in our favour. The ground was still frozen. It would make landing a possibility. I saw a patch of clear white. "There sir, to the north and west."

"I've got it."

I could now hear the engine struggling. I had no doubt that when the German train reached a halt they would let everyone know that there was a damaged bird behind their lines. I wondered if I would be joining Stan and become a prisoner. The engine became even more laboured as the field grew closer. I was just happy that we landed without cartwheeling. As soon as we stopped I leapt from the cockpit and threw the Lee Enfield to the captain. He stood in the cockpit and scanned the edges of the field. It seemed unnaturally quiet.

I ran around to the engine hardly daring to look at what might have been damaged. If it was the propeller then we would not be able to take off again. If the bullets had penetrated the engine block then we would have to burn the aeroplane and try to get back to our own lines. Not an easy feat with trenches going from the English Channel to Switzerland!

The propeller had been nicked but it was not dangerous and the engine block looked whole. As soon as I looked down I saw what the problem was. There was a pool of oil. An oil line had been cut. I opened the hatch which held my tools and other bits and bobs. I found some spare rubber tube and I used it to repair the cut. The tube I used was bigger than the one which had been cut and I was able to force the broken ends into the whole piece.

Suddenly I heard the crack of the Lee Enfield. "Hurry up Bill! Huns at the edge of the field."

I glanced up and saw a line of infantry climbing the fence. "Nearly done sir." There was an oil can we used to lubricate the joints and pistons. It was not perfect but it would have to do. I emptied it into the oil filler cap and then said. "Right sir, let's try it."

"Contact!"

The approaching Germans gave me added strength and the propeller flew around. It coughed and spluttered but it caught. I ran around to the front of the moving aeroplane. There were no chocks to hold it. The Germans infantry were less than two hundred yards away and they were firing at us. The captain's Lewis was not pointing at them and they advanced quickly. I had to run alongside the moving aeroplane and haul myself on board. As soon as I was in the cockpit I cocked the Lewis and sprayed the infantry. This was no short burst; I emptied the magazine and then reloaded while we were still on the ground. We were now bouncing along the icy white field and the fence was rapidly approaching. The infantry were lying down and firing and I felt the bullets zoom and zip over my head. The infantry were behind us now and I emptied my Lee Enfield at them. The front of the aeroplane suddenly lifted. I heard the sound of breaking branches as the undercarriage clipped the top of the hedge but we were aloft.

I turned to give the thumbs up at the captain and saw him mouthing something. I connected my tube. "Good flying sir."

"Yes, we were lucky. The thing is old chap, I appear to have been hit."

That was the worst news I could have heard. If he succumbed to his wounds then the aeroplane would dive to its and my death. "Is it bad sir?"

"I don't know. It's my leg and it hurts like buggery! How is the engine doing?"

I saw a thin plume of smoke coming from the engine. It did not like its new oil but it would survive. "It was an oil pipe. It is repaired and should get us home."

"Right then. It's up to me. How far away are we?"

"I reckon fifteen miles, sir." I readied the Very Pistol. I would need to signal the field that we needed the doctor and a fire team. I kept watch on the captain. He looked a little pale beneath his helmet but he was smiling. "You'll make it sir. Just hang on. Think of the pretty nurses who will see to your every need."

"Knowing my luck she will have a moustache and breath like a week-old dead pig!"

I glanced around. "Airfield ahead sir." I fired a flare into the air. It would tell the field that we had wounded and the doctor would be standing by. "Hang on sir, the doc will be waiting for you."

I watched as the wings wobbled. I did not risk a glance astern for fear it would unsettle the captain. It was in God's hands now; God and the captain. I was just the passenger. One wing seemed to be lower than the other. I prayed that we would not cartwheel. I had seen what it had done to the other observer. The quick death I had so blithely dismissed now seemed a little more painful. Inexorably the ground approached and I watched as the wing tip came up a little. We bumped down and then sprang up but the second bump saw us roll towards the huddle of anxious-looking people.

As soon as we stopped I leapt out and went to the captain's assistance. He had passed out. The doctor and the medical orderlies were there in an instant. "He has been shot in the leg."

The doctor nodded, "Thank you Flight Sergeant, we'll take it from here."

The major glanced at the unconscious captain as he was taken away and then came to me. "What happened?" I told him, describing the machine guns on the train. "You were damned lucky then. Well done Flight Sergeant." I gave him a pleading look. He smiled, "Don't worry, I will tell you any news as soon as I get it."

Gordy and Ted came over. I could see from their faces that they felt guilty. We had been alone. I told them what had happened. Ted went around to the engine. "I'll sort out the oil. She will need draining and refilling." He glanced at the propeller. "You'll need a new one of these too. You two sort out the holes." He shook his head, "Looks like a piece of Swiss, bloody cheese!"

Gordy and I began to assemble the canvas and glue for the repairs. "He is right you know, Bill, you are lucky. Not many can land, repair a crate and then take off again."

"I wish we had dual control aeroplanes, Gordy. I hated being helpless in the front. I kept remembering poor Stan."

"Aye, I know. The thought had crossed my mind." He shook his head, "I think I shall put in to become a pilot. I would rather be in control than being a passenger."

"What will the major say?"

"I think he would be happy about that. It saves getting a new boy from home. At least we have combat experience and know how to fly out here. Anyway, I'll give it a go."

It took two days to repair the F.E. 2 and about the same length of time for us to find out about the captain's wound. The captain's leg was saved and he was sent to the same hospital in England where I had been hospitalised. I went to see him the day he left. "How is the old bus?"

"She is all repaired, sir. As good as new."

"Well, I hate to leave you in the lurch like this." He hesitated, "The major is letting Captain Dixon fly the bus until I return." I could see in his eyes that he wanted me to cooperate.

I smiled, "Righto sir. I'll look after them both."

"I know you will. They say I'll be away for a fortnight or so. If I can I'll try to get you a decent coat."

"You don't have to, sir."

"I know, Bill. I want to. I know that it was you who saved our bacon out there and I am grateful."

As I passed the squadron office I noticed that there was a letter from home for me. It had been some time since my mother had written. I knew that letters were low down on the priorities of the war department but to us, they were a lifeline home.

Boxing Day 1915
Dear Bill,

Merry Christmas! I hope you are managing to celebrate. It was quiet this year, just Albert, Alice and Kathleen. Kathleen wanted her young man to come but I told her that until they are engaged then there are rules.

We have been reading about all the poor soldiers wounded and killed in the trenches. I am glad that you are in an aeroplane. We never hear about any of those coming to grief.

Did you read about the shelling of the East Coast? Some German ships sailed up to Hartlepool and Scarborough. They killed 78 women and children. They are evil those Germans. I didn't agree with this war at first but if this is the sort of thing that they do then you need to sort them out and teach them a lesson. It was bad enough when they shot those poor Belgians but these were English families!

Your sister, Sarah, suits marriage. We don't see a great deal of them as she and her hubby, Cedric, live in the big house. There's more room for the girls but I miss her. And I miss you. Take care, my dear boy, and come home safely to us. I pray for you every night and hope that God watches over you and all the other brave English boys.

Your loving Mother
xxxx

And so I had to work with a new pilot. I wondered how Captain Dixon would cope. He had not flown combat since before Christmas and I thought that the crash and his dead observer would be on his mind. They were certainly on mine.

Chapter 18

Captain Dixon turned up the next morning as I was running through the early morning checks we performed. He was older than Captain Burscough and he was a serious-looking officer. He came towards me with hand outstretched. "I just wanted to say that I am honoured and delighted to be flying with you. I'll try to keep up Captain Burscough's high standards." His lordship had more kills than anyone else and was still the only pilot to have a confirmed kill on an enemy aeroplane.

"Don't worry sir, you'll do all right. Are we up this morning?"

"Yes, we will be with Captains Dundas and Devries. We are to be tail-end Charlie."

I patted the rear-facing gun. "That's because we have a sting in our tail sir."

I would be lying if I said I wasn't nervous. I was petrified. You get used to a pilot. The take off seemed edgy and the flight not as smooth. It was probably my imagination but I had a queasy feeling in my stomach. Perhaps he would get better as the flight progressed. I kept turning to look behind us. Gordy, in the lead aeroplane, would be spotting the enemy targets. I was looking for the Hun in the sun.

We headed for the observation balloons. They had been absent since we had destroyed them earlier in the year. The effect on their artillery had been dramatic and they had not had the same success. We were told that they were back up and our job was to destroy them. We were given the ones in the middle of the line.

As soon as we neared them we could see that they had beefed up their defences. There were now machine guns and other weapons firing directly up at us as we approached. It made it much harder to concentrate on the enemy balloons. I was the last to fire and it afforded me the opportunity of observing their defences. I saw that they had erected sandbags around their winchmen. They could not be hit quite as easily. They also had machine guns there too. They had learned their lessons well. Then I had to concentrate on the balloons as the other two aeroplanes peeled away. Captain Dixon was not making life easy for me and the aircraft was moving up and down too much for me to concentrate my fire. I managed to puncture the balloon but I missed the observer.

As the captain wheeled away I saw, out of the corner of my eye, German aeroplanes heading in our direction from the east. "Sir, German aeroplanes!" I stood and pointed.

He nodded and began a slow bank. Once we were heading west I stood on my seat and cocked the Lewis gun. We would be the target for their first attack. There looked to be something different about the leading Albatros. As it came close I could see that the machine gun was no longer on the wing but over the engine and there were two of them. We had been told they were working on a machine gun which fired through the propeller. Was this one of those? Speculation was an idle luxury I could ill afford.

The first of the four planes began its roaring descent. I saw Captain Dixon glancing nervously over his shoulder. "Fire, Flight Sergeant! He's almost on us."

"Not yet sir. I have to be sure." I had no idea why the captain was so nervous; the Albatros had not even opened fire yet.

The machine guns ripped into action when they were a hundred yards away. It was too far to be effective and I saw only one bullet strike our tail; the rest flew harmlessly through the open fuselage. At fifty yards I fired a burst. I struck the propeller and the engine. As the Albatros wheeled away I could see smoke but it was not a fatal wound. The second aeroplane had also fired too early. Our aeroplane was not flying as straight as Captain Burscough would have flown it and that mistake saved us as the machine gun stitched a line through the wing. I gave a second burst and struck the undercarriage. I saw a wheel fly off and the aeroplane began to fly slightly more erratically as its balance shifted. I took the opportunity of putting another burst into the fuselage and I managed to hit the observer.

The third aeroplane and the fourth came at us together. They both fired their guns from two sides and lead struck the engine and the wings. I emptied one magazine at one and I quickly changed the magazine. I had just done so when Captain Dixon panicked. He went into a steep climb whilst rolling the aeroplane. It was a good manoeuvre but not when you had a gunner in the front and he was not attached to his seat. I was suddenly upside down and clinging to a Lewis gun which was held in place by a piece of wood. I felt like a trapeze artist at the circus. I thought my arms would be wrenched from my sockets and I was amazed that the gun did not tear away from the aeroplane. I saw the look of horror on the captain's face. He corrected his roll and my feet found purchase on the seat again.

We had briefly lost the other two Germans but also our companion aeroplanes. We were isolated and there were still three enemy aeroplanes which could hurt us. Once I was secure again I lined up on the nearest German. This time he held his fire as did I. When he did open fire he hit the tail which suddenly shredded. I saw pieces fly from our propeller. We yawed to one side and it gave me a perfect shot at no more than forty yards range. I fired a short burst directly into the pilot. His head was struck and I saw the blood and brains spray the observer. The aeroplane went into a vertical dive. I saw the fourth German line us up and then I saw bullets strike him from both sides as our two companion aircraft struck him from both sides. They must have emptied their magazines and hit the fuel tank for the aeroplane exploded in a fireball. The shockwaves made all three of us bounce up and down.

I reconnected the speaking tube. "Time to go home, sir. He hit our tail and our propeller. I think I have used up all of our luck for today."

There was silence and I wondered if the tube had broken. "Sorry. Flight Sergeant. That was my fault. I could have killed you!"

"We can talk about that when we land sir. I am still in one piece."

As tail end Charlie we were the last to land and the other crews were waiting for us. I saw Ted shaking his head at the propeller. It had barely got us home and I was impressed with the captain's skills for he had landed us without a real tail. He might panic but he could fly. His earlier crash must have really damaged his confidence.

After he had climbed down he walked over to me. "I am sorry about that. I was convinced they were going to hit us and I forgot that you were just hanging on to the gun." He looked up at the contraption. "How did you stay on board?"

"I wasn't ready to die."

He shook his head and walked off with the other two pilots.

Gordy and Ted looked at the aeroplane shaking their heads. "Lucky, lucky, lucky!"

"I know Gordy. I can't believe that a piece of scrap wood kept me in the aeroplane."

"Did he panic?" I nodded. "I thought so. You had it under control. Captain Burscough would have flown straight as a die."

"I know but I guess I will have to get used to Captain Dixon."

In the end, I didn't. He went to the major and they had a long talk. He left the squadron the next day. The major had me in the office to explain. "You did very well the other day Flight Sergeant and I appreciate your attitude. Many other men might have said something. I am pleased that you did not. Captain Dixon is returning to England for a while. He will train young pilots. He is an excellent pilot you know."

"I do sir. It was just one mistake."

The major leaned back and nodded. "Very philosophical of you however the fact remains that both of you could have been killed and a valuable aircraft destroyed. How long will it take to repair it?"

"If we had a propeller then we could be flying by the end of the week. We just have to rebuild the tail but the quartermaster tells me he is waiting for spares."

"Yes, I know. Well repair it and hopefully, Captain Burscough will have returned by then. Dismissed."

I turned to go and then turned back, "Sir, may I ask you something?"

"Of course. You have earned that right."

"Would it be possible, at some time in the future, for me to become a pilot?"

He smiled, "I see you and Flight Sergeant Hewitt have been talking." I nodded. "I'll tell you the same thing I told him. Take me up in the Avro and let me see what you can do. He is going up the day after tomorrow. Is that fair enough?"

I grinned, "More than enough, sir. Thank you."

When I saw Gordy I looked at him askance. "And just when were you going to tell us about becoming a pilot?"

Ted's cigarette almost dropped from his open mouth. Gordy looked embarrassed. "When I actually became one. Sorry lads. I didn't want to put a hex on it."

I smiled, "Don't worry you will pass and, just so you know, I am having a bash too."

"You don't mean I will have to sir the two of you?"

"Ted, we aren't even pilots yet let alone officers."

Ted shook his head, "I can see it happening already. Yes sir, no sir, three bags full sir."

Gordy looked at me. "When are you going to try out?"

"I thought I'd see how you do. But I wouldn't mind a couple more lessons over the next few days." They both gave me a quizzical look. "Captain Dixon is returning to England to become an instructor."

"That is probably for the best. Not everyone is cut out for combat and he is a good flier."

None of us resented someone who did not have the nerve to be an air warrior. It was a hard job and not everyone was cut out for it. Our attitude was that a man should admit to his limitations before others got hurt. The memory of Lieutenant Ramsden came to mind. He had hidden his flaws and men had died. I respected Captain Dixon far more. He was a real man.

As it turned out we were all grounded for a week by vicious storms. No one moved on either side of the lines. It meant the aircraft were all serviced and we even managed to replace the propeller. We rigged rear-facing Lewis guns on the other two aeroplanes of the flight although neither Gordy nor Ted relished having to fire them in action.

Gordy said, "I have even more incentive to become a pilot now. Bill here is the amazing trapeze artist but I am not."

The sergeant's mess had enjoyed teasing me by singing the music hall song about the young man on the flying trapeze. When I walked in the mess they all sang:

He'd fly through the air with the greatest of ease,
That daring young man on the flying trapeze.

Surprisingly they never tired of it. Even some of the officers thought it was amusing. I took it in good part; if I had shown any kind of discomfort they would have taken it as a sign of poor character and so I smiled and I bowed each time they sang it.

When the skies did clear we all watched as Gordy took off with the major as an observer for his flying test. He had been given clear instructions: take off, perform a figure of eight around the field, a barrel roll to port and one to starboard, climb to five hundred feet and then dive to fly across the airfield at one hundred feet. Basically the major wanted to know not only if he could fly but also if he could handle combat situations. From the ground, it looked immaculate but we knew that the major was a fussy judge. Nothing would get by him.

The major gave nothing away as he walked away from the aircraft. We all crowded around Gordy. "Well, lads, I am now a pilot!"

It did not change things immediately. We were still short of aeroplanes but we had volunteers from training depots in England who wished to be observers. My attempt to become a pilot had to be deferred. There was to be a new offensive and we had been tasked with photographing the area around Neuve Chapelle and Auber. Lorries arrived with cameras and the observers were all given lessons in photography. Later these would be attached to the aeroplanes but as March 1915 approached, we had to take the photographs by leaning out of the aeroplane. They were a little blurry. We now had wooden buildings. Some Royal Engineers had spent February constructing barracks and messes as well as workshops. We used one of the new workshops to learn how to take photographs.

As luck would have it Captain Burscough returned from his convalescent leave. I did not need to have the trauma of a new pilot. He was fully fit and keen to get back into action. He had a brown paper parcel with him and he proudly handed it to me. "Here as promised, a leather flying coat."

"Sir, you shouldn't have."

"Of course I should but perhaps you won't need it now that you have learned to be a trapeze artist." He was grinning as he said it. Word had soon reached him of my feat.

We took off as a squadron and headed south-east. We had rarely visited this quiet area of the front and it was new territory for us. The Germans had no aerial defences in the region so we had few machine guns and no aeroplanes to contend with. It was actually a pleasurable experience and we spent a couple of hours flying as low as we could go photographing the railways and the trenches. Others would analyse them but we all knew that our next task would be to support the attack.

Our next flight was on the morning of the 9th of March. We were to destroy any enemy aeroplanes and balloons as we could. For that reason, we flew as a squadron with five aeroplanes being supported by six much higher up. We had learned to protect ourselves once we were in enemy territory.

It was my first flight with the rest of the newly armed aeroplanes. Our aircraft had been nicknamed the Gunbus for we all now sported three machine guns. We might not be either the fastest or most agile of aeroplanes but we were the most dangerous. We bristled with weaponry. The armourer had even got us some small bombs. We had had a demonstration of their use but, so far, we had not used them in action. There were racks fitted to a couple of the aeroplanes to hold the deadly projectiles.

We reached the German lines and quickly destroyed the four balloons that we found. Our foray with the cameras had alerted the enemy and we saw a Jasta of Aviatiks and Albatros heading for us. We flew in a line abreast of five aeroplanes. As the senior officer Captain Burscough and I were in the centre. Above us, Major Brack and the rest of the squadron were waiting to pounce on any aeroplanes which attacked us. The enemy formation was three wide and four deep. Against our firepower that was a mistake. We flew directly at them. Each aeroplane fired their two Lewis machine guns and a wall of bullets tore through the poorly armed Germans. The captain and I managed to destroy one almost immediately and a second, from the second tier, headed home with smoke trailing.

The major's attack completely destroyed the Jasta. We shot down three aircraft and all of the others were damaged. We had done our job and we returned home elated. Our infantry attack would be a surprise. The enemy were blind and would not be able to discern the troop movements.

After we had landed we saw that there were tables laden with bombs. The armourer grinned at us. "Right lads, you have shown you can use a machine gun. Now let's see if you can use a bomb. There are four for each aircraft. My lads will fit racks to the outside of your cockpits."

He laughed wickedly, "The last thing we need is for one to go off during takeoff."

While the pilots all went to their briefing we helped the mechanics and armourers fit the racks to those aeroplanes which did not have them yet. The balance of the aeroplane was vital and no-one wanted them in the wrong place. I insisted that they be put slightly behind me towards the pilot's seat. I had enough weight in the front already. We finished by noon and the bombs were fitted. All we had to do was to detach the bomb from the rack and then throw it towards the ground. The fins on the back helped to steer the device and it would explode upon impact. We had no idea what our targets would be but we were like children on Christmas day with a new toy. This was exciting and new.

We took off at dawn and headed south-east. Other squadrons could be seen to port and starboard. Our target was the railway lines we had photographed. Once the attack of the infantry began the generals wanted no support to reach the beleaguered Germans. Having photographed them then we knew where they were. We were not the leading flight this time. The major did not anticipate any German aeroplanes and so we flew in line astern. That way we could go to secondary targets if we were successful with the primary.

There was a little anti-aircraft fire but it was not enough to cause us concern. It would have taken a very lucky strike to hit one of the bombs. We found the railway and the major led the attack. The first three aeroplanes managed to destroy the track and the major waved us further east. We saw smoke in the air; it was a train. The aeroplane ahead of us dived and the observer threw his bomb. I saw it explode at the side of one of the freight wagons. Then it was our turn. I deliberately threw it early and I aimed at a point ahead of the train. As we pulled up I saw the track as it was flung in the air and I heard the screech of brakes as the train tried to stop. Glancing over my shoulder I saw that Gordy had managed to drop his bomb on the engine. There was an enormous explosion and we could hear the screeching of the railway cars as they slewed off the wrecked track.

Once again the major waved us up into the air and we bombed a marshalling yard. This was almost too easy. They had no defences and we had time to aim our bombs. When it was wrecked we all had bombs left and we were waved west, towards the battle. We could see the smoke in the distance and hear the crump of the heavy weapons. The Germans knew they were being attacked. We found a road and it was filled with a German column of infantry. We dived and threw out bombs at the helpless infantry below us. They had nowhere to escape. Once our bombs had been thrown we flew up and down machine-gunning the road until our magazines were empty.

Oddly enough I did not feel elated but deflated. We had slaughtered the Germans with impunity. I knew we were saving British lives but it did not seem right somehow. It was not playing the game. The Germans had had no chance to fight back.

The mood in the squadron was, however, one of unbridled joy. We had done our job and more. The major came into the sergeant's mess that night with a wonderful boyish grin all over his face. "Well done boys. Thanks to your efforts we have broken through. The Germans are retreating."

We found out that the canals we had seen to the south had been attacked by the other squadrons. Nothing had reached the front. For the first time in the war, the Royal Flying Corps had had a decisive effect. The soldiers might have only gained a few miles but this was the first gain since October and promised to be a sign of things to come.

At the time we all thought that the war would soon be over but that was not the case. Still, that night was one of celebration. We had suffered no losses and the enemy had suffered a bloody nose.

Chapter 19

We were brought down to earth the following day when the Germans counterattacked. We had no more bombs to use; we later discovered that the artillery had also run out of shells too. We were forced to fly with just our machine guns. As we headed over the trenches we found a hotter reception that we had had the previous day. Roaring dangerously low over the trenches, newly prepared by the enemy, we found that they had machine guns aimed into the sky. I saw at least three of our eleven aircraft turn back with damage from ground fire. We pushed on until we saw another column of infantry hurrying to get to the front.

Once again we had been given the role of attacking. The three of us had a reputation for steadiness which the major appreciated. He knew we would not deviate from our line and would hold our nerve. The Germans were always quick learners and they had mobile machine guns which they hurriedly set up. As we roared across the treetops we were met by machine and rifle fire which was most unnerving. Standing at the front to the Gunbus, you felt dreadfully exposed. Short bursts were not effective and I held down the trigger until the bullets had all been used. When the captain saw me change the magazine he pulled the nose up to get us out of the line of fire while I reloaded. The third pass would allow him to fire his fixed machine gun. I had the advantage that I could traverse my gun through a hundred and eighty degrees he could only fire at whatever was in line with the front of the Gunbus. As we flew for our second pass I saw a mobile machine gun to the right. I fired a steady stream and saw the crew cut down and the gun knocked over. I hoped I had damaged it enough to stop it firing at the other aircraft in the flight. I finished off the magazine by firing at the motor car which was on the roadside. I reasoned that it would have officers, probably high ranking, on board and their loss was worth more than their men.

When I had emptied the Lewis Captain Burscough began to fire his fixed machine gun. I took out my Lee Enfield and aimed at those who looked to be in command. I was not certain if I hit any but I knew it would have an effect. Soaring into the sky and the relative safety of the higher altitude I saw that one of the other aircraft was pouring smoke from its engine. Lieutenant Hanson would be lucky to get back to the airfield. We went into a defensive formation as we headed back to our lines.

I turned to cock the rear Lewis and watch behind us. I could see the major with his surviving aeroplanes spread out in a thin screen as they, too, made their way home. Then I saw black dots appear. They were being attacked by German aeroplanes. We could do nothing about it; they were behind and above us. We had to escort our damaged comrade back home and besides that, we were all getting low on fuel. This was not a steady flight at the same altitude. We had climbed and dived numerous times. Running out of fuel behind enemy lines was not an option.

It was with some relief that we saw the damaged aeroplane land safely. The mechanics raced across to deal with the small fire and then we all landed. There were just four of us left from the original five. The major, I feared, had fared worse.

After we had climbed from the cockpits I noticed a colonel walking towards us. I did not recognise him but his lordship did. He snapped a smart salute, "Colonel Sykes, sir." We all stood to attention and saluted. He pointed to the black dots approaching the field. "Is the squadron commander with those aeroplanes?"

"The major is on his way, sir. That is his flight."

The colonel's features changed and he smiled easily. "Don't panic, Lord Burscough. I am not here to chew you out but rather to find out some facts."

I saw the relief in his face as the captain said to us, "I think you chaps can check the aeroplanes over. I am not sure what damage we suffered back there."

"Sir!"

Even though we were curious as to know why we had been visited we knew that we had to work on the aeroplanes. The battle was not over; that much we knew from the number of reinforcements being rushed to the front. We would be in action again the next day. I worried about my Gunbus. It took punishment day after day and we repaired the canvas and wood every day. Soon it would be no longer original but an aeroplane of repaired parts.

As usual, we had suffered the most damage. We had been in the centre. I left the mechanic, Joe, to check the engine and refill the oil while I began to assess the parts which needed replacing and the ones which needed mending. Out of the corner of my eye, I saw the major's flight land. The colonel and Captain Burscough whisked him away and we were left alone on the field. We would be lucky to have five serviceable aeroplanes for the next day.

It was almost time for food by the time we had repaired the three aircraft from our flight. They would all fly the following day but only the major and Captain Brown would be able to fly from the rest. Some of the ones which had returned would only be fit for spares. From twelve aircraft we now had just five; such was life in the R.F.C.

After we had washed up we piled into the mess for food. Now that we had a wooden building it felt cleaner and it was certainly warmer. There was a fug of hot food and cigarette smoke as we trudged in. Flight Sergeant Lowery waved us over to sit with him at his table. We were now the four senior flying sergeants in the squadron and there was a bond between us. Sometimes the armourer and quartermaster would join us but that night both were busy ordering spares and repairing guns.

"You know that big wig who was waiting for the major?"

"You mean the colonel?"

"That's right. Well, he is second in command to General Henderson, he's the bloke in charge of the Flying Corps."

"Phew. Are we in bother then?"

"Nah, just the opposite. They were talking while I was in the outer office. The door was open and I heard every word."

He waited expectantly. Gordy shook his head, "What are you waiting for? A round of applause."

He looked miffed, "Just building up the tension."

"Don't worry, pal, we have had more than our share of tension lately."

"Well, it seems we are the only squadron who send out the planes as a squadron. The rest just send one or two out or a flight at most. We have had the most success and, until today, the least casualties and damaged aeroplanes."

"Are we getting a bonus then?"

"Ted, you never fail to amaze me. When did the army every pay you for doing something well? The officers might get promoted but we will get bugger all."

Raymond looked at me, "They want his lordship to start a new squadron and use the same tactics. Those Germans you two managed to shoot down make him one of the most successful British pilots on the whole western front. You could well be leaving."

I don't know why but that disappointed me. I was happy here and comfortable. I did not relish the thought of starting afresh. It would be especially bad as we would be seen to be bringing new ideas and I knew that a lot of the men would like to see us fail. "When does he leave?"

"Not for a couple of weeks. The major said he couldn't afford to lose his most experienced pilot in the middle of an offensive. Besides we have still a job to do here."

The captain did not say a word as the five of us took off the next day. I heard his first words when he told me of our task that day. "Right, Flight, we are heading back for the road and then the railway. We will machine-gun any infantry and then harass anyone trying to repair the railway line."

I had a bad feeling about the whole thing. This would be the fourth day we had done exactly the same thing and the Germans were many things but stupid was not one of them. As we crossed into German territory we were jumped by a number of aeroplanes. They swooped down like hawks. Luckily we saw them before they opened fire but we were slow beasts and the Gunbus took forever to climb I fired at the Aviatik which was attacking the major's plane. I didn't hit it but I forced it to climb and Major Brack was able to continue to evade the enemy. I felt the floor judder as the undercarriage was hit by bullets from an Albatros heading at our starboard side. I swung the Lewis around and gave him a short burst. I saw pieces fly from his propeller. The fragments must have struck the pilot for he suddenly fell back, jerking the joystick as he did so. Alarmingly the Albatros began to climb above us. I grabbed my Lee Enfield and, as it appeared above us I fired five bullets into its underbelly. I saw flames appear and begin to spread down the aeroplane. Even as it climbed I knew that it was doomed. Sixty feet above us the fuel tank exploded and we were all shifted in the air by the concussion.

There was no time for self-congratulation. The captain's Lewis suddenly opened fire. It was always worrying when that happened as it was right next to my head. I saw that he had seen an Aviatik turning in front of us and he managed to hit the tail. I fired the last of my magazine and saw my bullets stitch a line towards the cockpit. The whole aircraft wobbled. Between us, we had hit some of the control wires. Captain Brown's aeroplane had been hit and I saw him heading to the ground in an attempt to land. I hoped he landed on the correct side of the front.

I changed the magazine and fired at an Albatros which was firing at Gordy's engine. I saw smoke begin to pour from the back of Gordy's Gunbus and I held my fingers on the trigger. The observer gunner slumped forward as my bullets struck him and the Albatros took evasive action.

In my ear, I heard, "Time to go Flight. We are the last bird in the air."

I looked around and saw that the rest of our aeroplanes were heading west and the surviving Germans were limping east.

"Righto, sir. We have ridden our luck again."

"I know, I know."

We allowed the others to land before us. We watched as Captain Devries tried to land the damaged Gunbus. He made a valiant attempt but one of the wingtips caught the ground and, to my horror I saw the aeroplane cartwheel. There was a cloud of smoke and I could not see anything. I hoped that Gordy had survived but the one who normally died in such a crash was the observer. I felt sick to my stomach as we taxied by the smoking shell of the Gunbus.

As we stopped I shouted. "I'm going to see how Gordy is."

When I reached the scene and the doctor I was amazed to see Gordy smoking a cigarette. There was a sheet covering something. Gordy pointed with his cigarette. "Captain Devries. He caught one when they hit the engine. He must have landed it and died or landed it already dead."

"How did you survive?"

He pointed at the pole holding the rear-facing Lewis gun. "That stopped me from breaking my neck and the seat belt actually held. If we hadn't had your device then I would be dead now." As they took the body of the young officer away I reflected that he had grown up as a pilot at the front but it had still not saved him from a premature death.

It was decided that we didn't have enough aeroplanes to operate the next day which was a relief to us all. I was busy repairing the bus when the major and Captain Burscough wandered up. I wondered if they were going to tell me about the new squadron but they surprised me. The major said, "I thought you wanted to try out as a pilot, Flight Sergeant Harsker?"

"I did sir but we have been so busy."

He nodded, "You aren't busy now are you?"

"Not really sir."

"Good. The Avro is fuelled and ready to go."

I ran to my tent to get my flying gear. When I reached the Avro the captain said, quietly, "You can do this, Bill. You are a natural."

I was not so sure but I climbed into the cockpit anyway. It had been some time since I had flown and I hoped I would remember what to do. At least I had an idea what would be required of me as I had seen Gordy's test.

As soon as the engine fired I focussed. I heard the major's voice in my ear. "Take off whenever you are ready and fly a circuit of the field at two hundred feet."

"Sir."

The test was like a blur. Even as I performed the various manoeuvres I couldn't remember the last one I had done. It made no difference that I had seen Gordy do the same thing. Everything just blended into one huge blank. When he said, "You can land now," I breathed a sigh of relief. The ordeal would soon be over.

I waited until the major had climbed out and then I joined him. Captain Burscough walked slowly towards us. The major had a very serious face. "Flight Sergeant Harsker did you know that Captain Burscough is going to be given the command of a new squadron?"

There was no point in lying. I nodded, "Yes sir, I heard a rumour." I knew what was coming now. I had failed the test and I would be going with the captain as his gunner.

"His new squadron will not be flying the Gunbus but a new single-seater fighter, the Bristol. Now, as a new pilot, which would you rather fly?" It took me a moment to hear his words and realise that I had passed my test. I hesitated and I saw the major smile, "Well?"

"I think I would like to stay with this squadron, sir."

There was palpable relief on the major's face. "I hoped that you would say that." He turned to the captain. "Sorry James, he wants to stay here."

To be fair to his lordship his smile was genuine. "No hard feelings Flight, and well done. I shall miss you but I understand why you want to stay. I was tempted to refuse the colonel." He suddenly looked like a boy again as he grinned, "I held out for a majority!"

"Congratulations to you, Major Burscough. When do you leave?"

The grin went. "Tomorrow. Back to Blighty. I have to go to the factory. I need to find out about this new aeroplane before my new pilots arrive!"

The two majors went over to the mess. I suspected they would be celebrating. Gordy and Ted ran over to me, "Well!"

"I am a pilot like you now Gordy!"

"Well done. What was the major saying?"

"He offered me the chance to go with Lord Burscough and fly the new single-seater scout."

"And you turned him down? That's daft that is."

"Always half-empty eh Ted? I know the Gunbus and I like it. I would not be confident in a single-seater; not yet anyway." I waved a hand at the airfield. There were just three aircraft fit to fly. "There are no aeroplanes left here to fly anyway."

We now only had the young lieutenants left as pilots and they had the heavily damaged aeroplanes. Until we received either spares or new aeroplanes then we would not be truly operational. This last offensive had hurt us.

We waved a hungover and bleary-eyed Major Burscough goodbye. He was driven in a staff car sent for him by the colonel. As we turned to go back to our aeroplanes, the other officers who had just waved his lordship off, began to clamber aboard a lorry driven by Quartermaster Doyle. Major Brack waved us over. "Harsker and Hewitt; get your flying gear. You are to go with the officers and pick up replacement aeroplanes and crew from England."

As we ran to our tent I heard Ted grumble, "I have no luck. I shall have to stay here and repair these wrecks while you get to go to England. There's no justice in this world."

Chapter 20

There were just six officers in the back of the lorry. We both felt self-conscious as we clambered aboard. It was only when we sat down and looked at them that I realised they were all lieutenants. Captain Dundas had stayed with the major. They all had less air time than we did. I also saw that they were a little nervous too. Gordy made everything comfortable, "We hope you fine gentlemen don't mind travelling with a couple of grease monkeys like us."

They were young but they were pleasant chaps. Lieutenant Donovan said, "No, of course not, Flight. Besides, you two have more kills than us lot put together. We were hoping you could give us some pointers on the way back."

And so the journey to Calais was a pleasant one. Gordy told many stories about flying and then they all asked me about my trapeze stunt. By the time we reached the sea, I felt as though I knew them all far better than I had done. They were not lords; they were ordinary chaps and they were keen to learn. That was all that you could ask. I had been worried that they would turn out to be versions of Lieutenant Ramsden.

We had an hour before we could board the boat and Gordy managed to buy a few bottles of French brandy for the voyage. "We can enjoy ourselves now, Bill!"

In the event, we did not. The ship was taking home many of the wounded from the battle of Neuve Chapelle. When Gordy saw the plight of some of the soldiers who had lost arms, leg, even eyes he could not, in all conscience, drink alone. Most of the brandy was doled out to soldiers who had a bleak future ahead of them. They would be cripples in a world which only valued the whole. He shook his head as we poured the last drop down the throat of a boy, who looked to be younger than my brother Albert. Gordy said, "I am coming round to your way of thinking Bill. We should have killed more of the bastards on the road. It's now our lads or theirs and from now I will save our boys if I can."

There was a lorry waiting when we reached Dover and we were driven to the same aerodrome at Dartford. It was dark when we arrived and we were billeted in the sergeant's barracks. It was a grim place. I suspect it was always used for transitory pilots and there was no sign of anyone leaving a mark upon it. After the depressing crossing, we both went to bed with sunken spirits. The euphoria of the first part of the journey had been forgotten after the horror of the boat and soulless barracks.

We were summoned the next morning to the briefing room where the station commander, Captain Dawes, sat at a table with a pile of papers before him. I noticed a group of men in new uniforms sat together. I guessed they were our replacement crews. We were told to sit and Quartermaster Doyle plopped himself next to us. He turned to speak to us. "I get to take back the new boys who aren't flying! What a depressing journey that will be."

"Are you taking anything else back?"

He tapped the side of his nose, "As many spares as I can manage to lay my hands on." He chuckled, "They have so many aeroplanes and parts coming through here that they haven't the first clue what we have signed for. I will pack the lorries to the rafters."

The captain stood up. "Gentlemen we have a little paperwork to do here. The pilots," he glanced in our direction, "will need to sign for their aircraft and check that they are airworthy." Gordy and I groaned while the loots looked confused. They would soon find out what that meant. Three hours of walking around the aircraft with a checklist.

"When I call your name then come here and sign for the aeroplane. You will pick up your checklist and logbook and then the Squadron Sergeant will allocate you your observer."

The captain looked to be a man who did things by the book... no matter how long that took. Gordy and I were in the middle of the alphabet and I was called before him. The captain gave me a supercilious look as though I could not read and then said, "Sign here, Flight Sergeant Harsker." He emphasised the Flight Sergeant part.

I smiled, "I'll just read it through, sir, if you don't mind."

As I was reading it I heard him say to the young lieutenant next to him, "We must be scraping the barrel if we are letting sergeants fly now."

I gritted my teeth and ignored the barb. If this man had been any good he would have been in Flanders. "Thank you, sir. That appears to be in order." I signed and picked up my documents.

As I passed the squadron sergeant he shouted, "Private Sharp. Here's your pilot!"

I saw a young and eager looking boy who picked up his bag and threw it over his shoulder. "Right private let's go and find our aeroplane." As we wandered out into the cold spring morning I asked, "Have you flown much?"

He looked embarrassed. "Today will be my first flight, Flight Sergeant."

That somehow brightened my day. I had been in his position a few months ago and now I was a pilot.

"Don't worry son, you will love it." I saw that the aeroplane had just two Lewis guns fitted. When I looked inside I saw that there were no spare magazines. "Stow your gear here in this front cockpit and then have a wander around it. It will all seem strange at first. I have to do something."

I saw Quartermaster Doyle at a large building loading his lorry. He turned when I ran up. "What do you want? Coming back with me now that you've seen your crew?"

"No Quartermaster, it's just that there are no spare magazines. Any chance of getting one?"

He grinned, "You'll get me shot." He nodded to a box. "They are there but only take the one!"

I felt much better when I reached my aeroplane. I handed the magazine to Sharp. "Know how to change one of these?"

He smiled, "Yes Flight."

"Then change it now and humour me." He did so successfully and I rubbed my hands. "Right grab the checklist while I do the guided tour," I remembered that Captain Burscough had not really shown me the aeroplane when I had been in Sharp's position. I did not want him to look the fool I had when I had tried to start the beast. In the end, the checklist and the tour went hand in hand. I discovered that there was not enough oil in the engine. That could have been a disaster over the Channel. I hoped that the young lieutenants would be as diligent as I knew Gordy and I were. We had the advantage that we had worked on the engines and knew what to look for. They were just chauffeurs. Everything else appeared to be in order. Private Sharp appeared to be diligent and keen. He paid attention to everything I said and his questions were intelligent. I had been lucky; they had assigned me a decent observer.

When we were finished I sent Sharp to wash up while I returned with the checklist. The captain did not appear surprised that there was oil missing but by the same token he did not appear to be bothered. I handed him the signed checklist and he gave me a lazy wave. "Have a good flight then, Flight." He seemed amused by his own wit. I shook my head and returned to the bus.

Gordy was on his way in. And he waved a thumb at the others. "Do we have to wait for them?"

I shook my head and laughed, "Do you want the poor sods to end up in the drink? Of course, we wait for them. We have, at least, done this once before."

"I suppose. The same route?"

"It is safe."

He shook his head. "Not any more. The Hun has been bombing Dover with Zeppelins and Aviatiks. One of the new lads comes from there and he was telling me."

"In that case, we will have to arm the guns well before the coast. I'll go and tell the loots what we are about."

They were all in a huddle watching the mechanics and observers checking the aeroplane. They would soon learn that you did that sort of thing yourself. "Sirs!" They all turned.

"Yes, Flight?" Lieutenant Donovan appeared to have the most about him.

"I have just heard the Hun has been bombing Dover and that is on our way home. We might run into Zeppelins or aeroplanes. I would suggest we all have our gunners cock their Lewis guns when we have taken off. It will just be a precaution but we don't want to get jumped do we?"

"Thank you for that suggestion, Flight Sergeant."

They looked at each other with a mixture of fear and excitement. I knew that some of them would fancy their chances against a Zeppelin; for me, I wanted a quiet trip back. However, I was a mere Flight Sergeant and they all outranked me. I looked at the sky. It was getting on for afternoon. "And we had better get a move on, sirs. Unless you fancy landing in the dark."

All thoughts of Zeppelin hunting disappeared as they began to chivvy their crews into action. I returned to our aeroplanes. Gordy was there with his observer. "Well?"

"I told them. I guess they will hurry up now." I saw Sharp looking intently at the Lewis gun. "If we have to fire this on the way back then wait until I give the order."

"Sir."

"And just a short burst; four or five shots at a time."

"Sir!"

Gordy laughed. "I see becoming a pilot has made you an old woman now."

"Better to be safe than sorry."

The officers returned. Lieutenant Donovan approached us. "None of us have flown over the sea before. We wondered if you chaps could navigate?"

I nodded, "It is simple enough. We head down the Thames and then fly south to Dover. Once there we head directly for Calais and then we are almost home."

They looked relieved. Gordy said, "Better keep it at six hundred feet unless we get low cloud cover, sir."

"Righto, Flight."

There were more mechanics at the aerodrome and Sharp was saved the ordeal of spinning the propeller. We had not rigged up the tubes and so I said, "Keep the map open and follow our route. It will be good practice. I will tap you on the head when I want you to do anything. If you have to open fire then you will hear me, believe me!"

As we bounced and trundled down the grass I could feel the butterflies in my stomach. I was not just leading three aeroplanes this time, I was piloting one. I had only flown the Gunbus once before but I knew that every aeroplane, even the same type, had their own idiosyncrasies. I was relieved when we pulled up into the air and I steadily rose to six hundred feet. As we flew down the Thames, slowly reaching the correct altitude, I listened to the engine and played with the controls. I needed to know the different sounds the aeroplane made. I wondered if Sharp was worried by that. I noticed that he had tightened his belt and held on to the sides as we had taken off.

Once we reached six hundred feet I tapped him on the head. When he turned around I mimed cocking the gun. He nodded. I tried to keep the aeroplane as level as I could. He had to take off his belt and stand to do so. I remembered what an ordeal that was. When it was done he turned and grinned boyishly. I smile back my reassurance. I mimed for him to sit down and I saw the relief on his face.

I cocked my own Lewis. I hoped I would not have to fire it for I had not briefed Sharp about keeping his head to one side.

When I saw the sea ahead I waved my left hand from the cockpit. Gordy would see that from his aeroplane and would know the turn was coming up. As we passed over Dover I saw the smoke and flames. They had been bombed. That was sad for Dover but good news for us. It meant that we would not meet any German aeroplanes or Zeppelins coming west. I used the harbour as my marker and turned east. As I did so I glanced astern and saw the line of aeroplanes. Gordy was perfectly positioned but the others were struggling to maintain their altitude. Some were higher and some were lower. Major Brack would not be happy with such sloppy flying.

We were approaching Calais when I saw smoke below me. It was an Albatros and it looked to have been damaged. It was wave hopping. We needed to descend anyway and I put the stick forward to get to a better altitude. We picked up speed as we did so and Sharp turned around in alarm as we drew nearer to the German. He mimed firing and I shook my head. I saw the observer turn around and then tap the pilot on the head. Gordy and the others had descended and the pilot waggled his wings to show that he would surrender. I flew next to him and mimed putting his aeroplane behind mine. I wanted Gordy's gunner to have him in his sights. As I overtook him I could see that his tail had been damaged and his engine had been struck. He wanted to make sure that he could land

and there were too many guns between him and home for that in such a damaged aeroplane. He was happy to sit between our buses.

As soon as we had passed Calais I turned the aeroplane and headed for the aerodrome. We were flying at three hundred feet. I put the stick down when I saw the field in the distance. I reached down and took out the Very pistol. I fired a rocket in the air. He might be a German but we needed to have the fire crews and medical staff on hand for his landing.

I slowed down so that I was flying level with him and I gestured for him to land first. He nodded and crabbed the stricken craft towards the greensward. He was a good pilot and managed to get it down in one piece. We were low on fuel and I wasted no time in getting down myself.

As I taxied I saw that the major himself was speaking with the captured pilot. There appeared to be no injuries. I was curious about the German aeroplane and I looked forward to inspecting it.

"Sharp, better bring your things and I will show you your billet."

"Sir." I could see the relief on his face that we had crossed the sea and landed safely.

As we passed the German pilot and observer, they clicked their heels together and saluted me. Major Brack smiled, "Well done, Sergeant Harsker."

The pilot's face turned to a snarl. His English was accented but understandable. "You are a sergeant? I thought you were an officer! You were leading the aeroplanes!" He said it accusingly as though I had deceived him in some way.

I was bemused, "Yes sir, I am a sergeant but I was leading the flight." He turned away and began to stomp across the field. "I would not have surrendered had I known."

I saw the flash of anger on Major Brack's face. "But you did, so behave with a little better grace." He shook his head and waved his arm at the two soldiers who held guns on them both. "Sergeant Davis, take them to the guardhouse until we can get them over to Intelligence."

After they had gone he gave me an apologetic look, "Sorry about that. So, you had an eventful flight. I see they all made it."

I nodded and then said quietly, "Some of their station keeping was a little below what you might have expected, sir." I suddenly realised that I was criticising officers. "Of course they are new aeroplanes. It takes time."

"Quite so, Flight Sergeant. There will be no operations tomorrow, we will practise formations."

"Sir." I was relieved. I needed to get to know Private Sharp."

Gordy and his crew reached me at the same time that Ted hurried over. "Our first capture! Do we share that amongst us all Bill?"

"I have no idea, Gordy. If he had flown off I would have let him. I think he thought we might jump him."

Ted threw his cigarette butt away, "Dozy bugger; I would have legged it home. Their aeroplanes are faster than ours." He pointed to the Albatros. "I wouldn't mind having a look at that one."

"Yes, I wonder what they will do with it."

Chapter 21

Sadly we did not get the chance to inspect the aeroplane and it was taken away on the back of a lorry. The major told me that it would be added to my tally as the pilot had said before he knew that I was a sergeant, that he had surrendered to me. The major told us of other men who had shot down a number of enemy aircraft and that those with five or more were called aces. I did not count those balloons and aeroplanes I had destroyed whilst a gunner and so this was my first. It seemed like a game to the major but to me, it was just a measure of how close we were to winning the war and the tally of one captured aeroplane would not make the war end tomorrow.

Two days after we had returned home our flight was given a patrol. The two days training had been spent in flying the aeroplanes in formation. They had proved immensely useful. Sharp was a much more confident observer now. He still had to fire his guns in anger but everything else was satisfactory. The sector was quiet now and the line had been stabilised after the battle of Neuve Chapelle. I discovered that all of the new observers had been trained in Morse code and we were equipped with a signal lamp. This was to allow us to communicate with the ground. As Gordy and I had the new observers we went on patrol with Captain Dundas watching us. For poor Ted, it was yet another affirmation that he had no luck. "Young kids still wet behind the ears and I have to be their babyminder."

Our improvised speaking tube still worked and I know that Charlie Sharp appreciated it. For some reason, he seemed in awe of me. I later discovered it was because I was a sergeant and pilot. It gave him hope that he could aspire to such lofty heights. We climbed to a thousand feet above the trenches. We were well out of machine gun range and it was too expensive to waste artillery shells on us. It made for safe flying. We rarely got balloons now as they had an early warning system and the balloons were already on the ground by the time we reached them. However, it did mean that, so long as we were about, their balloons couldn't be used to spy on our trenches.

It was sad to see the devastation caused by the shelling. Where there had been woods, hedgerows and buildings, now there was a sea of mud, albeit drying out after a brief dry spell. I glanced up. Ted's aeroplane was three hundred feet above ours flying lazy circles and seeking enemy aircraft.

Sharp's voice came in my ears. "Flight, if you fly along the lines for a mile or so I think I can see their artillery."

"Righto." I found myself using the same phrases that his lordship had. I wondered how he was getting on in his single-seater.

"Hold it there sir while I mark it on the map." Charlie was a meticulous draughtsman and far more careful than I had been when I had marked maps. After a few moments, he said, "If you fly over our lines I will signal the coordinates."

I knew that Gordy's observer would be doing the same thing and I did not worry that we would be out of contact with each other. Our babysitter in the skies above was our insurance policy.

"Hold her steady there, Flight." I saw the lamp flickering and, when it stopped I spotted the acknowledgement. "You can go up a little if you like and I will spot the fall of shot."

He was a cool customer. I was not sure how I felt about being in line with a target when there was an artillery barrage. I spiralled up a couple of hundred feet and positioned us above the area known as no-man's land. It looked bleak. I could see puddles and ponds amidst the wire and barriers. I did not envy infantry trying to slog through that lot.

"Any idea where Sergeant Hewitt is?"

A moment later he said, "A couple of miles to the north. It looks like he is doing the same."

I did not like that. Captain Dundas was our only protection. Being that far apart, he would have a difficult task to cover us both effectively. I saw the smoke and then heard the crump as the British artillery opened fire. They were just using one gun to make it easier for Sharp to spot the fall of shell. We both watched as the shell exploded just fifty yards short of the German artillery. We saw the crews racing around as the dust settled.

"Back again, Flight."

I took us down and back to the British trenches where Sharp relayed the information. Once it was acknowledged then we resumed our lofty perch. This time the bang and the smoke were much louder. Even as they were hurtling towards the German 42cm guns the Hun was firing blindly in the hope of hitting our guns.

I heard a scream in my ear as Charlie saw the first German gun disappear as it was struck. "Steady on Charlie."

"Sorry Flight. They are bang on. If you go back I can signal them and then we can leave."

Even as we spiralled down I could see, to the north, that Gordy was under attack. Captain Dundas had been between the devil and the deep blue sea, he was a long way from Gordy.

"Send that now Charlie. Sergeant Hewitt is in trouble."

"Right sir."

As his lamp flashed I banked to starboard. Gaining height had meant that we would now have more speed as we hurtled north to try to come to the aid of my two friends. I could see that there were three aeroplanes attacking them. Suddenly Charlie shouted, "Three German aeroplanes sir."

"Where away?"

"South and east sir, about a mile away."

It still made sense to go to the other two. Isolated we could be picked off but together we had a chance of defeating these six aeroplanes.

"Charlie, you will have to fire the rear Lewis." I knew that he was afraid and I saw the colour drain from his face as he stood and faced me. I mouthed, "Open your legs wide!"

He nodded. It actually made it easier to keep your balance but, more importantly, it allowed me to fire my fixed Lewis. I could see that Gordy was heading back over our lines and his gunner was pouring lead into his pursuers. Ted had not opened fire which told me that he was still too far away. The moment he could Ted would add his firepower to that of Gordy. I hoped Charlie remembered what I had said about short bursts and firing late. We were now level with Captain Dundas but approaching from an oblique angle. The nearest German was two hundred yards away and we were only gaining slowly. The Gunbus was just not fast enough.

I saw Charlie gesticulate with his arm. They were on us. I nodded and he gave a short six-shot burst. The German had the disadvantage that like me, his machine gun was fixed but he was even worse off as his gun was on the top of his wing. He had to adjust for the height difference. I saw the line of bullets as they flew high wide and handsome. I was tempted to jink to the right but I remembered Captain Dixon. I kept it straight. Charlie would not fall to his death on his first combat mission. There was another burst from Charlie and then I concentrated on the aeroplane before me. It was the second in the line. I cocked the Lewis and flew directly for the engine of the Albatros. The observer suddenly whirled his gun around to fire at me but it could not get a shot at us and I saw the bullets as they flew beyond our tail. At a hundred yards I fired a short burst and then again at fifty. The German pilot saw me and banked hard right. I kept on going. I would have to make a slow gentle turn or risk my gunner's life.

I saw Ted give a burst from his Lewis and the German flew back into my sights. I fired again. It was a snap shot but I hit the pilot. He slumped forward and the aeroplane began to dive into the ground. There was no cause for celebration as the Germans chasing us stitched a line of holes along the wing. One of the cables sheared. We could not take much more damage. Sharp tapped the magazine of the Lewis- it was empty. I mouthed at him to sit down. I would have to fly my way out of trouble.

It was now five against six and as Charlie sat and I was able to bank I saw Gordy's gunner and Ted combine to hit another Albatros which wheeled away with a smoking engine. My manoeuvre had thrown the aim of our pursuers and I began a climb. I knew it made us slower for a short time but it also meant that at least two of the aeroplanes chasing me flew by, unable to slow in time. At the top of my turn, I banked to port, towards the German lines and it fooled my last pursuer.

Charlie had connected the speaking tube again. "Charlie get ready to give this German everything you have."

We were diving towards the tail of the second of our pursuers. My move had confused him and, losing us in the sky, he was heading after Captain Dundas. His gunner spotted us and his Parabellum LMG began pumping bullets in our direction. They were steel-tipped projectiles and could pierce our engine. Luckily we had two bodies protecting ours! Charlie held his nerve. I saw the German gunner trying to reload his gun and Charlie gave him a long burst. He slumped to his death and the gun was silent. The German was now helpless. Charlie's shots had struck the engine and, with smoke pouring, the pilot headed east.

My dogged pursuer was still there and more bullets appeared in my wing. I glance at the damaged cable and saw that another was fraying. I would have to keep the aeroplane as stable as possible. I head Sharp's voice in my ear. "He's leaving sir. Captain Dundas has hit him."

"Then let's go home. Keep your eye on the damaged cable."

"Will do."

I saw Gordy, now well ahead of me, and his engine was smoking. The flare he set off showed me it was serious. Our fairy godmother still hovered behind us but I could see from the bullet holes that it had suffered as much damage as we had. This had been an expensive patrol. Gordy's landing was not the best but I saw two of them climb down from the much-damaged aeroplane. Then it was our turn. I landed her as gently as I could but there was an almighty crack and one of the struts gave way as we touched down. Miraculously the top wing just lay on the bottom wing and we rolled to an ugly halt.

The mechanics raced to us and pushed us out of the way of Captain Dundas' machine which rolled to a halt between us and Gordy. I climbed out and waited for Charlie. He looked unsteady as he touched the ground. I shook his hand. "Well done, young 'un. You did well."

"Thank you, Flight. I thought we had bought it." He lowered his voice. "Thank you for flying straight. The lads told me about the time the pilot flew upside down with you hanging on the Lewis."

"You never know Sharp, that may happen sometime but not on your first mission eh?" I looked at the damaged Gunbus. "Well, we have our work cut out tomorrow."

He looked at me in surprise. "But you are a pilot!"

"All the more reason for me to fix my own machine. I don't mind getting my hands dirty. But that is for tomorrow. Let's get washed up and then you can take your maps and reports to the intelligence officer."

Lieutenant Marshall had been promoted to Captain and given the role of Intelligence officer. It suited his organised mind.

Gordy and Ted caught up with us. Ted put an arm on each of our shoulders. "I'll tell you what lads, that was bloody good flying out there." He jerked his head at Captain Dundas. "The dozy bugger wasted time worrying which of you to help. It would have been a disaster."

I laughed, "But it wasn't, so forget it. We have learned a lesson today. Next time Gordy and I will stay closer together."

"Amen to that brother." He grinned at me. "Another two and a half and you will be an ace!"

"Don't be daft. I was just lucky."

Gordy shook his head, "I should be so lucky."

Major Hewitt was delighted and, when we made our report we saw that he had a blackboard in his office. Our names were there and next to them the number of kills. As I went in I saw him putting my new successes up there. My name was at the top. I was the leading pilot in the squadron.

Major Hewitt nodded, "You two could have been flying for months you know." He stared at Ted. "How about you, Flight?"

Ted backed off, "No sir. I am quite happy doing what I do sir!"

Major Hewitt said, "There is something a little incongruous about you saying you are happy, Thomas, you always look as though you have the worries of the world on your shoulders."

Our aeroplane took three days to repair during which time our flight was stood down. All three aircraft had suffered damage. It left just the major and the seven lieutenants to patrol. He divided them into two flights and he led the one with just three aircraft. The first day was a milk run. They came back without firing their guns at all.

Poor Ted was beside himself, "How come those lucky buggers get to swan around the German line and don't even have to fire their guns and we look as though the mice have been at us! There's no justice!"

Those words left a sour taste the next day when two of the young fliers failed to return. They had both been in the flight of four and the Germans who had jumped them had been flying Albatros aeroplanes. They had had a disaster. One of them, piloted by Lieutenant Cox, had tried to bank too steeply when the gunner was firing the rear Lewis and the unfortunate gunner had fallen from the aircraft. The Germans had easily destroyed the defenceless aeroplane. As the second one had tried to climb out of trouble, its engine had been hit. It had crash-landed in no-man's land and we did not know the outcome.

The major had Gordy and me in his office that evening after the meal. "Sit down boys." I smiled to myself, Gordy was at least ten years older than the major and I was about the same age. He took a bottle of whisky from his drawer and three glasses. He poured us a healthy glass each. I was not a spirit drinker but it would have been rude to refuse. "Cheers!"

"Cheers."

It burned as it went down but I enjoyed the taste. I noticed that the major had emptied his own glass and he refilled it. He gestured with the bottle but we shook our heads, "There's no getting around it, today was a disaster." He looked at me. "You lost men on the Yser, Harsker. How did you tell the families of those who died?"

The memory made me frown a little and I sipped the whisky. "It was different for me sir, I had grown up with most of the lads so I either wrote a letter or, in the case of the brothers, I went to see the mother."

Both of them looked surprised. "You had to tell a mother both of her sons were dead?"

"Yes sir and she was a widow too."

"How did you do it?"

"I told the truth but left out the pain the boys had suffered."

The major nodded and finished his whisky. "That isn't the reason I brought you both here. I intend to offer you both a commission. It seems the general thinks highly of us and so we can do this. Your flight, with Captain Dundas, is the best flight in the squadron. I can't be a babyminder all the time. I need to split the flight up and use each of you as a Flight Commander. You will need to be an officer. The young lads will listen to you. They respect you, I know that. Well?"

I looked at Gordy who said, "I didn't become a pilot to be an officer sir but I understand what you are saying. I accept." He put his hand across the table and they shook.

"I am honoured that you want me as an officer sir. I accept too." He shook my hand.

"We will be getting replacements soon so, for the time being, you two need to take one of the young lieutenants under your wing so to speak and teach them how to be a flier. You are both experienced gunners and that is what this will all be about soon. We will become fighters. Captain Burscough and his squadron of Bristols is a picture of the future. They need what you both have, flying sense. Your new rank and pay grade will begin immediately. I would get the tailor to make you a new uniform each. It will cost you a couple of bob each but it will be worth it." He stood as did we, "I'd like to thank you both."

When we got outside we both kept a straight face and marched back to the sergeant's mess. Ted was sat, nursing a beer. We sat opposite him. "What did his nibs want?"

Gordy leaned forward, grabbed Ted's ears and pulled him forward. He planted a kiss on his forehead. "What the bloody ..."

He was clenching his fists when I said, "He made us officers. We are Second Lieutenants." I waved my arm around the mess, "We'll be in the officer's mess soon so let's have one last night here eh? We won't be flying tomorrow anyway."

He actually smiled, "Well done but don't expect a salute. And as you have more money it's your shout." As I got up to go to the bar I heard him say to Gordy. "One thing's for certain. I am going to become a pilot. I feel like a granddad with these young gunners."

Chapter 22

Private Sharp was delighted. "That's better sir, a pilot should be an officer."

"But you want to be one don't you?"

"Yes sir and you have shown us the way."

I was still working in overalls despite the new uniform which was being made for me. The uniform and the salutes would not change the man within. I had got where I was by being me. If I changed then it could all crumble.

Lieutenant Murray was one of the survivors and he was told by the major that he was in my flight. I honestly think he was still in shock after the earlier debacle and he just nodded. His Flight Sergeant, Walter Hibbert, was also new and he, too, appeared to have less confidence than Charlie Sharp. It was a strange situation. With my bus all shipshape I took the three men who would be serving under me for a walk down the French lane towards the small village of Breteuil, a mile or so away. I wanted informality. I would do things my way.

"We are a team now. We are C Flight. In a few days, we will be getting more replacements and then we will have our third member of the flight. I am new to this game so I am going to do it the way I think will work best." I stopped and looked at them each in turn. "Feel free to ask any questions about why I am doing what I do but I want things done my way." I stared at Lieutenant Murray. "I do not want to have to write a letter to anyone's parents. Right?"

They all nodded soberly. I knew there was a small bar-restaurant in the village and I assumed it would be open. It was and there was an empty table outside.

"Let's sit here." A woman came out and gave a perfunctory wave of her cloth at the table, "Monsieur?"

"Vin rouge si vous plais. Pour quatre."

I knew that both my accent and my French were awful but that was all I had learned. I smiled at the three of them. "I just wanted to sit and talk with you off the base. If you don't like red wine then just nurse it. I am not keen myself but the beer is, frankly, awful."

For some reason that made them smile and I saw Lieutenant Murray begin to relax for the first time. The wine came and I paid. I knew they would allow me to run up a bill but I wanted to be able to leave when we needed to. I held up my glass, "Here's to C Flight," I paused, "and those absent friends who would love to be raising a glass right now."

"C Flight."

"Right, let's get down to basics. Here are my rules. John, you will always follow me and do whatever I do. The new boy will do the same. Walter, did you see the young observer fall out of the aircraft?"

"Yes, sir."

"Well that was nearly me and I hung on so if the worst happens then hang on to the Lewis. I am a big bugger and it held me. Right?" I saw him smile and relax. "But John, when Walter is using the rear gun you have to fly straight and level; even if you are being fired upon. That rear gun is our sting in the tail. Until we get another aeroplane then when we fly as a pair Walter's job is to watch astern. Charlie here will keep his eye on the front." I drank some of my wine. "Charlie you have flown combat with me. Any tips for these two?"

"Yes, sir." He held up a finger as he itemised each point. "Spare magazines, rifle in the cockpit. Fire in short bursts as close as you can get to the enemy."

"Good. Couldn't have said it better myself."

"Sir?"

"Yes, John?"

"Is it true that you have shot down a number of aeroplanes and balloons?"

"Yes, why?"

"You only have two and a half on the blackboard in the office."

I smiled. "The rest were when I was a gunner. I have been reinvented. Besides, I don't care who shoots down the bastards so long as we shoot them. I would rather their pilots died than ours and that goes double for you John. A little tip Captain Burscough and I discovered is that, because the Albatros has a gun on the top wing unless he is attacking from below all you need to do to avoid being hit is to dip your nose a little. He can't aim at you then. That also allows the gunner to fire into the belly of his aircraft."

"What if he is below you?"

"Then you bank and climb. It is a risk but the enemy would have to second guess which direction you will climb. Never repeat the same bank. Keep them guessing. Right. Let's go through some other little points. Hand signals…"

The time passed swiftly and they began to question me. I was happy for I wanted them to know my mind. I wanted John to be able to turn when I did and climb at the same time. It would not happen straight away but when we achieved that then we would all have more chance of survival. As we strolled back to the aerodrome I felt much happier. For a few centimes, I had learned more about my flight than a week of drills.

Our first patrol was two days later and I was eager to see how we fared over the trenches. It was a strictly observation patrol. I took us as high as we could manage without having breathing difficulties. The trenches and no-man's land were quite obvious, even from that altitude. I signalled with my arm and we began a slow descent to a better altitude for observation. As soon as we swooped down we saw the balloons beginning to make their descent. I had no idea about the other sectors but in ours, they were wary of our attacks.

I signalled to John to keep a watch for Germans and I was pleased to see Walter watching our stern. The patrol had been a success already. Lessons had been learned. As we flew along the lines of trenches Charlie marked positions on the map and then sketched new defences. He was a much better and neater draughtsman than I had been. This would be valuable intelligence.

Suddenly John appeared next to me and pointed astern; there were three German aeroplanes above us. I signalled to return to base. With John tucked in astern I began to climb. We had discovered that we could go marginally faster at a higher altitude and it was harder for them to hit us with their wing-mounted machine guns. The day that someone invented a machine gun to fire through their propeller we were in trouble. The German aeroplanes were faster and more manoeuvrable. Our only advantage was forward firepower. Once we reached four thousand feet I levelled out and looked behind. The nearest Albatros was less than a hundred yards astern of John. This would be a stern test of his first lessons. Walter was braced against the side of the cockpit. I had told them both that they did not have to fly directly astern when we were under attack. He used that discretion at that moment. As the German came in for his attack John lifted the nose slightly and began to climb. When I saw that I tapped Charlie on the head and he manned our rear Lewis.

John's aircraft was going slower but Walter had a clear view of the German whose gun was now facing fresh air. Walter gave a burst and I saw the holes appear in the fuselage. I banked right slightly and also climbed. Charlie fired a burst from his gun. The Germans were now in a narrow channel and were being fired upon by two guns. Their gunners could not fire and the pilots were hampered by the position of their gun. Their superior speed also worked against them as they overtook us. Two magazines were emptied into the three aeroplanes.

Once they were beyond us their rear guns began to fire. We dived below the guns' trajectory. Walter and Charlie were in the front with a full magazine each. Their two guns rattled a destructive tattoo and I saw holes and smoke appear from the three aeroplanes. They limped away, now being fired upon by our infantry from the trenches. We had not shot any down but there were three aircraft which would need a lot of work before they flew again.

Back at the aerodrome the lieutenant and his gunner positively bounced from their aircraft. "Did you see that? Two against three and they ran!"

I pointed to his wings, "Yes, John but we did not escape unscathed. We have repairs to do but you are right; it was a successful mission." I turned to Charlie, "Give me your maps and drawings and I'll take them to the adjutant."

I left the three of them congratulating each other as though they had downed the three rather than just winging them. It was a start.

The major was with Captain Marshall. The major asked, "Well? How did it go?"

"Better than we could have hoped sir. We were jumped by three Albatros and we damaged them all."

"Well done! I shall see if I can do as well this afternoon. Is Hewitt not back yet?"

"He hadn't landed when I came over sir." I handed the maps and the sketches to the captain.

He nodded approvingly, "These sketches are excellent. They are almost as good as a photograph."

I smiled and said slyly, "Yes sir. It's a shame he is just a private."

"You want him made up to Flight Sergeant?" This was the first time I had exercised my authority and I felt Major Brack's searching gaze upon me.

"Yes sir, I think he deserves it."

He smiled, "Good, so do I. Captain Marshall see to the paperwork. I'll let you tell him, Lieutenant."

As I walked back I reflected that Charlie was a far better observer and mechanic than I was but I knew his skills with a machine gun were not as honed as mine were. I was, by nature, a hunter. It did make us a good team. When I told him of his promotion he was both excited and embarrassed. "Thank you, sir. I'll try to live up to your expectations of me."

I shook my head, "Don't worry, you have earned it." I smiled at Walter. "And there is a target for you, private. See if you can get promoted as quickly as Charlie here eh?"

"Yes, sir!"

The replacements arrived the next day and I met Lieutenant Campbell, for the first time. The impression I gained of him was not a good one. He reminded me, in his manner, more than a little of Lieutenant Ramsden. In voice and in looks he could have passed for Lord Burscough. After we were introduced I wondered if he would be the grit in the machine which would make it break down.

The major introduced us as Flight Commanders. It seems none of the new pilots were familiar with either the term of the concept. The major was always quick on the uptake and he explained.

"We have a reputation, in this squadron, of having a high rate of success combined with a low number of losses. We have devised the flight system to continue that. Each Flight Commander is in charge of three aircraft. They may operate as a flight or in conjunction with another flight. It gives us flexibility. You will all fly when your Flight Commander deems that you are ready."

My first warning sign came with the scowl which passed over Lieutenant Campbell's face. He was not happy. I decided that a trip to the village would not work with this one and so I led him, along with John, to the three aeroplanes. I let Charlie and Walter take his gunner, Private Fletcher, to be given the rundown on their duties. I trusted Charlie now. His promotion had enabled me to have a chain of command.

"How many hours do you have in an F.E.2 Lieutenant Campbell?"

"Today was my first time so just from Dartford to here. To be honest with you I was rather disappointed. I had hoped for one of the new Bristol Fighters. The Gunbus is too old and slow."

I had never heard such an attitude. It was like a cavalryman criticising his own horse. I saw John frown. "I think you will find it a good aeroplane and it certainly has the beating of the Albatros and Aviatik aeroplanes we come up against."

"The thing is, I have been told that this squadron does a great number of flights to observe. Quite frankly I want a little more action." He grinned in what I think he thought was an engaging manner but it left me cold.

"We are here to win a war, Lieutenant Campbell, not to win glory." I saw his face fall. "Anyway, we have no time to waste in debate you are in C Flight and that means we fly my way. John here flies astern of me and you astern of him…." I gave the same talk I had done in the village but I knew that I was being less considerate and understanding. He had got under my skin.

When I had finished he looked unhappy, "You mean I can't attack an enemy without your permission? I have to fly behind Lieutenant

Murray here." He smiled at John, "No offence but I may be a better pilot than you are."

I saw John redden. I had this man's measure now. "In which case being the last man in the flight is the most important and requires the best pilot. For you protect us from an attack in the rear. Until we got these rear-facing Lewis guns we lost too many aeroplanes. Of course, that means that you have to fly straight and level even if the enemy are firing at you. Erratic flying will result in the death of your observer and then you."

He laughed, "I don't think I am dependent on my observer."

This was getting worse and I felt myself losing my temper. "John, explain to him what happened to Lieutenant Cox and his observer."

John had been there and had also been a close friend of the dead pilot. His words were far more powerful than anything I could have said. It appeared to have little effect. "Well, dashed sorry and all that but this Lieutenant Cox sounds like a poor pilot. Believe me, I am very good. I was top of my class at flight school. That's another reason why I can't understand them sending me here. I am wasted in a Gunbus."

I snapped, "Let's see how you do in a week of patrolling in a line and then we will see. Check your aeroplane. We fly at dawn and we will be observing."

I turned and began walking to the office. I didn't know if we were scheduled to fly the next day but I would press for us to do so. This arrogant young peacock needed his feathers plucking. When I reached the office Captain Marshall had a strange smile on his face. "Problem Lieutenant Harsker?"

I forced myself to calm down. "It's that arrogant young prig. He thinks he is too good for a Gunbus. I want to take my flight up at dawn."

He laughed, "That is not a problem." He picked up a file and threw it across. "This is interesting reading. He was the top pilot in the training school but the instructor suggested that he be sent here as he did not like his attitude."

"That sounds like a good instructor."

The captain nodded, "He is and you know him. It was Captain Dixon. He recommended he work with us here to, as he said in his letter to the major, '*teach him how to do the job properly*'."

As I left with the maps for the following morning's patrol I thought of what a small world it was. Captain Dixon had nearly caused my death and now he was sending us men to make real pilots of them.

Chapter 23

The sector we were to patrol was closer to Ypres than we had been for some time. I knew that I could rely on Charlie to observe accurately and, with an extra aeroplane we should be somewhat safer. As we went to the field I pulled John to one side. "Look, John, Charlie can observe for all three aircraft. Use Walter to keep his eyes peeled behind and to the sides. This is Lieutenant Campbell's first flight. It may be a little more traumatic than he expects."

John's face darkened, "He had no right to say what he did about David. He was not a bad pilot!"

"And I know that. But we both know that everyone pays a heavy price for any kind of mistake here. So no mistakes, eh?"

"Yes, I won't let you down, Flight."

As I climbed into the cockpit I reflected that I was still Flight, despite my promotion. Except now I was Flight Commander. I checked my two weapons and then the Lewis. I did not expect to have to use any of them but it was a routine which, so far, had worked.

I led the three aeroplanes to the take off point. I would have liked to watch my new pilot take off but I would have to rely on others for that. I knew that the major, Gordy and Ted would all be watching. I would get a report later on. Both of my pilots knew that we would get to a high altitude first. It used more fuel but it was safer in the long run. The day that someone invented heavy guns capable of shooting down high flying aeroplanes would be the day that aeroplanes would no longer be any use in war. I knew that they were far too flimsy to be able to stand up to shells exploding near them. I was just grateful that machine guns had such limited range.

I tapped Charlie on the head and gave him the signal to look astern. He took off his glove and held up three fingers and then moved the hand up and down. I nodded and he sat down. Our perfect pilot was not keeping station! As we had not been in this sector for a while I was cautious and we spiralled slowly down to our allotted patrol. The balloons were all down by the time we reached five hundred feet. I flew due north while Charlie beavered away with his maps, notebooks and pencils. I felt happier knowing that there were two observers who were scanning the skies for enemies.

The Germans fired their weapons in the air but they had little chance of hitting us. I risked a glance astern and saw that Lieutenant Campbell had taken his aeroplane up another hundred feet. I had no way of communicating with him and I just became angry. We turned at the end of the first leg and I banked to come south. As I did so I waved the errant aeroplane to get back in formation. I was ignored and he stayed at the same height.

I was the one who saw the German aeroplanes. This time there were five of them and two of them looked like the French monoplane, the Morane-Saulnier. It had to be a pair of Fokker Eindecker aeroplanes. I had never come up against them but I knew they were good. They were highly manoeuvrable and fast. I signalled to go for home. I tapped Sharp on the head and pointed to the Germans. He nodded, put his maps and drawings in the pocket of his greatcoat and then cocked the rear-facing Lewis.

His face fell and he pointed urgently behind me. I saw that Lieutenant Campbell was heading for the five Germans. As much as I wanted to, I could not leave him alone. I began to climb and signalled for John to follow me. Charlie resumed his position on the forward-facing Lewis.

I watched as Lieutenant Campbell's gunner made the cardinal error of firing too early. His bullets were wasted. The three Albatrosses flew down either side of the Gunbus and I saw bullets stitch along the side of the aeroplane. As the smoke began to drift from the engine the agile monoplanes headed for the vulnerable rear of the Gunbus. We were drawing ever closer but we would not reach it in time. I wondered why his observer was not manning the rear gun when I saw him slumped in his cockpit. He had been hit.

I aimed the Gunbus at the rear monoplane. Charlie opened fire and I stood and used my knees to keep the joystick steady. I turned the rear-facing Lewis until it was facing forward and I, too, opened fire. Chunks flew from the tail and the pilot dived, whether out of control or in fear I do not know. The F.E.2 continued to fly straight and Charlie and I repeated our attack. This time I saw the pilot fall forward and the aeroplane dived straight into the ground.

One of the Albatrosses poured bullets into the side of Campbell's aeroplane and then I saw the German being struck from below by Lieutenant Murray's aircraft. I had just dropped to my seat, having emptied the magazine when the fuel tank of the Albatros exploded. The concussion blew all five remaining aeroplanes away from the explosion. Lieutenant Campbell might have been an arrogant fool but he could fly. He managed to control the stricken aeroplane and turn towards home. I swung the front of our aeroplane across the remaining two Albatrosses and Sharp fired on both of them. They were discouraged enough to return east.

I signalled to John to cover Lieutenant Campbell's port side while I watched his starboard. I could see no signs of life in the observer and it was a miracle that the aeroplane was still flying. The engine was coughing and spluttering. I could see oil dripping from the engine and smoke coming from the propeller. He would be lucky to land it. When I saw the aerodrome I fired a flare. It might be too late for the gunner but I knew that the doctor and his team would try.

John and I stayed aloft as the aeroplane touched down. If it had been the Avro it would have turned over for the wheels caught in the mud. Luckily the Gunbus has a third nose wheel and it bounced him back upright. As soon as it had stopped moving we began our approach. They had emptied the aircraft by the time we landed. The major was there looking very serious.

"His observer is dead and I think his aeroplane might be our first write off. What happened?"

With the help of our observers, we told the major the sequence of events. We did not ascribe blame and we spoke factually but I could see the major becoming more and angrier. When I had finished I said, somewhat to my own surprise, "But he is a damned good pilot, sir. I think only you or his lordship could have brought that aeroplane back."

"The difference is that neither of us nor you two would have put ourselves in that position. You did well." He forced a smile, "Your first kill Mr Murray, congratulations."

After he had gone I added my own congratulations. He shook his head, "It doesn't feel like I should be celebrating, that poor observer is dead."

"And we could do nothing about it. If anyone should feel responsible it is me. Obviously, I didn't train him well enough."

"He hadn't been with us long enough. Don't blame yourself."

Gordy was waiting for us in the mess. "I heard about today. I know that you are thinking it is your fault. I can see it on your face but you are not. When we are in our aeroplanes we are our own masters. I hope the boss throws the book at him."

As we sat down to our meal I said, "The trouble is we can't afford to throw away good pilots. We'll have to make him better than he is."

We looked up as Lieutenant Campbell walked in. Every eye was on him. Every officer had heard what had happened and there was no sympathy for the man. He kept his head down, collected his food and sat as far away from everyone as he could. Major Brack and Captain Marshall joined us. The Major looked tired. No one said a word as the two men ate. After they had finished they both lit their pipes and Major Hewitt closed his eyes for a moment.

"I suppose you are wondering what we are going to do about the careless Mr Campbell." We all remained silent and he gave a dry, humourless laugh. "It is written all over your faces. Well, I am not going to do what I intended when I first heard what happened. I am not going to court-martial him. It would not do morale any good and it would be a waste of time. Lieutenant Harsker, you said he is a good pilot and God knows we need them. I intend to use him as a gunner on my bus for a week and let him experience the front from the sharp end. Hopefully, he will pick up some good ideas and rid himself of this notion that he is a knight on a white charger and that this is some noble form of war." He shook his head and relit his pipe. "You know why he went towards those Germans?" We shook our heads. He thought he could outfly them and it was dishonourable to leave without, at least, firing his guns. Can you believe it?"

Captain Marshall asked, "Where did he get such ridiculous ideas from?"

"The damned newspapers at home. Apparently, because there are so many of the upper classes in the Flying Corps and the German Air Force the newspapers have got it in their heads that we are like knights jousting. There was some cartoon about it."

The others shook their heads in disbelief. I could believe it. "I suppose, sir, that it is easier to make up a lie like that rather than admit how many thousands are being slaughtered in the trenches. We have lost far fewer men since the war began than the infantry do in the first two minutes of battle."

The major tapped his pipe on the table and then looked seriously at me. "I keep forgetting that, alone out of any of us, you have experienced the horror of that war. Ah well..." He pocketed his pipe, "It will just be the two of you for a week but you will need tomorrow to sort out your buses."

John and I stood and saluted, "Sir."

"And get some rest. You both did damn well today."

Captain Marshall made his apologies and left. There were just the three of us at our table. It was the first chance I had had to speak with Gordy in some while. "How is your flight working out then?"

He gestured across the room, "Compared with him? They are superb. In reality, they still need work."

"We ran into the Fokker Eindecker today. They are very nimble and fast. They can fly rings around us you know."

Gordy shook his head, "That's all we need. Someone told me that there is a French monoplane which has a gun firing through the propeller. Once the Germans get that then we will be like dead meat."

"There may be a weakness with the monoplane."

I looked at John. He was the quiet type who rarely said too much. "What do you mean?"

"The reason we have two wings is for stability and strength. I wonder how they would cope with an inverted loop. We know we can do it but I wonder if they could."

"You might be right."

Gordy suddenly burst out. "Did I hear right? You fired the rear Lewis over Sharp's head?"

I nodded, "It gave us a better angle. The lower one has the same trajectory as the observer's gun. It just means you have a better chance of hitting something."

"How did you work that out?"

I confess, I didn't know and I just shrugged, "It just seemed to make sense to me."

Gordy nodded, "Well I may try that."

I noticed something else today. "When we landed I saw that the German bullets had gone through metal. They are steel jacketed. It explains why we suffer so much engine damage. We will have to watch out for the attacks from the stern. We need to keep the Germans in front. If we do then we have a slight chance that we might actually win."

Chapter 24

The last week in April was, mercifully, quiet. Perhaps we had hurt them more than we knew for we observed unhindered by the enemy. I heard that the Germans had launched an attack towards Ypres but we were not involved. That would come later. Lieutenant Campbell did his penance and he did see some action when the major was asked to patrol further south, towards the French Sector. I saw the bullet holes in the aeroplane. When he climbed down from the front cockpit I saw him running his fingers over them. He now knew what a gunner had to do.

Contrary to what the major believed the mechanics managed to repair the F.E. 2. We had many spares from previously wrecked aeroplanes. When the replacements arrived I was summoned, along with Lieutenant Campbell to the major's office. I had never seen the major as serious as that day.

"Lieutenant Campbell, you will never know how close you came to a court-martial. Your actions were reckless. In addition, you disobeyed orders. I am of a mind to let you fly with Lieutenant Harsker again but before I do so I need assurances from you that you will obey orders but, more importantly, I need to know if the lieutenant will fly with you."

I saw the look of horror on Campbell's face. His eyes pleaded with me. In all conscience, I could not refuse. How could I, a groom's son from Lancashire, ruin the career of an obviously gifted airman?

"He can fly with me, sir, if he obeys orders."

The relief was pitiful, "Oh I promise I will obey orders, thank you both."

The major nodded. "Then get a good night's sleep. You have the dawn patrol."

As we headed back to our quarters he was like a puppy which had been naughty. "I know you were right sir and when…" He stopped me and faced. "I thought we had enough firepower to destroy them. I had heard that you have shot down balloons and aeroplanes…."

"And if a sergeant could do it then a gifted pilot like you would be able to shoot down even more."

He hung his head, "Captain Dixon said that you were an uncanny shot and the coolest gunner he had ever met."

"That is very kind of the captain but remember this, Lieutenant Campbell, our job is easy compared with the poor sods down there around Ypres. They have to advance through mud and barbed wire and face many more machine guns. Our job is to win the war and make life easier for them. It is not to put little marks on a blackboard. This is not a public school and you are not going for the headmaster's prize!"

I went into my room without another word. I had said enough.

The quiet ended the next day. The major summoned all of us to the briefing room. "Gentlemen, the Germans are attacking Ypres and they have used poison gas!"

We all gasped. When I had been in the cavalry we had laughed at the thought of having to wear gas masks. I still remembered trying to get Caesar's mask on. I was grateful he had been spared a gas attack. Now the unthinkable had happened the Boche had used that despicable weapon. It was not war it was murder.

He waved his hands to quieten us. "As you might expect they have made advances against both the French and ourselves. Tomorrow morning we are going on a bombing raid against their lines of communication. Unlike our last raid, we will not be flying as a squadron but as flights. We need to cause as much disruption behind their lines as possible." His gaze seemed to settle on Lieutenant Campbell. "You will have no protection from enemy aeroplanes. When you have dropped your bombs then use your guns to disrupt the reinforcements the Germans will be sending up. I do not need to tell you of the importance of Ypres. Enough brave Englishmen and Canadians have died there already. Let us not waste their efforts. The armourer is taking the bombs out to your craft as we speak. Your Flight Commanders have all used them before." Again he looked at Lieutenant Campbell. "Listen to them and heed their advice about how to use them effectively."

As we were walking out I turned to my two wingmen. "They will be affixed to the outside of your aeroplanes. Your observer will throw them from the aeroplane towards the target. Now we only have four each and we should not waste them. Follow me in but wait to see the effect of my bombs. If mine have not done the job then you drop yours. Hold your bullets until the bombs are gone unless, of course, we are attacked by German aeroplanes." I could see the intense concentration on both of their faces. I smiled. "It is not as hard as it sounds. You do not need to dive to release the bombs but your observer needs a good eye to hit the target. The railway lines are the easiest target. If we destroy the rails then they cannot reinforce the front. It is as simple as that."

I realised that Charlie was also a virgin when it came to bombing. I had an idea that he might be quite good at that. He had a mathematical mind and that helped. He was looking in some trepidation at the bombs being fitted.

"Don't worry Sergeant Sharp, you can get rid of them over the German lines." The armourer grinned as he went to John's aeroplane. I went to the rack and pulled the first bomb from its mounting. "See, just give it a tug and it comes off." I fitted the deadly projectile snugly back into place. "Here are the maps." I had circled the first target in red and written number one next to it. The others were similarly marked. "That is the order we will strike them." He nodded but still looked worried. "I have done this before. So long as you have us lined up over the railway I can tell you when to drop the bomb."

He looked a little more relieved. "Right sir."

It took time to fit all of the bombs but I was pleased that both observers and pilots watched with rapt attention. Gordy and I left to wander back to the mess. "I have heard we have some mail!"

"Excellent." That brightened my day. It had been some time since we had had letters and it was always good to hear from home. My letters always made me feel more secure as though the world was still as I had remembered it. Mother in the cottage and my sisters all working at the big house. I could picture my dad quietly seeing to the horses and it made all the death and destruction somehow worthwhile.

Gordy had two letters and I had two. We sat in silence and read them.

The first one was a short one from my mother.

February 1914
Dear Bill,
Just a short letter I am afraid. Your dad was over the moon with his pipe and tobacco. He was really touched. It came a fortnight ago. Thank you for my photograph of Princess Mary. Your dad made a frame for it and it is over the fire with the photograph of you in your uniform.

The reason it will be a short letter is that our Alice has come down with something and I have to look after her. Albert is still desperate to join up but he is listening to your dad and still working for his lordship.

I pray that God continues to watch over you.
Your loving mother,
xxx

It was short but welcome for all that. The fact that they appreciated the presents was not a surprise. I did not know she had a copy of the photograph. Major Burscough must have given it to her. He had had the photograph taken when we had first arrived in France. I was secretly pleased. I like the way I had looked in the photograph.

The second one was from our Sarah.

March 1914
Dear Bill,
I pray that you are still safe. I feel awful for not writing before but I knew that Mum wrote to you and I have terribly busy. I have been

promoted to housekeeper now which is a great responsibility. It means I cannot get home as often as I would like.

Kathleen is still seeing the curate. I am still not keen on him and even Mother thinks he is a bit wet but Kath likes him. I think there will be wedding bells there before too long.

Alice got over influenza. She was lucky. A couple of girls in Liverpool died of it. I was worried that Mum and Dad might get it but they are a couple of tough old birds. They keep going despite everything.

And now the news I didn't want to give to you. Albert has joined up. Mother was in tears for a week and Dad has aged ten years. The trouble is that he wants to be just like you. He has joined the Royal Engineers. Our Alice told me that they are really keen to get Albert's type; he can drive and he knows engines. I suppose the only consolation is that he won't be in the trenches. He will be training for a while and we all pray this war will be over soon.

Sorry to have dropped that on you. I only found out a couple of days ago.

You take care of yourself,
Your loving sister,
Sarah xxx

I folded the letters up and tucked them into my tunic. The news about Albert was to be expected and I felt happy that he would be with the engineers. Their job was not easy and they could come under fire but they would never have to charge across no-man's land and face machine guns. In some ways, the letters hardened my resolve to do the best I could for the people back home.

I said goodnight to Gordy and headed back to my room. The next day would be important and I hoped that Lieutenant Campbell had learned his lesson.

We were breakfasted before first light and, as the first rays of the sun peered over the horizon we started our engines. We had more weight to carry and I made the whole flight keep their engines running until they were thoroughly warmed up. When the light was good enough to see the end of the airfield I led my flight up.

We flew due east. Our route would take us south of Ypres. I was worried about this poisoned gas. I assumed the Germans had sent it west on prevailing winds which meant that south should have been safe. I had no idea of the effect of even dissipated chlorine gas. To the north, we could see the smoke and hear the thunder of heavy guns. In the lulls between salvoes, we heard the chatter of machine guns too. Ypres had been a lovely town, in the early days of the war; I dreaded to think what it would look like now.

We had crossed the German trenches and were flying over strangely undamaged countryside. The war had yet to touch this green and healthy land. When it did it would become the polluted and sterile mound of mud that marked the trenches. Sharp said, "Time to head north, sir."

"Righto."

I banked to port. Glancing behind me as I did so, I was delighted to see that both of the other two aeroplanes were in the correct position. Today, of all days, that was vital. I began to descend to three hundred feet. We risked machine gunfire but it meant a more accurate bombing run.

"Time for north, northeast sir."

"Righto." This time, when I banked to port I lined up in the smoke ahead which marked a train heading to the German front lines some four miles ahead. We passed a station and freight yard. That would be our secondary target. I flew straight down the railway line. The train was a mile ahead.

"Sergeant Sharp, we'll have a go at that train. Try to throw the bomb so that it lands about fifty feet in front of the engine. Hit the rails. I will take her down another hundred feet to give you a better chance. We'll swing around and approach from their front."

"Sir."

I banked the aeroplane and quickly flew down the length of the train. They had men and guns on the railway carriages and they were firing at us. The problem they had was that we were a small target. We were flying head-on and would be like a large bird to them. It would take a lucky shot to hit us from a moving train. As we approached I saw that they had armoured the front of the train. That would not help if we could derail it.

"Now, Sharp!"

He hurled the bomb and I jerked the nose up. I heard the explosion and the screech of brakes behind me as the engine screamed to gain height. As I banked to port I saw Private Hibbert hurl his bomb. He might have miscalculated but he was lucky for the bomb struck the tender. Both engine and tender flew into the air and the carriages slewed across the ground spilling troops and freight. I saw Lieutenant Campbell and I signalled for him to drop a bomb on the devastation below. He nodded and he hit the middle of the train damaging rails and freight.

I headed back north to the station. "Right Sharp. Have a go yourself. It is the rails we need destroying with the first bomb."

"Sir."

We zoomed down to a hundred feet. The bomb flew straight and true and the rails were ripped apart. John followed a minute later and another vital section of rails was destroyed. I signalled for Campbell to bomb the wooden station. It exploded spectacularly and was completely destroyed. There was no need for my bomb.

I was looking for a target when Sharp said, "Sir, I can see the flashes from their guns. They are to the northeast; close to the barrage balloons."

Here they were using barrage balloons to stop us from diving on to the gun crews and machine-gunning them. However, we could fly up and bomb them from a greater height. We might not be as accurate but we would disrupt their fire. I began to climb. We reached four hundred feet. I saw that we were well above the barrage balloons. I started to circle.

"It's your target Sharp. Drop your last two bombs whenever you are ready."

"Sir."

He leaned over the side and I saw him take great care as he dropped one bomb and then, twenty seconds later his second.

"Bombs gone sir."

I couldn't resist watching the fall of the bombs. As I looked his first exploded close to a German 42cm and killed the crew. The second must have struck some ammunition for we were sent into the air with the concussion. I signalled for the other two to drop their bombs. "Get on the Lewis, Sharp, we'll have company soon."

Perhaps Sharp was just lucky but the other four bombs from the other aeroplanes exploded without hitting ammunition. I did see one gun struck. As I led us west I could see that we had devastated their artillery position. They would not be firing for some time. For some reason, I headed north by west. We had not patrolled this sector. Perhaps I was hoping that the German Albatros and Eindecker aircraft would assume we had headed due west.

I heard Sharp's voice in my ears, "Sir, there is a convoy of German vehicles on the road. "

Whatever they were transporting would be valuable to the Germans. The vehicles alone were expensive to manufacture. "We'll turn east and then fly along the road. If they have guns they will be facing forwards."

"Righto!"

I hoped that the other two would realise my plan. As I glanced over my shoulder whilst banking I saw that they were both keep station well. Perhaps the lesson had been learned. I brought us down, on my slow and gentle turn, to one hundred feet. It would make our ground speed higher and that would inhibit anyone trying to fire at us. I cocked my Lewis in case I had the chance to fire too.

I did not need to prompt Sharp and at fifty yards he opened up. The noise of the vehicles must have prevented the convoy from hearing us as there was no initial reaction to our attack. As the .303 rounds ripped into the trucks the crews began to bail out. It seemed strange to me. I glanced down at the first one we had hit and could see no flames. As Sharp sent a burst into each vehicle so the crews jumped and seemed to evacuate the vehicles as though they contained explosives. There was something strange going on. I glanced behind and saw that the other two had begun their run and the vehicles and their cargo were systematically destroyed. As we passed the last one Sharp changed the magazine and I banked to starboard to support the other two. It was when I saw the drivers writhing around on the floor that I realised what the vehicles contained- chlorine gas. It was too late to alert my pilots and I had to pray that they would come to no harm.

I completed a loop and flew next to them. I could see that all four of them were coughing in distress. I signalled for them to get home. "Right, Charlie, we are tail end so get on the rear Lewis."

It pained me to watch the two F.E. 2 aeroplanes as they bobbed up and down. It showed that the pilots were suffering and were struggling to control their aeroplanes. How could I have known what the vehicles contained? If I had gone in higher we would have still damaged them but my flight would not be in danger.

"Three Eindeckers, sir."

"Righto, I shall climb, to port, while they are approaching and then level out. Keep a tight hold."

"Yes, sir."

The German aeroplanes were faster than we were and they gained on us, inexorably. Once we reached five hundred feet I levelled out. I could see, some way ahead, the other two Gunbuses. If the Germans tried to follow them I would be in a good position to come astern. The monoplane had no rear-mounted gun. As I expected they followed us.

"One on the port side and two on the starboard, sir."

"Righto. Empty your magazine at the one by itself. If you sit down I will reload your Lewis and you should be able to fire at the other two."

"Sir."

I had four spare magazines in my cockpit. I could change the magazine so long as I was extremely quick.

"Here they come!"

They came in at the same time. I saw the determination on Sharp's face as he emptied all forty-seven bullets at the Eindecker. The fuselage of our aeroplane was largely air and many of the bullets missed. The danger would be when the steel-tipped bullets hit the engine. That was a bridge I would have to cross later. I could see the German trenches approaching. I was thirty miles from home. I might as well have been three hundred. It was three to one odds that we would not make it home.

I saw Sharp sit down and I banked to starboard. I had caught the two planes unawares. The first one came into our sights. Sharp fired first and then his gun jammed. "Duck down!"

I fired a short burst and saw the bullets stitch a line along the cockpit. The pilot was hit but not dead. I continued the turn and the second monoplane dived down to avoid the same treatment. I could see that Sharp had damaged the first aeroplane which was limping home. I quickly changed the magazine on the rear-facing Lewis as Sharp cleared his blockage.

"I'm heading for home. Keep an eye on the Huns."

It looks like there is just one but he is below us."

That was dangerous. We had no defence from such an attack. "Hold on I am going to dive." My manoeuvre took the monoplane by surprise. He fired a burst at us as we crossed in the air. I felt the bullets hit the engine but the sound did not alter. "Keep flying old girl."

"What sir?"

"I must be cracking up Charlie, I am talking to the bus now."

We were now travelling over the German trenches and they popped away at us with their rifles and machine guns. They would be extremely lucky to hit us but that day had not been lucky for us so far. As we cleared the lines and zoomed across no-man's land I said, "Get back on the Lewis, Sharp. See if you can discourage him again."

He quickly stood up. The German must have been close for he fired immediately. I felt the aeroplane judder as the German's bullets ripped huge holes in our port wing. The aeroplane dipped alarmingly and I had to correct it. We were now just forty or so feet above the ground and I saw the faces of the soldiers in the trenches as they raised their guns to fire at the German Eindecker.

"The footsloggers have frightened him, sir. He is heading east."

"Well done Charlie. You had better sit down now. Our port wing looks a little fragile."

I saw him glance over. "Bloody hell. How come we are still flying sir?"

"I have no idea but if we can keep her in the air for another ten minutes we should be home."

I did not dare risk climbing; I could have torn the wings from her. Equally, I could not bank. The landing was going to be a difficult proposition. "Better get a flare ready."

I assumed that the other two would have landed and the emergency crews would have been alerted but I was taking no chances. When the airfield hove into view Sharp sent the flare high into the sky. I did not have to go down very far but I did it by inches. I needed the gentlest landing I could manage. Even though it was like the touch of a butterfly's wing it was too much for the Gunbus. We rolled along the ground for fifty yards and then the top port wing collapsed, followed a moment or two later by the lower. The aeroplane slewed around but we were going so slowly that it teetered but remain upright. As I had been told by Captain Burscough many months ago now, '*Any landing you can walk away from is a good landing.*' We walked away.

The major met me. "How are…"

He held his hand up. "They are fine or they will be. It seems you hit some chlorines gas canisters. They both flew through them but the gas had only just started to rise and they were only slightly affected. The doc has sent them to the hospital."

My face fell. He shook his head. "You could not have known what the convoy was carrying and even if you had then your duty was to destroy them. Even if your whole flight had died then that would have been a small price to pay for the lives of the infantry that they would have saved."

"I suppose so." I glanced behind me at my wrecked aeroplane. "That will take some fixing."

He smiled. "And while it is being fixed I am giving you a two-week pass. You deserve some leave. You and Gordy both. The rest of us will manage. Besides we are getting some new buses next month so your old crate will just be for spares."

Sergeant Sharp was philosophical about my leave. "It will give me the chance to get to grips with the engine. I can strip her down and rebuild her."

Poor Ted was beside himself. "Well, I am definitely going for the pilot test. Sod this for a game of soldiers. You two get leave and I stay here looking after the wee bairns. It's not right."

We left that night with the Quartermaster who was driving to Dartford to pick up spares. We would get the train from Dover. It would take me a couple of days to get home but it would be worth it.

1914

Epilogue

Gordy was with me until Crewe when he left to go to his home close to Stoke. On the journey home, we had noticed how many wounded soldiers there were both on the train and in the stations. "This war is not going the way they thought it would do, Bill, old son."

"Well if those bastards are going to use gas then we will have to find some other way to defeat them."

"Aye well, at least we are doing our job. We are more than a match for the aeroplanes they are sending against us." He smiled, "Especially with our first ace in the squadron."

"That last aeroplane was not confirmed. Besides Sharp helped with that one."

"Major Brack said you were an ace and that is good enough for me. My paltry two is nowt compared with your score."

As we said goodbye I realised that others set more store by my success than I did. All I wanted was to survive with as many of my friends as possible.

This time no-one knew I was on my way home. I got off the train in Burscough feeling dirty and tired. I had slept on the train but it had been uncomfortable. The food had been station food and the quality of that was in the lap of the gods. As I trudged along the road to the estate and our cottage I couldn't wait to have some of mum's food inside me and sleep in a comfortable bed. It came to me that, for the first time in my life, I would have the room to myself. Albert was away now. How strange would that be?

I did not see anyone on the road which was a novelty in itself and I wondered why. Normally there would have been carts and workers going to various parts of the estate but I saw no-one. As I approached the cottage I was surprised to see the curtains drawn and the door shut. More than that it was locked! What was going on? Mother never left the house.

I dumped my bags outside the back door and headed towards the big house. Perhaps dad was at work. When I reached the house the drive was filled with many cars just like his lordship's Lanchester. I saw liveried chauffeurs standing by their cars. I was wearing my officer's uniform and, when I approached them they saluted. I felt a little embarrassed.

"Excuse me what is going on here today?"

"Didn't you know sir? Lord Burscough died. It's his funeral."

It was like a slap to the face. I knew he had had a stroke some years earlier and he was old but he was the same age as my father. How could he have died? He would have had good doctors looking after him. He was a lord. That explained everything. The whole estate and village would be at the service for Lord Burscough was very popular. I knew where they would be; they would be in the chapel. I hurried there. I knew that I should have washed myself and cleaned up but I thought it was more important to be there to pay my respects to a man who had been good to me and my family.

I reached the chapel as the coffin was being taken out of the west door. I took off my hat and bowed my head. The first man following the coffin was Major Burscough. I saw the look of surprise on his face but he quickly recovered his composure. He gave me a brief nod and continued his long slow walk. The rest of the family followed: his wife, other son and daughters. The important aristocratic families marched after them. When they had all passed the servants emerged and that was when my family saw me. I knew they would be torn between happiness at seeing me and sadness at the occasion. I took my lead from my mother who gave me a gentle kiss on the cheek and then linked my arm. No-one said a word.

We walked slowly to the Burscough family graveyard. We all stood well back from the family and the dignitaries. I could see that not only my mother but my father too, had been crying. Lord Burscough had been their life. My father had been his servant during the South African War. They had both spent their whole lives working for one family and now the head of that family was dead. It was the end of an era. The world was changing and would never be the same again.

Once the coffin was in the ground and the vicar had shaken hands with Major Burscough my mother and the others relaxed.

"Why didn't you tell us you were coming home?"

"I only found out yesterday and I have been travelling ever since."

"Mother, leave him alone. You have been moaning on about not seeing your bairn and now he is here you tell him off."

The handkerchief came to her mouth, "Eeeh I am sorry our Bill. It doesn't matter, you are home now."

The others parted as Major Burscough came up to us. "Sorry for your loss, your Lordship."

He took my hand, "Thank you, Bill. I thought the old bugger would live forever." He shook his head. "Congratulations on the promotion. I see you are now a lieutenant. It won't be long before you are a captain, mark my words."

I shook my head, "I don't know about that, my lord."

He turned to my father. "Did you know that your son is one of the top pilots we have in the Royal Flying Corps?"

I could see that my dad was impressed. "I think you are being too generous, sir."

"Nonsense. The major keeps me up to speed on these things." He leaned in, "I think the finest thing I ever did was to get you to come to France with me as my gunner." One of his sisters tugged his arm. "Must go. How long have you got?"

"About ten more days."

He nodded, "I shall see you before then." He looked at my mother and father. "You two were the most prized of retainers. My father said that when they made you two they broke the mould."

Mother curtsied but I could see that she was pleased. Alice linked my other arm and we walked down the drive. I heard my dad say, "You're an officer now?"

"I am, Lieutenant Harsker; Flight Commander."

"Who would have thought that a son of mine would have become an officer? Your granddad would have been right proud of you."

My mum leaned in to me. "But we are more proud, our Bill. You are a credit to the family, God Bless you son."

And that was enough for me. My family were proud and his Lordship had praised me. You could forget being an ace or being an officer. I was truly happy as, on that saddest of days, I walked back to the cottage I called home with a huge smile on my face.

The End

Glossary

BEF- British Expeditionary Force
Beer Boys-inexperienced fliers (slang)
Blighty- Britain (slang)
Boche- German (slang)
Bowser- refuelling vehicle
Bus- aeroplane (slang)
Crossley- an early British motor car
Donkey Walloper- Horseman (slang)
Fizzer- a charge (slang)
Foot Slogger- Infantry (slang)
Google eyed booger with the tit- gas mask (slang)
Griffin- confidential information (slang)
Hun- German (slang)
Jasta- a German Squadron
Jippo- the shout that food was ready from the cooks (slang)
Lanchester- a prestigious British car with the same status as a Rolls Royce
Loot- a second lieutenant (slang)
M.C. - Military Cross (for officers only)
M.M. - Military Medal (introduced in 1915)
Nicked- stolen (slang)
Number ones- Best uniform (slang)
Parkin or Perkin is a soft cake traditionally made of oatmeal and black treacle, which originated in northern England.
Pop your clogs- die (slang)
Posser- a three-legged stool attached to a long handle and used to agitate washing in the days before washing machines
Pickelhaube- German helmet with a spike on the top. Worn by German soldiers until 1916
Shufti- a quick look (slang)
Singer 10 - a British car developed by Lionel Martin who went on to make Aston Martins
Toff- aristocrat (slang)
V.C. - Victoria Cross, the highest honour in the British Army

Historical note

This is my first foray into what might be called modern history. The advantage of the Dark Ages is that there are few written records and the writer's imagination can run riot- and usually does! If I have introduced a technology slightly early or moved an action it is in the interest of the story and the character. I have tried to make this story more character-based as I have used the template of some real people and characters who lived at the time.

As with all my books I have used fictitious regiments and actions. The organisation of the Lancashire Yeomanry and the Cumbrian Hussars is compatible with actual regiments. Their role is exactly that of the real Yeomanry. Compared with the regular regiments and especially compared with the foot soldiers, the Yeomanry casualties were very light. The total cavalry losses for the whole war were 5,674 dead and 14,630 wounded. Compare that to the Northumberland Fusiliers who had 16000 casualties alone. The Yeomanry losses were even fewer.

There will be more books in this series. The next one will look at the dark days of 1915 when the Fokker Scourge descended upon the Western Front.

I used the following books to verify the information:
World War 1- Peter Simkins
The Times Atlas of World History
The British Army in World War 1 (1)- Mike Chappell
The British Army in World War 1 (2)- Mike Chappell
The British Army 1914-18- Fosten and Marrion
British Air Forces 1914-1918- Cormack
British and Empire Aces of World War 1- Shores
A History of Aerial Warfare- John Taylor
Thanks to the following website for the slang definitions
*www.ict.griffith.edu.au/~davidt/z_ww1_**slang**/index_bak.htm*

Griff Hosker April 2014

Other books by Griff Hosker

If you enjoyed reading this book, then why not read another one by
the author?

Ancient History

The Sword of Cartimandua Series
(Germania and Britannia 50 A.D. – 128 A.D.)
Ulpius Felix- Roman Warrior (prequel)
The Sword of Cartimandua
The Horse Warriors
Invasion Caledonia
Roman Retreat
Revolt of the Red Witch
Druid's Gold
Trajan's Hunters
The Last Frontier
Hero of Rome
Roman Hawk
Roman Treachery
Roman Wall
Roman Courage

The Wolf Warrior series
(Britain in the late 6th Century)
Saxon Dawn
Saxon Revenge
Saxon England
Saxon Blood
Saxon Slayer
Saxon Slaughter
Saxon Bane
Saxon Fall: Rise of the Warlord
Saxon Throne
Saxon Sword

Medieval History

The Dragon Heart Series

Viking Slave
Viking Warrior
Viking Jarl
Viking Kingdom
Viking Wolf
Viking War
Viking Sword
Viking Wrath
Viking Raid
Viking Legend
Viking Vengeance
Viking Dragon
Viking Treasure
Viking Enemy
Viking Witch
Viking Blood
Viking Weregeld
Viking Storm
Viking Warband
Viking Shadow
Viking Legacy
Viking Clan
Viking Bravery

The Norman Genesis Series
Hrolf the Viking
Horseman
The Battle for a Home
Revenge of the Franks
The Land of the Northmen
Ragnvald Hrolfsson
Brothers in Blood
Lord of Rouen
Drekar in the Seine
Duke of Normandy
The Duke and the King

New World Series
Blood on the Blade
Across the Seas
The Savage Wilderness

The Reconquista Chronicles
Castilian Knight

The Aelfraed Series
(Britain and Byzantium 1050 A.D. - 1085 A.D.)
Housecarl
Outlaw
Varangian

The Anarchy Series England
1120-1180
English Knight
Knight of the Empress
Northern Knight
Baron of the North
Earl
King Henry's Champion
The King is Dead
Warlord of the North
Enemy at the Gate
The Fallen Crown
Warlord's War
Kingmaker
Henry II
Crusader
The Welsh Marches
Irish War
Poisonous Plots
The Princes' Revolt
Earl Marshal

Border Knight
1182-1300
Sword for Hire
Return of the Knight
Baron's War
Magna Carta
Welsh Wars
Henry III
The Bloody Border
Baron's Crusade
Sentinel of the North

Lord Edward's Archer
Lord Edward's Archer
King in Waiting

Struggle for a Crown
1360- 1485
Blood on the Crown
To Murder A King
The Throne
King Henry IV
The Road to Agincourt

Tales of the Sword

Modern History

The Napoleonic Horseman Series
Chasseur a Cheval
Napoleon's Guard
British Light Dragoon
Soldier Spy
1808: The Road to Coruña
Talavera
The Lines of Torres Vedras

The Lucky Jack American Civil War series
Rebel Raiders
Confederate Rangers
The Road to Gettysburg

The British Ace Series
1914
1915 Fokker Scourge
1916 Angels over the Somme
1917 Eagles Fall
1918 We will remember them
From Arctic Snow to Desert Sand
Wings over Persia

Combined Operations series

1914

1940-1945
Commando
Raider
Behind Enemy Lines
Dieppe
Toehold in Europe
Sword Beach
Breakout
The Battle for Antwerp
King Tiger
Beyond the Rhine
Korea
Korean Winter

Other Books
Great Granny's Ghost (Aimed at 9-14-year-old young people)

For more information on all of the books then please visit the author's web site at www.griffhosker.com where there is a link to contact him or visit his Facebook page: GriffHosker at Sword Books

Printed in Great Britain
by Amazon

67004777R00119